FIND THE RIVER

A Novel

The House in the Horseshoe, Moore County, North Carolina

A Novel

LAURA KELLY CAMPBELL

Low Country Press
Savannah, Georgia

Low Country Press, Savannah, Georgia
www.lowcountrypress.net

Low Country Press Trade Paperback ISBN
978-0-9883044-0-6

Excavations and RECONSTRUCTIONS

ABOUT THE TURN OF THE LAST CENTURY, a British archeologist began excavations on the island of Crete. Bits and pieces of a grand Minoan palace at Knossos were uncovered by his diggers. Sir Arthur Evans chose to reconstruct palace rooms and murals, using the fragments and his best guesses. He was criticized by purists, but praised by those who found that his recreations brought life to a long-dead time.

Like Evans, in my diggings into the past I have found wonderful bits and pieces. There is much of fact in my account. I know the name of Drew Smith's horse. It was there in his will: "My gray horse called Punch." There are also logical surmises on my part. Although I found no record of Temperance Alston's marriage to Mitchell Griffin, there is a record of their marriage bond, so I chose to assume that they were indeed married. And, finally, in those cases where there was nothing left of the past, I have invented. In doing so, I may have altered the past, and possibly flattered or libeled people who were undeserving.

Some parts of this book, therefore, are fiction.

Dedication

To my mother, Hulda Kelly, whose delving into our family history
helped form the foundations of this story.

And to my daughters, Laurie, Victoria, and Carol.
A river of strength runs deep within them.

LINN: ONE
Three weeks ago

T HE SKIES WERE AN UNCOMPLICATED BLUE. Linn, wedged between
the window and an imposing older man in a white dress
shirt and red and gray striped tie, watched Atlanta growing smaller
as the plane gained altitude. Was that the Chattahoochee below?
Her great-grandmother's sudden death three weeks before
semester's end had brought her home, and now, three days later,
after the blur of faces at the funeral home visitation, the odd
combinations of pick-up meals from food brought in by family
friends, and the solemnity of the burial service at St. Margaret's,
she was on her way back to college in New England.

Pushing her backpack further under the seat in front of her,
Linn cast a surreptitious look at the man beside her. He'd been
among the last to turn off his phone before take-off, and was now
highlighting phrases in a sheaf of papers in a folder, his elbow
overlapping the armrest. She'd watched him carefully fold his suit
jacket and stow it in the overhead compartment. That must be
uncomfortable, she thought, the way his shirt collar cut into his
throat. He reminded her a little of Dad. Oblivious to everything
around him at home most of the time. As long as the household
ran smoothly, Dad was content. As long as his word was law. A

corner of Linn's mouth twitched. Law. *The* law. That was all that really mattered to him. Oh, maybe she was being unfair. Dad loved her and Mom. More than anything. She sighed.

She wondered if her seatmate had a family. Yes, there was a gold band on his left-hand ring finger. The hand was attached to an arm with an elbow that was now well into her space. She scooted as far to the left as she could. Sometimes she felt invisible. It was going to be a long flight. She sighed again and closed her eyes, leaning her head against the window. Ooh, uncomfortable. And it was warm in the cabin. Unzipping the hooded sweatshirt she was wearing, she struggled to pull her right arm out, bumping the arm beside her.

"Can I help you with that?" a deep, male voice asked.

"Oh, thanks." Mr. Businessman held the jacket while Linn extracted her arms.

He was smiling. She smiled back. Not such a bad guy, then. She wadded the hoodie into a makeshift pillow and put it between the window and her head. Mr. B. turned back to his folder, and Linn closed her eyes again.

Once Linn was back at school, there were finals coming up, and she concentrated on her assignments and the term paper that was due. The three weeks passed somehow. There was a new parcel of sadness that she shoved into a back corner of her chest, where she could feel it crowding her heart.

And then she was home again. The director of the community recreation center had called during spring break to offer her the lifeguarding job again for the summer, and she'd accepted, with no clear idea of how to tell her dad she wouldn't be filing papers in his office after all. When Gran phoned the morning after she got home to ask for help in sorting through GeeGee's genealogy work, she'd agreed, readily.

I should have tried harder to talk to Dad while I was home for spring break, she told herself. I just couldn't figure out what to say. "Dad, I hate school. I'm just not fitting in. I shouldn't be there." He'd be so disappointed in me.

She walked to her great-grandmother's house. It was just a few blocks from home, and Linn had made the trip on foot so many times through the years. She remembered the first time she'd been allowed to walk it alone, with her mom standing at one end and GeeGee waiting on the other. "Remember to look both ways!" She could almost hear her mom's voice.

GeeGee's little house smelled musty to Linn, and sadly empty. Gran had worked with her usual efficiency, and a For Sale sign was planted in the front yard. Linn's mother, Anne, and Gran's other daughter, Sue, and son, Michael, had claimed what they wanted of the contents of the house, and Linn knew from talking with her mother that there had already been an estate sale. GeeGee's jewelry had been divided according to her carefully written instructions among her children, grandchildren, and the great-grandchildren of the family. Linn got the topaz ring she'd admired as a child, and a little gold locket with a loopy "L." The clothes had been packed off to Good Will, and Habitat for Humanity had expressed a willingness to take whatever was left of the household goods. All of the shabby furniture that Linn remembered was gone now.

What remained were cardboard boxes, stacked in the little living room, two filled with loose photos and albums and several filled with manila file folders. "The folders are what I'd like you to help me with, Linn," Gran told her. "Let's get these boxes to the kitchen, and we can take a look at what's here, and then you can help me load up my car."

Together Linn and her grandmother, Susan, carried the boxes into the familiar kitchen. While Linn lifted the boxes of photos onto the counter, Gran went out to the car to bring in a tin of cookies and an electric kettle. She ran some water into the kettle and plugged it in. "Get the cups." She pointed to the cabinet to the left of the sink. It was empty except for the last two of GeeGee's thin china—two cups and saucers and a sugar bowl, with a broken top, carefully glued together. There was a box of ginger-peach tea bags next to the cups. Linn's heart lurched when she picked up the sugar bowl.

"Gran, I miss her."

Susan Sullivan looked at the nineteen-year-old standing at the cabinet. "I know, sweetheart. So do I."

"Holding her things makes her seem so near. She asked me to make the tea for us when I came to see her the last afternoon of spring break. I remember how apologetic she was that she didn't feel up to making it herself. She said she'd been so tired lately."

"Linn, you know she didn't suffer at all. Doctor Vann said her heart just wore out. She was ninety-three, honey."

"But she was always right here, and ready to listen to me. I wish I'd known it was the last time I'd be with her. I wouldn't have rattled on so much about school and classes and the blind date that girl lined up for me the weekend before spring break." Linn's voice dwindled off. Now I'm glad I didn't tell her the whole story, she thought. I just told her what a jerk he was, taking me to a party and leaving me alone while he talked to other people.

"You know she loved hearing what was going on in your life! It kept her young. Don't feel bad about that, Linn. She adored you, and not just because you were her only great-granddaughter and her namesake." Susan studied her granddaughter. Linn was taller than Susan by several inches and had the physique of the competitive swimmer she'd been in high school. Susan noticed that Linn had lost a few pounds. Her jeans were loose. And she was biting her nails again.

The kettle steamed, and Linn poured boiling water over the tea bags in the cups. Gran opened the cookie tin and held it out. "I made shortbread. GeeGee's recipe."

Linn took a cookie, and, munching, pulled the nearest box closer. It contained folders. "Drew Smith" was written on the tab of the one on top. "Who's Drew Smith, Gran? One of our ancestors, I guess."

Gran was leaning over an album filled with black and white pictures from her childhood. "Hmm? Oh, yes. The Smiths were from North Carolina."

Linn skimmed through the papers in the folder. "Here's a photocopy of a will. Wow, it's dated 1762. 'I, Drew Smith, being sick, but of perfect sound mind and memory, and calling the uncertainty of this mortal state to mind...' Gosh!"

Susan looked up. Linn's shoulder-length honey brown hair hid her face as she leaned over the paper.

"Gran, he even mentions his horse! 'My will is that my gray horse called Punch should be sold to the highest bidder...'"

On the banks of the Roanoke,
May, 1762

"**P**unch, WHAT A GOOD BOY YOU ARE!" Temperance Smith stretched herself along the neck of the gray horse and crooned in his ear. Punch whuffled and shook his head. Temperance laughed.

"I'm going to miss you so much, boy." The brown-haired girl atop the big horse slowed him to a walk as they neared the barn. She loved these morning rides, with the rough coat of the horse scratching her bare legs. And the air was so sweet to breathe! A brief drenching rain just before dawn had left the grass glistening. May, she was thinking. The perfect month. Cool mornings, pleasant days.

Ahead in the road near the stable gate stood a tall man, watching her as she approached.

"Good day," he called out. "You must be Mistress Temperance. Your stable hand said I'd likely find you and the horse coming down this road."

"And you must be Mr. Brumble," she answered, holding her head high. "How do you do? We weren't expecting you until this afternoon." That Mingo! He should have sent Mr. Brumble into the house to wait. Mama will be most displeased, she thought. I'm in my oldest gown, and my feet are bare. And my hair!

"No, I'm not Mr. Brumble," the man responded, with a hint of a laugh in his voice. The child had poise! She was dressed like a serving girl but spoke like a lady. "I'm Philip Alston. I heard about your horse at the tavern in Scotland Neck last night and decided to ride out and have a look. I might consider buying him. I watched you jump the fence. He's a fine jumper. How's his stamina?"

Temperance's dark brown eyes widened in surprise. Philip Alston! Good thing Papa couldn't know that the son of Joseph John Alston was standing here on the very land the senior Alston had tried to take from him. She had been young, but she remembered the lawsuit and her father's delight when he'd won. The senior Mr. Alston was a powerful man. "He can gallop for miles," Temperance said, collecting her thoughts. Her pride in the horse showed in her voice. "He never seems to tire. Perhaps you'd like to ride him?"

"I should be delighted to, after dinner. Your mother has very graciously invited me to stay and share your meal."

Temperance was surprised again. On second thought, though, that was just like Mama. One does the proper thing, and extending a dinner invitation to a stranger here on business was what one should do. And then, too, Mama had never paid much attention to Papa's land dealings.

The tall slim gentleman in the light blue knee breeches and high shiny black boots was speaking again. "May I assist you in getting down?"

Mingo usually helped her, or if he were not close to hand, she'd walk Punch alongside the fence and climb down that way. But there was nothing to do but accept Mr. Alston's offer. "Thank you, sir." She slid one scratched leg over the horse's back and jumped down into Philip's waiting arms.

Holding her face to face, Philip realized she was even smaller than he had thought, and a great deal prettier. She was barely five feet tall, almost a foot shorter than he was. Her eyes, he thought, are very nearly black. He revised his estimate of her age upwards. She was likely nearer fifteen than twelve. Her hair had tumbled loose from its pins, and there was a twig caught in her brown curls, just above her right ear. And she was wearing no stays! His hands, catching her just under her armpits, felt only the firmness of her ribcage and the tender swell of the sides of her young breasts.

"Sir!" she said. Philip realized he was still holding her above the ground and lowered her quickly.

With great dignity, Temperance said, "I shall see you at dinner, sir." She turned and led the gray stallion away, her bare feet splashing through the puddles as she walked. Philip watched her slender figure as she made her way into the barn, Punch following with the devotion of a puppy, his reins slack.

Temperance took the back stairs two at a time. In the room she had shared with her sister Priscilla all her life, until Prissy's recent marriage, Temperance shed her mud-stained dress with the help of Rose. "Miss Temp, they's gonna be waitin' for you downstairs. They's comp'ny for dinner."

"I know, I know, Rose. Just hush and help me get dressed." Temperance pulled her stays over her shift, and wiggled impatiently as Rose laced them. She ducked into the waiting petticoat Rose held, and then the skirt and bodice of her buttery yellow dress sprigged with tiny pink and white blossoms.

Rose handed her a wet cloth, and she washed her face and neck quickly. "What can we do with my hair?"

"Jes' stan' still, Miss Temp. Stop all that jumpin' around. What you so excited for?" Rose's deft dark hands pulled the twig out gently, then drew a comb through Temperance's light brown curls and pulled them up in a twist on top of her head. She quickly secured the topknot with bone hairpins and fastened on a small lace-edged cap. "There now. You looks jes' fine. Now hurry! Wait, Miss Temp! Your slippers!"

Temperance, hopping first on one foot, then the other, pulled yellow silk slippers onto her bare feet and ran out the door and down the hall. At the top of the stairs, she slowed to a walk and made her way down the mahogany staircase, one hand resting lightly on the banister.

At the bottom, in the hall, her mother stood with their guest. Elizabeth Smith, Temperance's mother, was well groomed as always. At thirty-seven, she was still the beauty she had been when she had married Drew Smith, but it took much of her time now to maintain that beauty. Temperance's younger sisters, Millie and Anne, neat and clean in their second-best dresses, watched from behind the adults as Temperance descended. Millie nudged an elbow into Anne and pointed silently to Temperance's unstockinged feet, in the dainty slippers. A large smudge of mud was visible on her right instep as she came down the stairs.

In the dining room, their guest held Mistress Smith's chair. "Why, thank you, Mr. Alston." The girls took their seats at the table, while their guest seated himself at the end of the table next to Temperance.

Philip looked around the room. Well-lit and airy, with windows extending to the floor along one wall that overlooked the front grounds, it was not nearly so grand as his father's dining hall, but it was well appointed. A tall sideboard held a shiny silver tea service, but no decanters. Ah, yes. The late Mr. Smith had not partaken of spirits—a well-known and much-discussed fact in Halifax County, where most gentlemen of English descent enjoyed their brandy.

Jacob brought in the first dish, a tureen of soup, and lowered it in front of Mistress Smith. She filled a small bowl from the stack in front of her with a rich fish chowder, and handed it to Jacob to take to Mr. Alston. Temperance watched him as the others were served. His hair, tied back in a neat queue, was such a glossy walnut brown. And his eyes were the gray-blue of a winter sky. And, goodness, how modish he was. His white shirt under the dark blue jacket was stiffly starched, and his stock was knotted precisely, with a black ribbon tied into a bow around it. He looked up and catching her gaze, gave her a quick smile, lifting one eyebrow. A dimple appeared, denting his right cheek.

"So, Miss Temperance. Your mother tells me you've been seeing to it that your gray horse gets enough exercise since your father's death."

"Yes, Mr. Alston. Papa was so very proud of Punch. That's how he got his name. Papa bought him a year ago when he was a colt and said, "I'm proud as punch to have this beast." So I said,

"Let's call him that. Punch, I mean. We wouldn't be selling him if Papa's will hadn't directed us to. He wanted Punch to have the chance to race, and of course, with just us here—four daughters and no son—he wouldn't be likely to have that chance."

"Mr. Smith couldn't have known that our eldest daughter, Priscilla, would be wedding Thomas Hunter so soon after his death, or he might have left Punch to Priscilla. But then, Mr. Hunter doesn't seem to have much interest in horses or racing," Mistress Smith concluded. Anne and Millie, seated next to each other, exchanged glances. Tom was a dull bird, to their way of thinking. But so was their sister Prissy!

"Papa and I spent much of his last year with the horses," Temperance said. "Until he took sick. Since then, Mingo and I and the stable boys have worked them every day. If you decide to purchase Punch, I think you'll find he's very well trained, though he's never been raced."

As the meal progressed, and the serving staff removed and brought in dishes, Philip found his interest piqued by the talkative young woman to his right. The soft yellow of her dress was very becoming, he thought, as he admired the gentle swell of her breasts in the deep square neck of the bodice. She ate neatly, but with appetite, the game pie and fresh green peas that followed the soup. Cornbread was passed around, with butter in small pats. "Millie shaped the butter," Temperance said. "She and I like to help Lucy in the kitchen. Lucy's the best cook in these parts. Her cornbread is just wonderful. And I think we're having her dried peach pie for dessert."

"There's a Lucy in my father's kitchen, too," Philip said with a small twitch of his full lips. "I don't know that she's all that good a cook, however."

Elizabeth Smith frowned at Temperance and shook her head just a little. Young ladies shouldn't admit to doing kitchen work, much less enjoying it.

Oh, I've done it again, thought Temperance. I just can't remember all the subjects I shouldn't mention. Casting about in her mind, she asked, "Does your wife enjoy riding, Mr. Alston?"

"I'm afraid there is no wife, Miss Temperance."

Anne forgot a rule, too, that children were to be seen and not heard, and blurted out, "Oh, did she die?"

Over Mistress Smith's shocked gasp, Philip laughed and said, "No, Mistress Anne, there never *was* a wife. I'm unmarried."

Temperance giggled, caught herself, and said, "Do try this honey on your cornbread, Mr. Alston." Unmarried, she thought. Wonder why? He's well of an age. And rich and very certainly handsome.

"Yes, do," her mother urged. "It's from our own hives, and is reputed to be among the tastiest in the Carolinas."

Jacob came in at that moment to say, "Mr. Brumble's here to see the horse, Mistress Elizabeth. Shall I tell him to wait in the parlor?"

"No, tell him it's already been sold," Philip said, before she could respond. "I think you'll be more than satisfied with my proposition, Mistress Smith."

Philip noticed that Jacob looked to Temperance for direction, rather than her mother. Temperance made her decision quickly. "Yes, Jacob, please make our apologies to Mr. Brumble, and offer him some refreshment before he leaves. Mr. Alston, we'll discuss this after dinner."

Philip looked with great interest at Temperance. This girl, who chattered so delightfully and rode her horse with the abandonment of a boy, spoke now with the quiet authority of a well-seasoned businessman. He looked forward to their talk later. In the meantime, he politely addressed the twelve-year-old to his left. "And, Mistress Millie, do you also ride?

Linn:Two
Tuesday morning

Linn woke early the next morning. For just a moment, she felt happy and peaceful. The sun was shining brightly, and a merry bird somewhere just outside her bedroom window seemed to feel that a celebration was in order. She sat up, swinging her legs over the side of the bed. Then the feeling of sadness came back. Oh, I can't. Crawling back under the covers, she pulled the bedspread up over her head. The air under the covers smelled stale.

I've got to figure out what to do. How to tell them I don't want to go back to school. How to stop thinking about what nearly happened. Linn stuck her head back out. Oh, God, she thought. What can I do? I hate feeling like this. She headed for the bathroom across the hall and shut the door behind her, turning on the shower to let the water run hot.

Shucking her pajama bottoms and t-shirt, she leaned into the mirror over the sink and while she waited, studied the face reflected there. Circles under her eyes, but on the whole, not a bad face. Nice teeth, thanks to the orthodontics clinic. A dimple in her right cheek when she smiled. She tried that now. Looks fake, she thought. But it's such an ordinary face. Brown eyes, normal-sized mouth. Plain nose. Not big, not little. Dirty blonde hair, a little oily. She hadn't washed it yesterday. But it'll be *clean* dirty blonde hair in a minute. That brought almost a real smile when she thought it, but no dimple.

There were footsteps coming up the stairs. "Linn, are you in there? I've got breakfast ready."

"I'm not really hungry, Mom. I'll get something after I shower."

"Are you okay, Linnie?" Her mother's voice was close. She must be standing just the other side of the door.

"I'm fine, Mom. I'll be down in a little bit..."

"I'll leave some sausage in the microwave for you. Gotta run. Don't want to be late!"

Linn heard her mother's quick footsteps on the stairs. Sausage! I'm just not hungry. Her stomach tightened every time she thought about that night and what she had to tell Dad. Got to stop thinking.

Back in her room after her shower, she rummaged through the drawers, pulled on underwear and shorts and a clean t-shirt. She looked down at the folder on the floor that she'd been reading last night, just before she fell asleep. She perched on the unmade bed and pulled out the top papers. GeeGee's tiny cramped handwriting completed a family chart.

Philip Alston.
Father: Joseph John Alston.
Mother: Elizabeth Chauncy/Chancy.
Spouse: Temperance Smith. Date of marriage: about 1763 or 1764.

And then the babies came. One about 1764 or 65, then others over a twenty-year span. The last was in 1785. And then Temperance was dead, soon after that, Linn knew, from reading the chart last night. But she was only about 40...

What did she feel, all those years ago? She must have been terrified, at seventeen or so, to be carrying a baby in her body. I'm nineteen, and I can't even imagine. But maybe she loved her husband, and he probably loved her. At least, I hope so. And I'm alone. All those Hallmark movies that Mom likes to watch when

Dad's not home—they make it seem as though there's a soul mate waiting for everyone, and that true love and happiness will find the way. The music swells, they kiss, and the credits roll. But I don't know if that's true. Take Mom and Dad, she thought, flopping back on the bed. They've been married a long time. Dad's nearly sixty now, and Mom not that far behind. They get along okay, as long as Mom keeps things smooth for him—and doesn't argue with him. There were some massive scary fights when I was little, but Mom seems to have figured out that arguing with Dad gets her nowhere. Wonder if they still are in love or if it's just easier to stay married than to split up? Temperance and Philip stayed married until she died, but who knows how they felt about each other.

On the banks of the Roanoke,

November, 1762

Temperance WRAPPED HER WOOLEN SHAWL more closely around herself and walked down the road that curved in front of the two-storied white house. Dry leaves crunched under her feet, and there was a bite in the air. Where *was* he? He'd said last week that he'd be here by dinner today, but dinner had come and gone.

Since Philip had met with her that May afternoon in the parlor to make his offer for Punch, she'd seen him nearly every week. He'd ridden over often from his father's plantation near Bear Swamp on the other side of the county.

She *had* been more than pleased with his offer. He'd proposed a very fair price for the horse, but asked if he could leave him to board at the Smiths' stable, telling Temperance he thought the horse would prosper there. He intended to race him as a three-year-old.

"I don't have a good spot for him at home, and I'm away so much he'd not get the attention he needs," he'd told Temperance that day, "but I'd be happy to pay you for his board and training. You and Mingo can work with him, and I'll ride over as often as I can to put him through his paces."

Since Drew Smith's death, Temperance had handled the day-to-day affairs of the plantation with the occasional advice of her father's brother, her Uncle James. Elizabeth Smith was content with this course of action. She had relied completely on her husband, bearing him four daughters who lived, and two sons, one stillborn and one who lived but two days. When Drew had sickened the previous fall, her helplessness was apparent. Her very existence was built on the pleasure she brought her adoring husband. Temperance's fifteenth birthday passed unnoticed, for Drew had been so sick. He had rallied after Christmas, but then died quietly on the last day of February, his big calloused hand in Elizabeth's small, soft one.

Tom Hunter had been courting Priscilla for more than a year, and they married quietly the Sunday after Easter with just their families present. Elizabeth had protested the unseemliness of their wedding coming so soon after Drew's death, but Temperance weighed in on that issue.

"They've waited long enough, Mama. Tom has their house built and furnished. With the slaves and the land Papa left her, they'll be fine. And if people gossip—well, let them. There will be something else for them to talk about soon enough!"

And today was her sixteenth birthday. Rose had waked her that morning with a hug and kiss for her favorite of the children. "You's sixteen, Miss Temp!"

Temp had hugged her old nursemaid in return. "Good day, Rose!" A little shiver of expectation had run through her. Philip had promised to come today! They had grown so close the last months. On his frequent visits, they spent mornings working with Punch, of course, but afternoons often found them riding down by the river, where they would let their horses graze while they sat on the grass in the shade of the trees. They would talk the time away, watching the Roanoke slowly make its way to the sea.

Some afternoons, during that magical summer, they took Millie and Anne on fishing expeditions, driving one of the carts down to the bank. Philip welcomed the company of the children, and in turn, the girls came to love him and added him to their prayers at night.

Occasionally, when Priscilla and her husband came driving over to visit from their home in Northampton County, Temperance and Philip took tea with Elizabeth, as her husband had often done when guests came. Elizabeth would preen in her finery, with powdered wig and jewels at her throat and ears. Philip was always first to compliment her.

Other afternoons, Lucy packed a basket with cold meat pies and fruit and bottles of ale, and they'd while the afternoon away until dusk. Then Philip would ride to the tavern in Scotland Neck to spend the night before making his way back to his father's house.

Temperance gradually came to know Philip's life. She learned that Philip was the second oldest of his father's sons. He and his older brother John and his younger brother William, along with his sister Pattie, had lost their mother, Elizabeth Chancy Alston, when Philip was eight, William not yet three, and Pattie still a baby. Joseph John had remarried within the year after her death, a Mistress Euphan Wilson, who had borne him four more children: Willis, who was about Temperance's age, Harry, Mary, and little Euphan, who was two now. The two little girls were dear to Philip, who often talked about them.

ONE GOLDEN MORNING, as Philip lifted Temperance down from Punch, he laughed suddenly. "I know what you remind me of. Your eyes are as dark and bright as the eyes of my grandmother Alston's little linnet bird that my grandfather had sent from England, and I vow you're not much heavier than a bird!" After that, he often called her "Linnet."

"Tell me about your mother," Temperance had asked Philip one day in early fall, when they had finished their picnic and were comfortably seated, Philip leaning against the broad trunk of their favorite tree and Temperance cross-legged on a blanket nearby.

"I remember her quite well," Philip said. "They called her Betsy. She was quiet and always loving to us. Her mother, Deborah

Symonds, was a Quaker, but married an Anglican, and that's how we were raised. Father always made sure we were in church on Sunday mornings, lined up in our pew, and that Mother was with us.

"John and I thought she was very pretty. I remember especially her hair. It was dark like mine. Sometimes at night she'd tell us stories, with her hair hanging over her shoulders. She spent a great deal of time with us. She loved to play with us and to listen to John and me recite our lessons. I recall Father getting very angry with her once when he found her down on her knees playing jacks with me. It seems they were expecting guests, and Mother had quite forgotten the time. When he came in, we were laughing, because our little gray kitten had gotten the ball and was batting it around the room. Father told her with fury that she was no better than the commonest slave to be down on the floor with the children. He kicked out at the kitten and broke its spine. I recollect the poor creature twitched for the longest minute until it died. It broke William's heart."

"Oh, Philip. How horrible! What did your mother do?"

"What *could* she do? She got up without saying a word, picked up the little furry body, and left, warning us with a shake of the head not to say anything to Father. William cried for hours that night. I finally crawled into bed with him. Truth be told, I needed comforting, too." Philip looked over at Temperance. Her face was white and still, and tears stood pooled in her dark eyes.

"I've made you sad," he said. "We can't have that!" Reaching behind her ear, he produced an acorn. "Good heavens, Linnet! The squirrels have already begun storing their nuts for the winter in that tangle of curls you call hair. Chances are they'll never find them again."

Temperance managed a giggle, but her heart ached for the blue-eyed boy who had held his little brother while he cried himself to sleep.

That night, as Temperance readied herself for bed, she thought again of the sad little boy who had grown into such a kind young man. Her prayers were fervent for Philip and his sister and brothers, and for the soul of Betsy Alston.

Philip occupied her thoughts when he was not with her. She found herself planning things to tell him. She always could make him laugh with her stories of just ordinary happenings. She remembered that dimple in his cheek and longed to touch it. She wondered how his lips would feel on hers. Sometimes her finger would trace "Philip" on whatever she was holding. "P" with a flourish, "h," "i," then a loopy "l," another "i" a final "p," with a long tail hanging, then back to dot the "i"s. A perfect name. Papa had taught her a little Greek, and she knew that "philos" was "love." And "Alston." She'd sometimes murmur "Temperance Alston" to herself, then blush and look around to see if anyone had heard.

She would have been very surprised to learn that the fashionable gentleman who listened to her stories so attentively and who teased her little sisters and shared their games was nothing like the Philip Alston others knew. He had earned the reputation throughout the eastern part of North Carolina of being a shrewd, even unscrupulous, businessman as he went about his duties as his father's agent, arranging the sale and shipping of the naval stores and tobacco produced on Joseph John's vast holdings. He was also a gambler, racing horses himself at the private tracks at the big homes of the colony and wagering on his horses and those of others.

And as Philip would ride back along the moonlit road to a tiny room above the noisy tavern, he thought with tenderness of the grief in his little Linnet's eyes as she listened to memories he had not shared with anyone else. He and William had never spoken of that night. It had been followed so soon by the sudden death of their mother, and the bleakness that had enveloped the household. It had seemed to Philip that all the colors of the world had turned to grays. Now Pattie at fourteen was docilely content with her role as the very eligible eldest daughter to a wealthy plantation owner. Whoever she chose to marry would be deeded an estate by her father. John was also busy with his father's businesses, married now to Ann Macon, raising a family of his own, and William was calling on Anne Yeargan, the daughter of Samuel Yeargan, who was making a name for himself preaching, and a match was being discussed by their fathers. His brothers and sister were at ease in the world. Why did it seem to be such a tight fit for Philip? The only comfort he found was in listening to his little Linnet chatter on so merrily, and in watching her animated face.

There had been times in the past, when, staying in taverns while on business for his father, that Philip would engage the services of a tavern girl. Now, for whatever reason, he was not tempted to pay for their company. The smiling face of a brown-eyed young woman filled his mind.

It's late. I should go back to the house, Temperance thought, and turned and started back down the road. Was that the sound of hoof-beats? Her heart gave a sudden leap, and she turned again, and peered into the gathering darkness. Yes, it was!

"Philip!" she called. "I'd nearly given up watching for you." He was alongside now, and swinging down from his black horse Demon, took her outstretched hands in his. In the dim light, she saw he was not alone. A thin dark-skinned boy was following on a roan.

"Temperance, this is Dave." Philip gestured towards the boy on horseback and handed him Demon's reins. "Dave, take the horses and go around to the stable. It's that way," he said, pointing to the road leading behind the house. "Ask for Mingo, and tell him Mr. Alston said to look after the horses and find you something to eat and a place to sleep tonight."

"I have something to talk to you about, Linnet." Philip tucked her under his arm as Dave rode off, leading Demon. "Are you too cold to walk with me a few minutes?"

"No, I'm fine. Are you all right, Philip?"

"Yes. No. It's better, now I'm here."

"Has something happened, Philip?"

"I've quarreled with my father. I won't go back there again."

"Philip! Why?" Temperance knew only what Philip had told her of Joseph John Alston. She had never met him. She knew him, from Philip's accounts, to be a distant man, obsessed with increasing his estates and his importance in the colony.

"We'll talk of that later, I promise, but now I need to know one thing. Do you think you could learn to care for me?"

"Care for you? I *do* care for you, as do my sisters. You are very dear to us." Temperance could feel her face growing hot, and her heart seemed too big for her chest. What was he saying? Oh, please, God, let it be what I think.

"No, little Linnet, that's not what I mean. Can you love me as a man, as your husband?"

Temperance drew back from the shelter of his arm to look up at his face. In the moonlight, his eyes were turned to hers. As he waited for her answer, his eyes were anxious.

"Oh, Philip, I could love you as whatever you choose to be to me. You have been my friend. If this is what you choose, then, yes. I can love you forever as my husband."

She felt a release of breath from Philip as he drew her into his arms. His head bent to hers, and his lips met hers in their first kiss, a kiss filled with the promise of a lifetime of kisses.

LINN: THREE
Tuesday afternoon

L INN WAS ALONE IN THE HOUSE. Although the high school was out for the summer, her mother Anne was enrolled in a weeklong staff development course for teachers, and she had driven away shortly after Linn's father, Bill McKinney, left the house for his office. The office was at the law firm of Sullivan, Drake, and McKinney, and the house was an older, two-story brick colonial, in a tree-lined suburb of Atlanta. Linn had spent most of the morning pacing the floor, trying to think, trying to formulate a plan. She had buried the sausage her mother left for her deep in the garbage can, and settled for some coke and crackers for lunch. After that, still nearly frantic with worry, she dragged the vacuum cleaner from the broom closet.

Their old dog, Moonshine, struggled to his feet from his regular afternoon spot in front of the window as she pushed the vacuum into the living room.

"Aw, come on, Shiny. The vacuum's not going to get you!" The elderly basset looked reproachfully at her from bloodshot eyes. He waddled out of the room and headed with great dignity for the kitchen. Linn's thoughts circled as she pushed the vacuum over the living room rug.

That awful night with that awful boy. On a Thursday, a girl she barely knew in her English Comp class had asked her if she was doing anything Friday night. "Why?" Linn had asked.

"My boyfriend's having a party. He's got a friend who needs a date."

"I don't know. What's he like?"

"He's a sophomore, on the football team. Maybe you've heard of him—Jake Munro?"

"Oh, okay," said Linn. Not that she'd heard of him, but, then, football didn't mean a whole lot to her.

"So, do you want to go?"

"I guess."

"Great! What dorm are you in?

"Winslow."

"Jake will pick you up around 8:30. Be out front. See ya!"

Linn hadn't really dated in high school. All her spare moments went to swim team practice and keeping up with her classes. She had friends. She and some of the girls from swim team were pretty tight. She knew she was considered sort of nerdy. Her grades were always good, and she was in AP courses. Prom was a blind date, too, arranged by Gran, who didn't want her to miss her prom—the grandson of her father's law partner, who came from his prep school out of town to take her. And who hadn't let her forget what a favor it was. He spent the evening talking about his school, his friends, and where they were going on vacation, and all the hot babes that would be there. Linn, in her beauty-salon hairdo and her uncomfortable, expensive prom dress, both paid for by her grandmother, could hardly wait for the night to end.

Linn asked around and found out that the party on Friday was informal. She went back to her room Thursday evening after dinner downstairs in the dining room and rooted through the closet. She tried on several outfits and rejected them before settling on a short khaki skirt that showed off what she considered her best feature, her legs. She chose a loose yellow sweater that she thought camouflaged her wide shoulders and her breasts—or lack of them. On top of that she added a jeans jacket and chose a pair of brown flats.

Friday after supper in the dining hall—at which she could eat very little of the baked fish—she hurried up to the fourth floor and showered, washed her hair, and shaved her legs. She tried several arrangements with her honey-brown hair before deciding to leave it loose.

Dressed, she was downstairs by 8:20. At 8:28, she went outside. At 8:45, just before she gave up looking both ways down the street, a car pulled up, a window was rolled down, and a voice said, "You Linn?"

"Yes. Are you Jake?"

"Get in, honey. Let's roll!"

The young man in the driver's seat was stocky. Linn stole sideways glances. Acne. Too bad. But the blond hair was okay. Could be worse.

They were only a few minutes from the house where the party was going on, so there was little time for conversation. He found out that Linn was from Atlanta and a freshman. She found out that he hoped to be a starter next year on the football team. She was pre-law; he was majoring in Phys. Ed. and planned on being a high school football coach. Maybe a college coach.

The party was a nightmare. Linn couldn't hear what was said to her, because the music and the hoots of laughter were so loud. Most of the girls were showing a whole lot more skin than she was. Jake abandoned her after the first fifteen minutes. After that she propped against a wall and tried to look as if she were having fun. She was near the punch table, which had a huge bowl of a sweet purple punch.

She'd had way too much to drink of it, and her head was spinning when her blind date, Jake—oh, yeah, that was his name— led her to his car. Linn leaned her head back against the headrest. Without talking, he drove to the park by the river and stopped the car in the shadow of a big oak, well away from the light-posts. In a fog, Linn didn't argue when he got out of the car and came around to her side and helped her out. His voice sounded far away when he said, "Let's get in the back seat. We'll be more comfortable."

In the back seat, he said, "Let me help you take off that

jacket." He tossed it to the front seat, and then his face loomed near. His lips met hers in a wet kiss.

"No, stop!" Linn said, and tried to push him away. "Please don't!" she said against his mouth, squirming. His body pinned her against the seat, and he pushed her skirt up with one hand, ripping her panties with the other. Linn was so dizzy. This seemed to be happening to someone else. What was he doing?

"No! I mean it. No!" She managed to get a knee up and drove it into his groin. "Stop it. Get off me!" She raked his cheek with her nails, trying to get a finger in his eye.

"Bitch!" he said, and climbed off. "To hell with this. You're not worth it. I'm taking you back to the dorm, and I'm going back to the party. There are other girls." As she sat up, there was a feeling of upheaval in her stomach, and she leaned out of the door and vomited.

When her stomach was empty, and she was shuddering, Jake handed her a piece of cloth. "Here, wipe your mouth." She did, and then looked down at the material she held. It was her panties.

"Get in the front seat. And tell me if you're going to puke again. I don't want my car stinking." She made several attempts to find a pocket in her skirt and finally located her jacket and stuffed the torn panties in one of its pockets. Jake started the car, and backed out from under the tree, gravel crunching under the wheels. After a silent ride, he pulled up in front of her dorm and called out, "Hey!" to a girl going in. "Can you get her to her room? She's pretty wasted."

The girl, Marcie, an R.A. on her floor, called a friend over, and supporting Linn between them, they got her to the elevator and then down the hall to her room. Meg was in bed, but got up when Linn was brought in.

"Oh, my God, Linn! You're drunk! Are you okay?"

Linn sank down on the bed and passed into oblivion. She didn't feel Meg and the other girls taking her shoes off and covering her with a blanket, before they turned out the lights.

THE NEXT MORNING WAS HORRIBLE, of course. She knew Meg was leaving early to go to go to an art show at a gallery in downtown

Boston, and she lay still, feigning sleep, until Meg was dressed and gone. Linn's head throbbed, and she sank in and out of sleep. About noon, she made it to the shower room down the hall. The mirror over the sink showed redness around her mouth, but what was more terrifying to Linn was the realization of how close she'd come to being raped.

Marcie, the R.A., came by in the early afternoon. "Hey, Linn, are you okay? You were in pretty bad shape last night. Sort of surprised me. It's not like you. What happened?"

"There was this purple punch at the frat house. It didn't taste too bad, and I drank a lot of it, I guess. I don't really remember. Then that guy, Jake Munro, took me by the river and . . ." the tears started again, "he tried to rape me." She was sobbing now.

Marcie sat down by her on the bed. "You need to report that."

"No, I can't. I can't! I just want to forget it ever happened. Promise me you won't tell anybody. Promise!" Linn was crying. "I'm all right, really."

"If that's what you want, Linn, but I still think...."

"No, I'll be okay. I just don't want to talk about it." She turned her face into the pillow.

Soon after that, Linn went home for spring break. She tried to put the whole thing out of her mind when she got back to school, but then Gran died, and she made the round trip home again. Back at school, she grimly finished out the semester. She saw Jake twice on campus, and both times he walked right by her without any sign of recognition.

The girls on her floor were all busy talking about housing for the fall. Meg was moving into an apartment with some friends. Nobody said anything to Linn. Guess they'll have to fix me up with another roommate, if I have to come back, she thought. She and Meg had little in common. Meg was an art major, and didn't spend much time in the room. She was usually off with friends or in a studio in the art building creating her sculptures.

And it wasn't that anyone was unfriendly to her. She just hadn't found close friends like the girls from swim team. She could hang out in the lounge on her floor and watch TV or a movie and nobody was rude or anything. I just don't fit in there, she thought.

Maybe I should have reported Jake. Wonder what would have happened? Would anybody have believed me? What could I have said? "He almost raped me?" That sounds dumb. And I was drunk. So it was partly my fault.

Shaking her head to clear it of the thoughts that chased themselves around in circles, Linn put the vacuum cleaner away, and, feeling a little empty, threw a slice of bread in the toaster and spread some chunky peanut butter on it to take up to her room. The boxes she'd brought from GeeGee's house were full of files. Gran had asked if she'd enter the data on her computer using genealogy software and then gave her the CDs for the program she'd already bought.

"If you weren't willing, Linn, I was going to try to do it myself, but you'll do a great job, I know! Keep up with your hours. I'm paying you for your time."

Sinking onto her bed, with the piece of toast in her mouth and scattering crumbs, Linn pulled out one of the files: "Joseph John Alston." She knew he was Philip Alston's father. She looked through some of the papers. Gosh, he owned a lot of land. Thousands of acres in North Carolina! And here was a copy of his will. She read it through. It was a long complicated document, and she was nearly at the end, with descriptions of pieces of land bounded by this creek or someone's property, before she realized that although other children and grandchildren were given big chunks of land and slaves, of all the sons, Philip got only "all the negro slaves which I allotted for him being now in his possession."

Slaves. Drew Smith's will had mentioned a number of slaves by name, also. So weird to think you could own people, as well as horses and cows and land. And sell them or "allot" them to your kids.

And what was *this* bequest about? "It is my will and desire that my negro woman Lucy, the cook wench, shall enjoy her liberty after my decease in the same manner as a free-born person."

Elizabeth SMITH HAD BEEN MORE THAN A LITTLE SURPRISED when Temperance and Philip Alston came into the house that evening hand-in-hand two weeks earlier to announce that they were to be wed, as soon as possible.

"I need to return to my father's to settle my business, Mistress Smith, but I'll be back by the end of the first week of December. Temperance tells me she can be ready to leave by then."

"To leave? But where are you going?"

"To Georgia, Mama!" Temperance burst out before Philip could answer. "There's land to be had for the asking. We'll build a house and settle down there."

Elizabeth was dumbfounded and wished heartily for the advice of her husband. Surely Drew could have talked Temperance out of this foolish venture. But, as the three sat in the dining room with Philip while he ate a bowl of warmed-up stewed chicken, she listened to Philip's confident plan for their future. He would go back to Halifax and claim his share of his inheritance. His father could give him some slaves and sell off some land if necessary. He'd be back in a week or so with wagons and oxen, as well as horses to ride, with supplies and household goods. In the morning, before he left, he'd go into Scotland Neck and post the marriage bond, if Temperance's brother-in-law and her uncle would act as sureties. And if Temperance could supply some linens and such, and be ready for a wedding in the Kehukee Chapel when he returned, then they could leave for Georgia before the winter weather set in.

Elizabeth sent for her brother-in-law James as soon as Philip left. Her misgivings were confirmed, and she dispatched Rose to summon Temperance to the parlor. But all of her uncle's warnings about Philip's reputation as reckless and hot-tempered had no effect on Temperance.

"You don't know him as I do!" Temperance insisted. "He's kind and funny, and I know he loves me!"

James could find no fault with Philip's plans for their future, and he knew Temperance as well as she knew Philip. She would not be swayed.

When James left the next morning, Elizabeth again called for Rose.

"Oh, Rose, you're going to have to talk to her about wedded life, as you did with Priscilla." Elizabeth's fair cheeks were pink.

"You jes' leave it to me, Miss Elizabeth. Miss Temp has been seein' animals all her life. She knows more' n you think she does." Rose smiled. She had not missed the signs of Temperance's falling in love with Philip. "It'll be jes' fine."

Rose and Temperance had a long conversation that night in Temperance's bedroom, while Rose brushed out her curls. "That first time may hurt a little bit, but jes' you be patient. The ways a man and woman can love each other are gonna be some of your bes' times. What you two do at night ain't nobody's business but yourn, and if you both is happy, then that's all that matters. Let him teach you what feels good. And never let Mr. Philip think you don't want to be with him, and don't never turn him down 'cause you're mad at him. I think he's a good man, deep down, and I think he'll learn to be an even better man with you."

And now it was morning on December 6th, the wagons were loaded with supplies and goods, and accompanied by five slaves, who had bedded down in the barn the night before. Elizabeth came out of the house with a small wooden crate in her arms.

"Temperance, take this with you to remember me by. It's the white pitcher your father had sent from England that last year before he died."

"Oh, I can't take that, Mama. He bought it for you. I know you treasure it."

"That's why I want you to have it. You have been such a blessing to me." Her voice broke. She handed the box to Philip and watched as he settled it carefully in one of the wagons.

"It will have place of honor on the mantelpiece in our new home, Mistress Elizabeth."

Temperance was wet-eyed but beaming with happiness, while she and Philip said their goodbyes to the family, and to Rose, Mingo, and the other household slaves.

"I'll write as often as I can, Mama!" The horses were saddled, and Dave held their reins. Elizabeth Smith looked again at the tall, slender, light-skinned slave who waited so stolidly. There was something about the way he carried himself. He seemed prideful for a slave. He caught her eyes and held his head a little higher.

ELIZABETH COULD NOT HAVE KNOWN, and indeed, would never know, the tale that Philip had told Temperance, as she lay in his arms after their wedding. The ceremony had been attended only by Temperance's immediate family, as was the dinner following. Temperance wore her best dress, a cream-colored silk with pink and blue flowers embroidered along the bodice. Around her neck she wore the pearls her father had given her. Her curls were tamed and pinned up on her head.

After dinner, Philip took Temperance to her bedchamber early, pleading an early morning departure. He missed the knowing smirk of his new brother-in-law, Tom Hunter.

Rose had helped Temperance out of her dress and stays, loosed her hair, and left her standing shivering in her shift, telling Philip, waiting awkwardly in the hall, "Miss Temp's ready for you now, sir."

"Dear little Linnet, how good it is to hold you," he murmured against her curls, having shut the door firmly behind him. "I've missed being able to talk to you.'

"You promised to tell me why you left your father's house. It's cold. Come to bed and tell me now, Philip." Temperance climbed up on the bed, crawled under the covers, and patted the pillow beside her. Philip turned his back to her, slipped out of his clothes, jumping on one foot and then the other as he pulled off his boots and jerked the hose from his legs. Temperance watched his clumsiness with a smile, and looked at the way his broad shoulders narrowed down to his waist. She blushed when he turned around, but although her eyes widened, she kept her smile. She patted the pillow again, and lifted the quilts so he could climb in beside her.

"You know that my mother died when I was a boy. I have only recently learned the circumstances of her death, and the part my father played in it. This is what happened." The words came tumbling out as he pulled a pillow up against the headboard of the cherry bed and settled his long legs under the quilts. Temperance leaned against him, and he put an arm around her.

"My father had arranged to sell Dave as a field hand to a neighbor who was moving west. Dave is just thirteen. Lucy, Dave's mother, who works in the kitchen, came to me to beg me to talk with my father to prevent the sale. I told her I thought I'd have little effect. Joseph John Alston seldom listens to advice from others."

'But Mr. Philip, sir,' she said to me. 'Dave is your brother! He belongs here on this place with you and the others.'

"I must have looked confused, because she said, 'Your mama knew about it. Why you think she killed herself?'

"Killed herself!" For a minute I couldn't think, and then it came to me. I remembered a night when I heard my mother sobbing. And then in the morning, they told us she was dead."

"I don't understand, Philip," Temperance said, snuggling closer against him. She felt the black chest hairs beneath her cheek. My husband! she thought.

"I went from Lucy straight to my father. I was furious. I found him in his office. 'You're Dave's father,' I said. "He just stood there and looked at me and shrugged his shoulders."

"It's true, then. And my mother knew about it."

"My father turned away to the window. 'Such things happen all the time. A man has certain rights with his slave women. I don't know why Betsy was so distressed when she found Lucy and me together. If she hadn't gone out to the kitchen herself that night to make a honey potion to quiet William's cough, instead of sending a slave—she spoiled you children— I told her it meant nothing, but she just kept weeping and weeping. She shut herself in her room and told me to go on back to Lucy. So I did. In the morning, we found the empty laudanum bottle by her bed. She was a weak woman, Philip.'"

"Linnet, I lost my temper. I called him a sanctimonious hypocrite and worse. I knew he was a harsh man, but I had always thought he was honorable. When I think of him sitting there in church every Sunday listening to sermons that he could not admit applied to him . . . Did he think his wedding vows meant nothing? And then, he was married again before six months had passed."

Temperance was very quiet. She reached for Philip's hand and held it tight. "Linnet," he said, "I swear to you that you will never have reason to doubt my faithfulness. I will love you and only you."

"I believe you, Philip. You promised in church before God..."

"God! God has nothing to do with it. God was not there when my mother was in pain. My promise is from my own heart to yours, and I will always honor that promise."

Temperance made a sound of protest, but Philip took her face in his hands and kissed her. "We'll talk tomorrow. We'll always talk to each other, but now..." This kiss was deeper. Temperance smiled and lengthened her body against his. Her arms closed trustingly around her husband.

LINN: FOUR
Tuesday evening

LINN OFFERED TO WALK MOONSHINE WHILE MOM COOKED. The meal was a childhood favorite of hers—Mom's special baked chicken with rice and butterbeans. Mom did most of the talking at the table. The course she was taking was interesting to her, and she chattered on to Linn about how she'd use what she was learning with her A.P. students. Dad, as usual, was quiet. Linn wasn't sure how much longer she could keep her Mom in the dark. Mom was usually pretty observant. Dad, now, that was a different story. She and her Mom had often joked that once Bill McKinney was home, he wouldn't notice a dead body in the house unless it was sitting in his recliner.

After supper she helped her mother clean up the kitchen. Then Anne brought her books to the kitchen table and started making notes on an assignment. Soon she was deeply immersed in the reading.

Linn stood in the door for a moment, uncertain. What should she do? She headed into the family room, where her Dad was watching a Braves game from the comfort of his leather recliner, Shiny snoring serenely at his feet. "Who's winning?" she asked.

"The Braves are ahead by a run right now, but the Phillies have men on base. No, you idiot!" he shouted at the TV. "Well, that's a home run. Three men in. Guess they'll take the pitcher out now. They should have pulled him at the beginning of the inning. Could you bring me a beer, Linn?"

"Sure."

Her mother looked up when Linn came back in the kitchen. "What do you need, honey?"

"I'm just getting Dad a beer."

"Well, take him that can of peanuts on the counter while you're at it."

After Linn handed her father the beer and peanuts and received a distracted "Thanks" from him, she headed slowly upstairs. When she was home for GeeGee's funeral, she had no time to spend with any of her friends, but she'd promised to call so they could all get together when she got home for the summer. Maybe she should call Julie and see if she'd like to hang out. No, Julie's counseling at Camp Mikell this month. She didn't really feel like talking to anyone anyway. I'll bet Dad's going to be asking soon when I'll start work.

Up in her room, she plugged in her earbuds and selected R.E.M.'s "Out of Time." Her cousin Rob, Aunt Sue and Uncle Jack's younger son, was a huge R.E.M. fan. He had gone to the University of Georgia and was in grad school in North Carolina now. Rob played guitar and had reluctantly given up dreams that his band, Penguins from Hell, would ever play at the 40 Watt where some of the great Athens bands had started out. Michael Stipe's voice informed her that the world was collapsing around his ears.

You don't know how right you are, she thought. My ears, too. What am I going to do? She caught a glimpse of herself in the mirror over the dresser. There were still deep circles under her eyes. Well, I don't want to think about it right now.

She turned to the laptop on her desk and pulled the box of folders nearer. There were some copies of petitions by Philip Alston for land in St. George's Parish. GeeGee's handwriting in the margin identified that as "now Burke County, Georgia." That was in

August of 1765, and Philip stated that he had had been in the province three years and was asking for 150 acres.

So Philip and Temperance had lived in Georgia. There were big atlases of North and South Carolina in one of the boxes, as well as one of Georgia. Linn pulled out the Georgia atlas. Burke County. Waynesboro was the county seat. The petition was asking for land on the Savannah River at a place called Boggy Gut. Linn looked closely at the map. Yes, there it was! Boggy Gut Creek, running into the Savannah River. She found the family record sheet on Philip Alston and looked at the list of Philip and Temperance's children. James. Born circa 1765, probably in Georgia. Then John, about 1767, and then, about 1770, Elizabeth. Both also born "probably in Georgia." Then five other children, including a Temperance and a Philip, were born in North Carolina.

Linn looked at the data she had already entered. If Temperance, the mother, was born about 1747, then she was probably 18 when her first son was born. Just a little younger than I am, she thought. And by the time she was 23, she had three kids. She remembered a conversation she and GeeGee had once about her genealogy research. GeeGee said babies came along pretty regularly in those days, and if there was a gap in birth dates, it probably indicated a baby who hadn't lived. Guess they didn't care any more about birth control than Jake apparently did. She was maybe a little foggy about that night, but she was absolutely sure no condom was involved in his attack on her.

I wonder if she was as scared as I was. I was probably the only virgin in that dorm. But she was in love with Philip. At least I hope she was. I sure wouldn't want anyone like Jake to be the first. But so far I don't have anybody to BE first. Wish I had someone to talk to. My life is so messed up.

There's Gran. Gran would listen. Without freaking out. Maybe I can talk to Gran before Mom figures out something's going on.

*T*emperance PUSHED HER HAIR BACK, tucking a wayward sprig behind her ear with her right hand, as she balanced little Elizabeth on her left hip. She could hear Philip calling brisk orders to the men. The wagons were loaded. She'd made sure the wooden box holding the white pitcher brought from home was safely nestled among some folded quilts. She'd kept the pitcher filled with something fresh or fragrant these years in Georgia—daffodils in the spring, daisies when they bloomed, roses in mid-summer, or just bright-colored leaves in the fall and wild holly at Christmas.

She looked back over her shoulder. The door stood open to the empty log house she'd called home for the last what? Nearly ten years. She was twenty-five now, no taller than she'd been at sixteen when she'd married, but certainly rounder. Childbirth had a way of adding curves to a woman's body. Philip, on the other hand, was no heavier, but Temperance had found the first gray hair at his temple and teased him unmercifully about it. "Your day will come, Linnet Bird, when your feathers will turn gray, too!" he'd said, with a rueful smile.

The journey to Georgia had been arduous, but she was so

warmed by Philip's love—and lovemaking—each night as they camped under the bed of one of the wagons, a discreet distance from the others, that it seemed an idyllic adventure. One of the men put together a supper when they stopped each night at dusk and handed out cold food when they paused briefly late mornings to rest the oxen and horses. Punch had been left behind, sold to Mr. Brumble after all. "He's trained to race, little Linnet," Philip had told her when she protested, and she had to agree he was right. Life on the frontier would not have suited the high-spirited horse.

THE WEATHER HELD, except for a stretch of bone-chilling drizzly days. Philip smiled at Temperance's red nose, which was all that showed when she pulled the hood of her brown cloak well down over her face. She kept her cheerful manner during the spell of bad weather, but when the sun broke through late one morning, she admitted to herself how miserably cold she'd been.

Philip had bought some land downriver from Fort Augusta near Boggy Gut Creek and in the next few years he petitioned for and received additional acreage adjoining his purchase, close to McBean's swamp. The first months were hard for Temperance. She was accustomed to meals appearing as if by magic on the table and clean clothing turning up fresh and sweet-smelling in the clothes press. Philip and the men he'd brought with them had quickly gone to work to erect a lean-to shed. Temperance realized with a shock that with all the men laboring from sun-up to sun-down, clearing and stacking logs, she was expected to provide food for them from the dried stores they'd brought along. Most evenings there was game—usually rabbit— to add to the beans or corn and onions in the pot. Water had to be fetched from the creek, and a fire kept going. At least the men provided the firewood!

There were no complaints from the men about the corn pone she burned, or the chewy meat, and she learned quickly, with Major offering quiet suggestions.

Spirits were high. Philip expected hard work from the slaves, but willingly worked alongside them. At first he raised blisters on his slim hands, but calluses formed. Temperance had gotten to know the men in the evenings on the journey to Georgia. The first few nights they sat respectfully at a distance from her and Philip, sharing the evening meal, but Temperance's friendliness drew them into conversation.

All but Dave, that is. She was still trying to figure out this light-skinned boy with the sprinkling of large freckles across his face. Philip treated him as he did the other slaves, and Dave was deferential to Philip, looking to him for directions when there was a decision to be made. She wondered if the other slaves knew that Joseph John Alston was Dave's father, and decided they probably did. She knew from what Philip had said that such happenings were common. Dave seldom talked and didn't enter into the banter of the other men around the campfire at night. He slept, rolled up in blankets, a little apart from them.

The other men were hard workers. She imagined Philip had chosen them for that reason. There was the one called Major, who told her he thought he was about fifty—old to be as tough as he was. And there were Joe, Silus and Cesar. Joe and Silus were brothers in their twenties, young and strong. Cesar was probably close to thirty, with a wonderful voice. He, if asked, would sing for them at night around the fire. Temperance learned the songs and joined in, her clear alto providing harmony.

AFTER THEY ARRIVED IN GEORGIA, the men cleared some land for crops to be planted when the soil warmed, built a lean-to, and then began work on the cabin. There was one large room, with a fireplace at one end. Within a month, Temperance and Philip were able to move in, and life became simpler. Being able to stay warm and having a fireplace to cook in made the chores easier. Enclosures went up, and then a smaller house for the men. Philip took Dave and a wagon and rode upriver to Fort Augusta to the trading post. He came home with a squealing wagonful of piglets and three cows roped to the back, trailing behind.

Rolled up behind Philip's saddle was a bearskin for the floor beside the bed. Philip laughed at Temperance's delight that night as she sat on the side of the bed and wiggled her toes in the fur.

"You're an easy woman to please," he said, and reached for her.

As the days lengthened, sometimes the men went fishing in the early mornings or late afternoons. Temperance went along when she could. She had always enjoyed fishing, and the catch made a change in the usual fare.

Crops went in. Philip rode off by himself in early June in a wagon, leaving Temperance in charge. She still remembered her initial misgivings. She knew very little about the actual work of farming and tending livestock. But Cesar kept the men busy, and her time at her father's side, and then managing the estate after his death, had taught her more than she realized.

When Philip returned, on a hot and steamy day towards the end of July, he had with him a rounded black woman driving the wagon, which was filled with dry goods and furniture. Cesar straightened from his work in the field with a slowly widening smile. Philip swung off his horse, with laughter, and stood braced for Temperance's assault as she raced to embrace him.

"Linnet, this is Dinah. I think Cesar already knows her."

Work began immediately on another little cabin. Philip told Temperance that night, as they lay together on the mattress of cornhusks, topped by the feather bed that Temperance had brought from home, that he had kept a promise he had made to Cesar. "I don't want to tell you how much my father's agent made me pay for her, but she'll be worth every penny, Linnet."

That proved to be true. Dinah took over the meals and washing. Temperance had suspected in late August that she was quickening. Dinah was the first one she told, even before Philip. Dinah smiled. "You been lookin' mighty green, Miss Temp, when I fry up the pork in the morning."

One rainy, cold morning in early April the next year, just before dawn, Dinah was able to lay a red-faced little boy in Temperance's arms. It had been a long night—and a long day before that—and Temperance was exhausted. Her ordeal was matched by Philip's, who was ordered from the house by Dinah. He hovered, within earshot, those long hours. Cesar tried to distract him. "It'll be fine, Mister Philip. Dinah's helped with a lot of birthin's. Come on. Let's go chop some wood."

But Philip was obstinate. For those long hours he paced. As the moon rose, he hunkered and shivered on the porch. Not far away, another figure leaned against a tree, waiting, too.

Temperance had spent some of her precious free hours since their arrival with Dave. She had discovered that, like the other slaves, he could not read or write, but unlike them, he was eager to learn. She had offered to have "school" in the evenings of the first summer, but Dave was the only one who was willing to take the time. He was a quick learner, and she enlisted Philip's help to teach him some simple math, as well as reading and writing. They had only a few books, but Philip liked to please Temperance, and he often brought a book or two when he returned from his travels, so their collection was growing.

That April morning, when he heard the baby's first squall, he rushed into the house. Dinah told him, "Go on out, now. I ain't finished here." But he refused. He knelt on the floor by the bed while Dinah tended to the cleanup of the birth.

Temperance smiled. She was sweaty, and her curls were matted, but to Philip she had never been so beautiful. "What are we going to call him? Shall we call him Philip?" Temperance asked.

"No, let's give him a name all his own. How about James?"

"For my uncle James. I like that. James it is."

"Miss Temp, that boy's on the porch. You want me to tell him to go on away?"

"No, bring him in, Dinah. I want him to see the baby."

A silent Dave approached the bed. Beaming, Temperance asked, "What do you think? Isn't he beautiful?" Dave nodded and backed away, bumping into a bench on his way out of the cabin.

Temperance was touched a few days later, when Dave came to the open door, his hand behind his back.

"What have you got there, Dave?"

Unsmiling, he brought out a little carved rabbit. "It's for your baby."

"It's lovely, Dave. It looks ready to hop away! You made this?"

"Yes, ma'am."

"Thank you so much. It's a wonderful gift!"

Little Jem was a strong baby, hungry all the time. The men—and Dinah—doted on him. In a basket, he oversaw the planting that spring. Philip made a trip to Savannah and brought back two young women and another field hand.

It wasn't long before the wooden rabbit had teeth marks in it. It seldom left Jem's pudgy fist. Dave brought Temperance a charming wooden mother bird, perched on the edge of a nest containing a baby bird with a gaping mouth. She put that on the mantel, next to her mother's pitcher. "It's too pretty to be chewed," she told Dave. "This one is mine."

Fifteen-year-old Dave was a difficulty. He didn't work well with the other slaves. He wouldn't take orders from Cesar, waiting instead for Philip's or Temperance's words. In the fall, after some discussion with Temperance in the evenings, Philip traveled again to Savannah and apprenticed Dave to a cabinet-maker.

Temperance found herself in charge of three women and the household affairs. The outbuildings sprang up, the fields grew larger. Philip became involved in selling livestock and naval stores, acting as agent for some of the other settlers in the area.

From time to time, some of the neighbors came to visit, or men who had business with Philip. Temperance welcomed visitors, but she saw few women besides Dinah, Jenny and Sall. Once, that first year, Philip took her across the river to George Galphin's trading post, a square brick building at Silver Bluff. Temperance was fascinated by the solemn Indians who came in to swap their deerskins for colorful cloth, shiny beads, and rum. George's little daughter, Susannah, a self-assured child of perhaps five, came to sit with Temperance in front of the fireplace. They were joined by Daniel MacMurphey, an Irishman a little older than Philip, who often went trading in the Indian towns scattered about the Southeastern colonies, and while Philip went about his bartering with George, she talked with Daniel, who answered her eager questions about his adventures with a delightful Irish lilt. Philip, watching her, smiled to see her excitement.

As they left, Philip steered her carefully around a group of Creeks outside the post, who were passing around a wooden cup filled with rum from a nearby keg. "That liquor will be the death of them," he whispered in her ear. "They'll not be taking a drop of it home with them. And I wouldn't want to be near any one of them come morning."

She came home with a bottle of hickory and walnut oil from the Chickasaws that added wonderful flavor to the thin cornmeal cakes that Dinah baked on the back of a hoe in the fire, and a length of brightly patterned cloth made for Indian tastes that she planned to incorporate into the quilt she was making for Jem. After that, when Philip went cross-river trading, he knew what to bring back for her.

IN THE SPRING OF 1766, she realized another child was on the way. This was an easier birth, and Philip was off on one of his trading trips, so she was already up and about the house when he came home one day in late fall.

As usual, she went out to meet him when the dogs alerted her to his approach. His eyes took in her newly slender figure, with Jem in her arms, and widened.

"Come inside and meet your new son!" she said, laughing. "He arrived a little beforetime, but he's just fine, and Jem is so glad to see you!" Jem was holding out his arms to his father and straining away from Temperance.

"Linnie! I should have been here. Are you well? How was it..." his voice trailed off as she reached up to pull him off Demon. He dismounted and took Jem from her.

"I'm very well. I haven't named him yet. Come on," she tugged impatiently.

Inside, Philip looked down at the tiny sleeping baby in the cradle that Cesar had made for Jem. "He's a fine-looking boy. Small. Linn, I didn't think he'd come so soon."

"I didn't either. He was a surprise. Are you hungry? There's stew and beans on the fire.

"Later. Tell me what happened."

"He was born last Tuesday. I woke up in the night to realize..." Temperance stopped.

"To realize what?"

"That my water was leaking." She giggled. "I very nearly ruined the bed. And he was born before midday. Poor nameless babe! So what are we calling him?"

Philip thought. "John? For my grandfather. Not for my father."

"John is good. I have an idea. You name the boys. I'll name the girls."

"My sweet little Linnet. I won't put you through this again."

"God decides when a child comes into the world," Temperance answered him.

"God," Philip said. "I don't want to hear about God."

Philip began talking about moving back to North Carolina after Elizabeth's birth. Her naming had been a matter of no discussion. "Elizabeth. For both our mothers," Temperance had said. Elizabeth was a frail child who fretted with colic. There had been a baby between John and Elizabeth, a girl, born tiny and still, three months before she was expected. Philip, silent and grim, had buried the perfectly-formed little body himself, in a hastily-nailed-together wooden box. He turned away, still holding the shovel, caked with gray mud, while Temperance and the women bowed their heads in prayer. He couldn't bear to see the silent tears rolling down his wife's cheeks. He wouldn't discuss a name for the baby, but Temperance called her Rachel in her thoughts and prayers, remembering the story of Benjamin's mother, who had died giving birth to him.

Temperance had been saddened to receive a letter from her sister Anne from North Carolina soon before Elizabeth's birth that her vain and beautiful mother had succumbed to a fever. Word from home was often slow in arriving, depending on who might be coming that way, so Elizabeth Smith had been nearly three months dead before her daughter in Georgia heard the news.

And Major had sickened with a fever and died in December, just before Christmas, in spite of Temperance's best efforts to reduce his fever with herb teas. She and Dinah made him as comfortable as they could in his little cabin, and one of the four women was always with him during his last days. He died as quietly as he had lived. He was buried by the grave of the tiny baby that Temperance thought of as Rachel, and Temperance wept, knowing how much she would miss the stocky gray-haired man who had kept Jem entertained with tales of a cunning spider who always bested his enemies. Temperance had laughed at the clever stories and tucked them away in her mind.

PHILIP MADE TWO TRIPS BACK TO NORTH CAROLINA to locate and buy property in Cumberland County on the Deep River at a horse-shoe bend. And now the time had come. Dave had rejoined the group, a young man of twenty-three. Philip had praised his skills, saying that Dave would be in charge of the woodworking for the house he was planning to build for his family. Privately, he talked about his doubts to Temperance.

"I don't know, Linnet. His master told me he's a talented carver, but he didn't make friends in Savannah, and he doesn't take correction well. He holds grudges against anyone he thinks may have wronged him or me. I'd sell him, but..." his voice trailed off.

"I think giving him responsibility for the woodwork in the house may be what he needs, Philip. And we can't sell him. This family is all he's ever known." Temperance had never forgotten what Philip had said on their wedding night about purchasing Dave from Joseph John Alston.

"There was just no place for him there," he'd said. "My father was already planning to sell him as a field hand. I promised Lucy I'd look after him. I don't hold her responsible for what happened to my mother. She wouldn't have had any choice in the matter."

Their group had changed. Cesar and Dinah had a little girl, Lindy, now. Jenny had been sold to the family on the next plantation so she could marry Jerry, who belonged to them. And Major was gone, of course. Philip had bought more slaves in North Carolina and left them behind to clear land and begin the building of what he was calling the "House in the Horseshoe."

LINN: FIVE
Wednesday morning

THERE WAS A BRIEF KNOCK AT THE KITCHEN DOOR while Linn was rinsing cereal bowls and coffee mugs and stashing them in the dishwasher she'd just emptied. Before she could get there, Gran pushed the door open with her hip and came in, carrying a cardboard box full of files, with a book balanced on top.

"Hi, honey. Is your Mom gone already?"

"Yes, you just missed her."

"Well, it was you I came to see anyway. I've got a book for you, and the rest of the boxes from GeeGee's. How's it going with the computer program?"

"Oh, fine. Slow. I keep stopping to read stuff."

"This book will slow you down even more!"

Gran handed Linn a thick book. It was entitled *A History of the House in the Horseshoe*, by someone named George W. Willcox.

"Wow," Linn said. "I saw on one of GeeGee's charts that Philip Alston built that house!"

She opened the book to find GeeGee's name, Linnie Anne Griffin Miller, and Mr. Willcox's "Best wishes" before his signature.

"I think one of the Alstons married a Willcox, so we're probably distantly connected," Gran told her. "I'm sure GeeGee would have known. I wish I'd had the good sense to ask her more about the family while I had the chance. Oh, well." She shook her head and went on. "How about coming to have supper with me tonight? I thought it would be fun to get together, just the two of us. I'll make that crab casserole that you and I like—and your dad hates!"

"Sure," Linn said, and then thought, Perfect. I want to talk to her alone anyway. Crab casserole. It does sound good. Maybe I'm getting my appetite back.

"Come over about 6:00. Now, come on out to the car with me and let's get the rest of those files. I've got to run. I'm due at Hospice in fifteen minutes." Gran volunteered at the local hospice on Wednesdays. She often complained that she was busier now than she'd ever been, but the whole family knew she enjoyed her "causes." Her special favorite was tutoring at the after-school program of the Boys and Girls Club.

Linn helped her bring in two more boxes, and waved goodbye. Good thing Mom was distracted right now by the class she was taking. Maybe if she talked to Gran tonight and told her how much she hated the university, how she wasn't fitting in, they could figure out a way to tell Mom and Dad. Her folks had been so proud when she'd been accepted by the prestigious school up north. She hated the thought of letting them down. Especially Dad. Ever since she could remember, he'd talked about her getting a law degree and coming into the firm with him. If only they'd had a son. Or even another daughter who would have wanted to be an attorney. Linn shook her head. I'm pretty sure that I know what I want to be, she thought. And I'm really sure I know what I *don't* want to be. Sometimes it's tough being an only child. At least, with a father like Dad.

Linn lugged the boxes up to her room and stacked them in a corner. She sank down on the edge of the unmade bed. Dad. He'd always expected so much of her. It wasn't that she wasn't capable of maintaining a near-perfect GPA in high school. That was really kind of easy, because she'd always been the good girl he wanted her to be. No drinking, no smoking—of any kind of substance. That kind of thing went on at the school. Just not with her and her friends. Not that they didn't have fun. There were movies and sleepovers. But Dad had always stressed the idea that major goof-ups could mess you up for a long time. Admitting she'd gotten drunk? What would Dad say? Maybe she'd never have to tell him about that. She shook her head. It was going to be tough enough to tell him about not going back in the fall. Since she could remember, Dad had always talked of the day when she would join the law firm.

Downstairs again, she pulled a container of spaghetti sauce from the freezer to thaw. The last thing Mom had said as she hurried out the door was "See if you can figure out something for supper." There were salad makings in the fridge, and Dad never got tired of spaghetti with Mom's sauce. You could always count on Dad. He was pretty predictable. And she was predicting he was going to be very disappointed with her.

Linn got a can of ginger ale from the fridge and pulled the pop top, enjoying the cheerful little metallic "cr-rack..." and headed for the sofa in the living room, *A History of the House in the Horseshoe* tucked under her arm.

Temperance LOOKED UP FROM WEEDING the rose bed in back of the house at the sound of hoof beats and a familiar voice calling, "Linnet!" Philip had a young boy on the saddle in front of him.

"Are we too late for dinner?" he said as he swung down for the saddle and lifted the boy off. "This is Hugh McDonald. Hugh, this is my wife." The red-haired boy, as Temperance got a better look, was perhaps thirteen or fourteen. His face was gaining the angularity of adolescence. He ducked his head at Temperance, and smiled, showing a gap between his teeth.

She heard the door behind her open.

"Jem, this is Hugh. Go to the kitchen house and ask Dinah to get dinner ready for your father and Hugh. Wait, take Hugh with you," she added as Jem jumped down off the side of the porch that ran the length of the front of the house. John was right behind him, as he always was.

"Tell me," she said to her husband as the three boys vanished on their way to the kitchen outbuilding. "You're gone a week, and you come home with a boy. Is there something I should know?" Philip laughed.

She took his hand and led him onto the porch as Dave came from the barn and took Satan's reins. Demon was an elder among the horses now and spent most of his days grazing in the pasture, but Philip took him out for short rides down by the river, often with Temperance alongside on her spirited mare, Brown Nell.

"Thank you, Dave. Unsaddle him and give him some water." Philip told the silent man. He knew Dave was sulking because he hadn't been taken along on the recruiting excursion.

"Linnie, the five of us were trying hard to raise some troops, but the word must have gotten out in front of us, because all the adult men had mysteriously disappeared, especially the ones who had fought with the British. We found Hugh pretending to plough a field near Bear Creek not too far from where Cagle, the Dutchman, lives, which is where we planned to muster. I say "pretending," because he sure couldn't handle that big horse and the plow. We'd found another boy earlier, young Tom Graham, to guide us, but he was worn out and already six miles from home. We wanted to send him on back, so Daniel Buie asked Hugh to take over and lead us to the next farm. He recognized Hugh—knows his father, I think. Hugh said his father would kill him if he went with us, but Buie put him up behind Jacob Gaster anyway and sent the other boy homeward.

"Hugh guided us from farm to farm, but when we thanked him and told him he could go back home, he wouldn't go. He said his father really *would* kill him, and he might as well go with us to the muster.

"I dismissed everyone at Henry Cagle's after the muster and brought Hugh on home with me. I couldn't figure what else to do with him."

"Oh, Philip," Temperance laughed. "Well, we'll figure out something. In the meantime, let's send word to Mr. McDonald, was it? and let him know Hugh's safe here. Maybe when he comes for him, I can talk to him. Surely he wouldn't *really* kill the boy for helping your militia."

"I'm not so sure of that. Hugh's pretty convinced he can't go back home. His father's one of the Loyalists who were paroled to come back home after the British and the Highlander companies were routed at Moore's Creek."

Jem and Hugh, with John tagging behind, reappeared. Jem said, "Dinah says she's sending Sall with some food, if you'll just go in the house and wash up, Papa."

Temperance invited Hugh to join her and the boys for their afternoon lessons after he and Philip had eaten, but he said, "I thank you kindly, Mrs. Alston, but I reckon I'll just go with Major Alston when he goes to Fayetteville tomorrow and join up with the Americans."

Temperance made a pallet for Hugh that night upstairs in the bedroom with her boys. With baby Temperance asleep across the big bedroom from her and Philip, she cuddled against her husband. It was good to have him here, if only for the night.

It had been a busy few years. Living in the house was such a change from life in the Georgia cabin. Gone were the days of hard work from dawn to dusk, but gone, too, was the freedom of dressing without stays and simply tying her curls back out of her face. She and the children had stayed with Tom Hunter and his wife, Priscilla, Temperance's pretty, fashionable sister, while the house was being built, and that had brought on a flurry of dressmakers, bonnetmakers, shoemakers—it seemed to Temperance that the fittings were endless. The children got new clothes, too. Little Elizabeth kissed herself in the looking glass, happy with her dress and ribbons. She was a pretty child and ruled her brothers with kisses and little pats on their faces when she wanted her way. Temperance smiled to think that she'd inherited some of her grandmother's nature, as well as her name and blonde hair.

The house built in the horseshoe bend was everything Philip had hoped. An itinerant Scotsman, a Mr. McFadden, had stayed around long enough to help Philip with the details of the design. The lumber had been sawed at the Irishman Connor Dowd's mill, a hub of local industry a few miles to the north. Dowd and his growing family also maintained a grist mill, a tannery, a distillery, a foundry, and a store.

Some twenty-five years earlier, Connor Dowd had arrived from Ireland to the Carolinas, bringing a motherless son, Owen, and nothing in his pockets. He was a charmer, and soon he married the very eligible widow Mary Overton Shields, who had two boys of her own and about 500 acres of property. Now you could take corn to be ground, get horseshoes fashioned, buy salt and come home with a bottle or two of whisky.

The Alstons' new white-painted house had two large rooms on each of the two floors, with a wide hall between, and an attic for storage under the eaves. A narrow staircase led upstairs from just inside the front door, which faced towards the river. The fireplace in the parlor was particularly handsome. Dave had done well with that. The downstairs rooms were painted a deep rich red, Philip's choice. Upstairs, the two bedrooms and the hall were gray. Philip had a small office built for himself on the front of the house, with an exterior door, as well as one leading into the main floor bedroom. "I can keep the accounts and do business without disturbing you," he'd said to Temperance, "but I'll be right there if you need me."

John Willcox's ironworks in nearby Gulf had produced the bricks for the two big chimneys, one on either end of the house. Philip had consulted Dinah about the design of the kitchen house, and she was proud of the two ovens built into the brick alongside its large deep fireplace. She had commandeered Sall to help with the cooking, and Sall, married to Joe and with two little ones, was becoming a fine pastry chef.

A row of cabins housed the slaves, except for Cesar and Dinah, who slept at the far end of the kitchen house so the fire could be kept going all night. Dave's cabin was nearest the house, set a little apart from the others, and was unique in its built-in bookcases on either side of the small fireplace. Dave had seen to that construction.

Temperance had time now to spend schooling her boys. Soon Elizabeth would join the morning session of classes. Jem was impatient, but quick, and John was an eager learner who strived hard to keep up with his brother. Several of the slaves had children, and Temperance had invited them to learn to read and write, and she made time for all who were interested. There was some quiet criticism of this by a few of the planters in the area, but none would have dared to talk openly about Philip Alston's wife. Philip would certainly not have countenanced such talk. And Temperance was well-liked by the neighboring wives for her friendliness and genuine concern.

PHILIP HAD PLUNGED HEADFIRST into the politics and law enforcement of the county. He relentlessly pursued horse thieves in the countryside, bringing charges against them in court. Tempers ran hot in Cumberland County. Men were choosing up sides; some, including many of the Scottish settlers, were siding with King George. Locally, Connor Dowd had sent supplies to the British Army. Others in the area, including Philip, felt their fortunes lay with the Americans, and Philip, once decided, threw himself into the cause.

Temperance, in talking about this with Philip, was in agreement that the king an ocean away did not govern the colonies fairly. Taxation was pinching everyone. Earlier there had been an attempt by a group calling themselves the Regulators to protest abuse by local British officials, but this was quelled. And then shots had been fired in the Massachusetts colony, and soon after that the war came south.

The decisive battle in February at Moore's Creek Bridge in which the British and the Highland Scots Loyalists were defeated had brought a change of government to North Carolina. Philip's appointment as Second Major of the Cumberland County Militia had sent him into a flurry of activity, recruiting and training men. Temperance was often left running the plantation during his absences.

Behind the house on a little rise a small stone marked a tiny grave. William, named for Philip's brother, had lived less a day. His birth came about a year after the family moved into the house, and Temperance had known from the moment that Dinah wrapped him in a shawl to hand to her that all was not well. His little body was limp and blue, he didn't cry, and he wouldn't nurse. She and Dinah frantically chafed his limbs, but nothing roused him.

Philip was away then, as he often was these days. He took his appointments seriously. When he returned late that evening, he was met by a solemn Dinah. She led him to the bed chamber, and through the half-open door, he saw Temperance, weeping, propped against the pillows, holding the shrouded body of their son.

Philip turned without speaking, went across the hall, gave orders for the digging of a grave and called for a decanter of whisky. He paced and drank in the parlor, cursing a God who would cause his Linnet such pain. It was nearly an hour before he was able to go and comfort his wife.

The new baby stirred now across the room, whimpering in her sleep. Her name had been a matter of some discussion. Temperance didn't want a daughter named for her, but once Philip had seen the baby, he would have it no other way.

"Just look at her, Linnie. She's the very image of her mother! She's got your eyes exactly. I'll bargain with you. If we have another boy, you can name him," he'd said.

Temperance listened now, her head on Philip's shoulder. Little Tempie was quiet again. She was a good child. She ate well, slept well, and laughed with delight when her brothers and sister played with her. She was unlike delicate and demanding Elizabeth, who was choosy about her food and pushed away dishes that didn't please her taste.

At her side, Philip whispered, "If she cries again, we'll give her to Nan. I'm only here for the night, and I don't intend to waste a moment of it." Nan, who was twelve, and daughter of Priss who worked in the house, slept on a pallet just outside their door when Philip was at home, and brought her pallet in the bed chamber near the baby's bed when he was away.

"Shhh," said Temperance, putting a finger to his lips, and turning to him in the dark.

LINN: SIX
Wednesday evening

LINN BORROWED HER MOM'S CAR TO DRIVE TO GRAN'S. Her summer job at Dad's office, the one she wasn't going to take—she rolled her eyes, thinking of that—was supposed to help pay for a car to take back to college in the fall, when, in theory, anyway, she'd be able to live off campus. Her dad was old-school. He was willing to pay the insurance, but Linn should be kicking in towards the car. All that stuff about "responsibility." She knew he'd come up the hard way, putting himself through law school. She'd certainly heard it often enough. Kids at school who thought she was lucky to be an only child didn't know her dad.

Linn pulled into the parking lot of the gated condo complex Gran had moved into following Granddad's death when Linn was thirteen. Gran opened the door before she could knock.

"I've been watching for you. Come on in the kitchen. The casserole's almost ready to come out of the oven. Sit, sit."

"Smells good." Linn perched on a stool and watched her grandmother slice a cucumber into the salad bowl. "You kept GeeGee's sugar bowl! I'm glad. How was your day at Hospice?"

"Oh, fine, I suppose. I didn't do much but sit at the front

desk and answer the phone. How was *your* day, Linn?" Her eyes watched Linn intently over the top of the reading glasses she'd donned to slice the cucumber. She kept a pair in every room. "When do you start at the Rec Center?"

Linn met her eyes. Crap. Gran knew. She took a deep breath. "I'm not going to be working for Dad this summer."

"Really, Linn? I thought that was all settled. I ran into . . . oh, what's his name? the Rec Center director? . . . in the produce section at Kroger. He told me you're going to be lifeguarding and teaching swimming this summer."

"Mr. Bartelli. Gran, I just had to say yes. You know how much I loved working there last summer. And this year he's going to let me teach the beginning swimmers. Those little kids are so much fun. And I really, really didn't want to spend the summer hauling files around at Dad's office. I'm just scared to tell Dad. I don't know what he's going to say."

"Oh, honey. You haven't told him yet?" Gran's brown eyes were full of sympathy.

"I'm afraid they're going to be really upset with me. Especially Dad. Uncle Jack's supposed to be looking out for a used car for me at his dealership, but I'm sure I won't make enough money at the Rec. They pay minimum wage. And it won't be full-time. Thirty hours, if I'm lucky. Maybe I can pick up some extra money babysitting or something. " She laughed. "But I get to use the pool free."

"Come on and let's eat. The table's all set. We'll talk after supper. Don't worry, Linn. We'll figure it out. How's the family history coming along? Are you keeping up with your time? Remember I'm paying you at least minimum wage." She smiled at her granddaughter's solemn face. "Really, don't worry."

Linn brought the salad bowl, following her grandmother into the living room and sat down at the little table, looking appreciatively around. Gran had put GeeGee's corner cabinet—GeeGee called it a "what-not"—in the dining area at the far end of the room by the kitchen, and a few of GeeGee's cups and saucers were on it. And the old white pitcher with the embossed daisy design was on Gran's console table, filled today with some cheerful yellow tulips. GeeGee would have liked that.

"You kept the pitcher, too. Where did that come from? I asked GeeGee once, and all she knew was that it came down in her family, like the what-not."

"GeeGee was a Griffin before she married, you know. She said it came through the Griffin line, but she didn't really know any more than that. An antique dealer told her it was English, from the eighteenth century. The what-not, according to the same dealer, was probably made in Virginia. Oh, have you had a chance to look at the book I brought over?"

"Mr. Willcox's book? Yes! Did you know we have an ancestor who was captured at the Battle of Brier Creek here in Georgia during the American Revolution and put on a British prison ship? And, who, I want you to know, escaped! Philip Alston! He and another man, a William Gipson, threw some pieces of wood out a porthole and used them to swim to shore." Linn's eyes were bright. Gran smiled. It was good to see her excited about something.

On the banks of the Deep River,
November, 1779

Temperance STOOD ON THE FRONT PORCH of the House in the Horseshoe. It was nearing dark, and there was a chill in the air after an unusually beautiful late fall day. The children had played games beside the house until she'd sent them in. She'd have to go in soon, too.

It seems as though I'm always looking down the road, she thought. Where *is* he? Word had come in September that Philip had escaped. Escaped! After all her frantic efforts to have him ransomed from the Roebuck, the British ship that held him captive, somewhere in the waters off Savannah. She'd swallowed her pride in late March, learning of his surrender at Brier Creek and his capture by the British, and knowing full well that Philip would be furious with her when he found out, had sent a plea to Joseph John Alston, Philip's estranged father, only to learn by a letter from Philip's brother William, who had served in the North Carolina Continental troops, that the old man was very ill. William, however, was going to Charleston and offered to contact the British authorities there to set up an exchange or to parole him. William had a thriving plantation in Halifax County and many acquaintances in Charleston, where he kept a house.

And she had waited. Time passed. Weeks, a month, another month. And another. And then finally a letter from William. The British were considering his offer to pay for a parole for Philip.

Before the British could make up their minds there came a rumor that Colonel Alston was no longer on the Roebuck. Then the official word, relayed by William, that his brother and someone named Gibson had managed to escape. No one was sure how it had happened.

Temperance only hoped it was true—that he really had escaped—and that the British were not merely concealing the death of a Patriot officer.

The door behind her opened. She could hear the laughter of the little boys in the hall, and Nan singing to the baby. She would need to go in and feed Philip, who would soon be a year old. His father had missed most of his first year, she thought. A small hand slipped into hers.

"Hello, little one," she said. She loved all her children, but secretly, her namesake Temperance had her heart. At four, she was thin and quiet and solemn, but her dark eyes watched. She was the only one of the five who seemed aware of her mother's worries. Jem and John talked of elaborate plans to storm the ship and kill the British who had captured their father, while Elizabeth wondered if he'd get home in time for Christmas and if he'd bring her a gift. And little Philip just gurgled and laughed, looking so much like his father with his blue eyes and his dimple, in earlier, happier days. Philip had left a bare month after his birth, rounding up his troops and heading off to join General Ashe in South Carolina.

"Come inside, Mama. It's cold out here. Come in and tell us a story."

A figure was approaching. It was Dave, who had taken to spending his nights sleeping across the front door on the porch, wrapped in blankets, since word had come of Philip's capture. Temperance had tried in vain to talk him into sleeping in the hall now that winter was coming on, but he'd refused.

Dave had been distressed by Philip's refusal to take him off to war with him. Philip had told Dave how much he was needed at home, but privately he'd told Temperance that Dave would be a hindrance. "You know, he's never been able to shoot anything. Anything. Even a rabbit. I taught him to fire a gun when he was young, back in Georgia, and he isn't a bad marksman, but hitting a target is not the same as killing a deer. And he doesn't let me out of his sight away from home. He's fine around here. He does an excellent job looking after me here, keeping my boots clean and waiting on table. But the real problem is that he won't listen to anyone but me. That would never do in the military."

Dave was about thirty now. In maturity, he was as slender as ever, and Temperance often noticed the similarity in his bearing to Philip's way of carrying himself—erect, head high. Dave was a little taller than his half-brother, and his reserved demeanor and watchfulness stood him in good stead when the Alstons entertained at dinner, and he waited on table. Other plantation wives had asked Temperance how she had managed to train him so well, and she could only answer that his behavior was natural to him.

"Good evening, Dave. Have you eaten?"

"Yes, Miss Temp."

"We may get a frost tonight. Are you sure you won't come in?"

"No, I'll watch the house from here."

"You're a hard-headed man, Dave." There was a hint of laughter in her voice.

"Yes, Miss Temp."

"Sweet dreams." This was from little Temperance, echoing her mother's usual good-night to the children.

"Good night, little missie." A rare smile from Dave. The four-year-old was his favorite of the children. Everyone knew that. She was the only one he had ever allowed in his cabin. He trusted her to be careful with his books and carvings.

Temperance gave a last look down the road and, still holding Tempie's warm hand, went into the house.

It was early afternoon the next day when she heard shouts from the yard.

"Mr. Philip!"

"Papa!"

She dropped her mending and ran to the door. Who was the thin, dirty, bearded man walking quickly up the steps? Was it really?

"Oh, Philip!" she threw herself into his arms. She could feel his ribs under the ragged cloak he wore. "Come in, come in! Children! Let your papa sit down."

Jem and John stood back, as befitted their years, as nine-year-old Elizabeth launched herself onto Philip's lap. Little Temperance came as close as she dared and gazed at the almost unrecognizable man. Philip winked at her, and she smiled shyly back. It truly was Papa!

"Philip, what can I get you?"

"More than almost anything, what I want is a bath, a shave and some clean clothes. Oh, and a glass of our very best brandy." He looked appreciatively around the tidy parlor. "It is so good to be home."

He counted, his eyes resting on each child in turn, "One, two, three, four. If I remember aright, there's one missing."

Temperance laughed, "You've lost some weight, but I'm happy to know that you can still count. Little Philip's napping. Do you want to see him?"

"Later." Oh, her laugh. Just as he recalled.

Dave was hovering in the doorway. "Mr. Philip, sir."

"Dave! Just the man I need. Can you see to it that there's bath water brought up, and find me some clothes? And I'll need a razor. Everything I took with me is long gone. And tell someone in the stable to feed and water that bony nag I rode in on."

"Yes, sir, Mr. Philip. Someone is already getting the water, and I'll go see about your clothes and a razor. The horse is being taken care of, too. What should we do with the blanket on her?'

"Burn it!"

LATER THAT EVENING, after Philip's needs had been met—the bath, the shave, the clothes, a good meal prepared by Dinah and served by Dave, and then a meeting with little Philip before handing him off to Nan, Philip sat comfortably in his usual place by the fire in the parlor, Temperance across from him, and little Temperance contentedly on his lap. Elizabeth had learned to her chagrin, that no, her Papa had not passed any stores on his way home, and that there were no ribbons or slippers for her. Jem had asked a few questions about battle casualties. Now the three of them were entertaining themselves with a card game in the corner.

Philip offered Temperance a glass of brandy, smiled at the headshake, "No," and poured himself another.

"We'd heard that you escaped with someone named Gibson. What has happened to him?"

"Gipson. With a "p'" Philip said. "Will. You may remember him. He signed up a couple of years ago, and was with me and Carroll and Irvin when we went looking for Hugh McPherson and his band. When he went home to Guilford County after his six months, he found his house had been destroyed by Tories and his mother had been tortured."

"Oh, yes. He's the one you wrote for who got here just before you and your regiment left. Tall, lanky young man."

"Yes, he'd been serving with Colonel Armstrong when Armstrong was wounded and then later died. He's fearless and vengeful. He helped capture Hugh McPherson and one of the Campbell brothers, and was present when McPherson was condemned and shot, and Campbell was tortured by spicketing."

Temperance said quickly, "So where is Will now?" She frowned and caught his eye, then nodded down at little Tempie, drowsy in her father's lap. Spicketing was a horrible practice—impaling a man's foot on a pin driven into a block of wood and then turning him on it. She didn't want her daughter hearing about it.

"I left him headed to Fagansville. He has some kin there. His mother's sister or some such. He'll be here in a day or two. I've promised him his discharge and some money and a horse so he can get on home. And I'll need to send that old horse back to Betty Jackson in the Waxhaws or some money to buy another. She'd probably rather have the money."

"Betty Jackson?"

"I'll tell you about that later. This little girl is yawning away."

"Elizabeth, take your sister and go to bed. It's past everyone's bedtime. And tell Nan to bring little Philip to me, and I'll feed him. I think I'm ready to retire, too." She looked at Philip and caught him looking at her, smiling, his dimple denting his cheek. She blushed.

Soon after, with the baby full and drowsy in his bed, she snuggled against Philip. "Tell me more. Were you and Will the only ones to escape?"

"As far as I know. Linnet, many of us died. Mostly from the flux. There must have been close to five hundred men on that ship. They fed us very poorly. Rice every single day, and tough, boiled beef only once a week. Oh, tell Dinah, it'll be a while before I want rice again! Every day or so, British officers came aboard and offered us gold to join the King's army. There were some takers, including some of my men. William Poplin, for one. He's from Chatham County. I wonder how he's faring with the British."

"Your brother William tried to arrange an exchange or a ransom for you. He was told they were considering his offer. Then we heard you'd escaped. Oh, Philip. I've been so worried and afraid! I prayed to God every day that you were safe, and my prayers were answered."

"You know I promised I'd always come back to you. I fail to see what that has to do with God." The tone in Philip's voice changed, hardening.

Now was not the time for an argument, especially one she knew she'd lose. Temperance said, "Tell me about when you were captured."

"They should court-martial General Ashe. He had us camped into a corner, river on one side, swamp on the other. And he rode off just after the British surprised us. We were short on ammunition. Many men didn't even have muskets, and those that did had no cartouches to keep their powder in. It was a rout. I thought of you and the children and coming home alive and tied my handkerchief to my sword and surrendered. Will Gipson was right beside me. They walked us all the way to the mouth of the Savannah, out on an island called Tybee, herded us into a building that had been built for a church, and kept us there several days, all crowded together. I imagine they were sending for a ship. I thought it couldn't get any worse, but they rowed us out in batches to a ship that was already full."

"I'm not going to describe how filthy it was, and the stench! Men got the bloody flux and died. Finally I'd had all I could take, and I talked to several of the men who'd come to Georgia with me about an escape. We pulled some boards off a bunk, but when it came down to it, Will was the only one who was brave enough to climb through the porthole and jump with me. By that point, almost anyone could have fit through the portholes. We'd all lost weight—those of us who were still alive."

"Will and I held on to the boards and paddled. It was a moonlit night, and the tide was with us. We came ashore in a marshy area, wherever the tide had carried us. I think it may have been the South Carolina coast, up from Savannah. We lay low, resting a little, and then we heard someone chopping wood. We crept near until we could see that it was a Negro, putting wood in a canoe to float it to where he needed it. I'm sure we startled him, two scrawny white men in ragged clothes, but he listened to our story and agreed to take us further inland. I told him I'd come back and buy his freedom, but he said he was already a free man. He lived in a little shack nearby and made his livelihood catching and selling seafood. He boiled us some blue crab and made some corn pone. The best food I'd had in months!"

"He took us as far as he could inland, and we left him with many thanks for his generosity. After that, we mostly travelled by night and slept in the day, avoiding towns. The British pretty much control the coastline now." Philip paused. "Are you sure you want to hear all this now?"

"Yes! Don't stop. How did you get food?"

"Various ways. People on small farms would feed us and let us sleep in the barn in return for a little work. Wood chopping, clearing land, plowing. It made me remember the days on Boggy

Gut Creek! I got my calluses back." Philip showed her his palms.

"And one day I heard we were near the Hughes's plantation. We have a connection there. One of my cousins married a Hughes. They gave us a horse and lent us a slave to guide us for a couple of days and keep us away from the British sympathizers."

"Eventually we ended up at the Waxhaws. That's a settlement of Irish immigrants right on the border of the Carolinas. A kind woman there, the Widow Jackson, Betty, took us in and fed us. She has every reason to hate the British. She had three sons, the youngest, Andrew—she calls him Andy—born just after the death of her husband. Her oldest son, Hugh, died at the battle at Stono Ferry in June. He was barely sixteen. The middle boy, Robert, and Andy were still at home. They are old for their years—they've seen a lot of hardship. Both want to enlist, and Andrew's even younger than John!"

"Oh, Philip, remember your promise when this all started. I am not ready for my boys to go off to war! I can only pray that this will be ended soon."

"The British are thick in the area around the Waxhaws. And Andy is already running messages for the Americans. I told Rob and Andy that their mother needs them at home, but I'm afraid I didn't help their mother's cause much by telling them how the British had treated Will and me."

"We stayed there two days. Betty Jackson gave us a horse— that old nag I came home on—and blankets. I really do intend to repay her for her kindness as soon as may be. She has very little but her sons."

Temperance was nodding at this. "Oh, yes! I'm so grateful for her generosity!"

"I left there figuring I was only about a hundred miles from home. It still took us ten days, taking turns on the old horse. Will took sick towards the end. That's why he was going to Fagansville. I don't think it's anything serious. He's tough as nails."

"Linnet, I think our boys may be a little sheltered. Perhaps their life has been too easy here in Carolina. Some of that's my fault. I've been away so much. I think it's time I took Jem and

John in hand." He felt Temperance stiffen beside him. "Oh, I just want them to learn a little about how to be men. I'm not sending them off to battle. I'll keep my promise to you. Not until they're eighteen. And you'll still have little Philip to coddle. At least until he's breeched!" He laughed and hugged his wife to him. "Now I'm going to stop talking."

LINN: SEVEN
Wednesday evening

Linn put the plates and silverware in the dishwasher while Gran washed out the wooden salad bowls and stored the leftovers in the fridge.

"Let's wait a bit for dessert. I shouldn't have had a second helping of the crab," her grandmother said. "Now tell me a little more about this summer job thing." Gran poured herself a second glass of wine. "Should I make coffee?"

"Not for me, thanks. I'm good." Linn followed her back into the cozy living room and sank onto the sofa. Gran took her usual spot in the armchair by the window. The little table next to it held Gran's current library book and a pair of reading glasses. Linn pulled her legs up under her, and looked at Gran, hesitating.

"Well? So you haven't told your dad you're not going to be working for him this summer?" Gran prompted.

"Not yet."

"You know you're going to have to, sweetie. And soon."

"I know, I know. Believe me. But Dad's going to be furious

with me, Gran. I'm not so worried about Mom. She'll have my back."

"So what made you decide you'd rather be outdoors at a pool with a bunch of kids than indoors shuffling papers?" Gran laughed. "Wait. I don't think you need to answer that!"

"You think he'd know me by now, right?" Linn's smile was rueful. "Gran, all year I knew I was doing the wrong thing for me. I don't want to practice corporate law. I don't want to spend my life trying to help some rich guy get richer. I'm not going back north this fall. It's a waste of Dad's money. Hey, there's a thought. Dad hates to waste money."

"You're saying you don't want to go back to college? Really?" This was serious. "Linn, are you sure?"

"Not back there. I want to go to college, of course, but I want to stay here, in Atlanta. Maybe one of the community colleges."

"So you don't want to be an attorney. Do you know what you *do* want to do?"

"I know I want to work with kids." Linn paused. "Pediatric nursing. That's what I've been thinking about. A lot lately. The nursing thing, I mean. I'm good with kids, you know I am." Linn's voice had become less tentative. "I really think I could that."

Gran smiled. She had a sudden vision of Linn in brightly-colored scrubs, with a zoo animal print, pony-tail bouncing as she walked down a hospital hall.

"It's certainly worth looking into. There are some excellent nursing programs here in Atlanta. But first we've got to tell your folks. I doubt it's ever occurred to Bill that you might not want to follow in his footsteps. He worked so hard to get where he is."

"I know, I know. I've heard it a million times. Growing up on the farm and having to convince his dad to let him go to college. Working to pay his way through, joining ROTC, and then how long it took him to get through law school, after he got out of his two years in the Army."

"Bill had just made junior partner when he met your mother. I remember the first time she brought him home for dinner. He was so nervous, even though he knew your granddad and me. He knocked over a water glass and dropped his salad fork."

"It's hard to imagine Dad being nervous about anything now."

"Oh, he's come a long way, but down deep somewhere, there's still that insecure farm boy inside him. You know, I'd about given up hope of your mother ever settling down. She had turned thirty by then. After they were engaged, your father tried to talk her into quitting work, but she stood her ground. She loved teaching."

"She still does," Linn nodded.

"After you came along, she did stay home until you started kindergarten. I'm sure the way Bill came up is the reason he's so careful with money. You know he didn't buy the house you live in until he had the full price saved up. Nobody but your dad buys a house that way."

"I remember the summer we moved out of the duplex. I was going into sixth grade that fall."

"He wanted you in the best school district, and when that house came on the market not far from GeeGee's, he went for it. Talked the price down and got the owners to put on a new roof, too. You have to give him credit, Linn. Whatever he's done, it's always been about your mother and you. He loves you both very much."

"I didn't understand when I was in middle school. Why I had to do chores for spending money, when the other kids got allowances."

"He was trying to teach you responsibility. I think it worked, Linn. I'm proud of how you turned out. How about if I come over tomorrow night, and I can be a little moral support when you tell them?" She saw relief on Linn's face, and a smile as she nodded. "Now, what about dessert? I've got some raspberry sherbet, or there are still some of the shortbread cookies left."

"Any chance of both? Oh, and I want to tell you about a brochure I came across about a battle at the Alston house in North Carolina."

"The House in the Horseshoe. Your uncle Michael and Mark

took GeeGee up there a few years back to see the reenactment they have there every summer. She really wanted to see that house. I'd almost forgotten about that. Michael might have some pictures. I'll have to ask him when he and Mark get back from wherever it is they've gone this time. Somewhere in the Caribbean."

Michael and Mark were frequent travelers, but they were beginning to talk seriously about adopting. Gran wondered if Linn had heard this bit of family news. "Mark and Michael are applying to adopt a child. Did your mom tell you?"

"Yes, we talked about it during spring break. I think Dad has some reservations, but he'll get over it. He likes Mark a lot. Says he's got a good head on his shoulders, which is about the highest compliment he can pay somebody."

"Yes, Mark's definitely the level-headed one in that partnership."

"I guess your head has to be level to be good on your shoulders?" They both laughed. "They'll be great parents," Linn continued, "Michael's so much fun, and Mark's, as you say, level-headed." Gran smiled at Linn's criteria for "great parents," but Linn was right. Michael's creativity and Mark's steadiness and patience had worked well in combination for ten years now.

Linn went on, "I'm looking forward to having a baby in the family. I've been the youngest all these years." Linn's cousins, Ben and Rob, Aunt Sue's boys, were grown now. "Hey, if I go to college in Atlanta, I can babysit!"

"Linn, I've known your dad even longer than your mom has. Let me think about this a little. We'll figure something out. Now, tell me about the Battle at the House in the Horseshoe."

Temperance SAT STRAIGHT UP IN BED. Beside her Philip struggled to his feet. The first light of day was coming through the open windows. And through the windows, the shouts that had awakened them were growing louder and more confused.

"Inside! Quick! Inside! Shut the doors! Get in! Get in!"

"Colonel! Colonel!" There were running footsteps. Philip pulled on his pants and ran to the closed bedroom door and threw it open.

"What is it?" Throughout the house now there were shouts. Across the room, the baby began to whimper, gearing up for a full-out bellow.

Temperance, in her shift, ran for the baby. She could hear the voices from the hall. In the growing light she saw Jacob Duckworth and Elijah Fooshee with Philip.

"It's Fanning and his men. They've got Folsome and Cutts. I think all the rest of us are in the house now," Jacob Duckworth was telling Philip.

Shots rang out from within the house, followed by answering shots from outside. Temperance put the screaming baby girl on the floor and pulled Nan, who was cowering outside the door on her pallet, into the room. "Take Winnie and stay low," she said. "Keep away from the windows." Her voice was muffled as she hastily struggled into her dress. No stays and petticoats today! As she left she looked back. Nan had the baby and was crouched on the side of the bed nearest the hall. Good.

Philip came back for his musket, leaning in the corner. "Nan, do what my wife tells you, and be quiet. She's gathering the rest of the children."

"Yes, sir, Mr. Philip."

It had been a hot night. All the windows were wide open, but there had been no breeze. Little Winifred had finally slept, her body beaded in sweat. Philip and Temperance had dozed on top of the covers, trying not to touch each other. His answer to her questions as they were preparing for bed had been, "Not now, Linnet. I'll tell you everything later, but not now."

Upstairs, Philip had quartered Jacob Duckworth and Elijah Fooshee in the boys' room, and baby Philip was bedded down with Elizabeth and Tempie. Jem and John were sleeping in the parlor. Captain Folsome had taken three of his men and settled down at the gate to keep watch. The rest of the men slept on the porches.

A small group of Philip's men had ridden through the gates in the heat of the afternoon the day before. Temperance had questioned them as to the whereabouts of the rest of the men, including Philip, and was told by Captain Duckworth that Colonel Alston and his slave would be arriving soon, that he'd sent them on to the house, since he was sending the rest of the men who lived nearby to their homes to rest. Dinah and her kitchen help had managed to provide ham, green beans, creamed corn and biscuits for all of them. The young boys especially were grateful. There were several about Jem's age in the regiment, and Temperance knew how hungry Jem and John stayed.

She had tried to learn their names, these thin young men— not much more than children, really—so far from home. She had sat down between two of them as they perched on the edge of the porch, wolfing down their supper. Bess and Dinah, on the porch behind her, were keeping an eye on their plates and cups, offering more biscuits or cider. Little Tempie, who was five now, stood behind her mother and listened to the conversation, as the boys responded to her mother's gentle queries.

Most were from Cumberland County, and she recognized some of the family names. Several said they were sixteen. There were two Stephens, Collins and Morris; two Williams, Smith and Cutts; but Cutts was noticeably older than the other privates. There was a John Spears and another John whose last name she didn't catch. Lowden Harwell, Jesse Mitchell and James Griffin were from Chatham County, recruited, she suspected, by Jacob Duckworth. She was sitting between James and Jesse, who said they were cousins. And there was a boy named—it sounded like "Reesa" Oliver. She asked him how that was spelled, and he said, "I don't rightly know, Miss. Mostly they call me 'Reesie.'"

She asked about how things were back home and learned that most had signed up to help their families. There was a bounty paid to join up, and clothing, weapons, and food were furnished. Two of the boys were substitutes for men who didn't want to go to war. She wondered, but didn't ask, if most were illiterate. They all nodded when she asked if they were being treated well. James, who was among the oldest at nineteen, volunteered that he was enjoying seeing other parts of North Carolina. He told her that when the war was over, he planned to go down to the Florida territory and see what it was like down there.

"Why Florida, James?"

"They got them some big scaly creatures called alligators, Missus. I want to see me one of them. I hear tell they get to be as long as two men laying end to end!"

"Oh, there ain't no sech thing!" said Jesse. Temperance stood up, smiling, and smoothed her skirt. She left them arguing and went in to nurse little Winnie. Tempie stayed, fascinated by the alligator discussion.

IT WAS NEARLY DARK before Philip and Dave came riding in. One look at Philip's face told his wife that all was not well. She caught his eye as he walked into the hall, followed by the officers who'd been waiting on the porch. An almost imperceptible shake of his head warned off her questions. Dave's usually inexpressive face seemed even more closed, if that were indeed possible.

Jem and John had come into the hall from the parlor to meet Philip, who was saying, "Dave, go tell Dinah to send me some supper. And John, ask your mother to come in and join us."

In the parlor, the officers sat with Philip while he ate. Dave waited just outside the hall door, alert to directions from his master. Temperance took a minute to pat her hair and make sure her cap was not askew, as it usually was.

"Have you had anything to eat, Dave?"

"No, Miss Temp."

"Then go to the kitchen and get something. I'll handle things here."

The men stood as she entered, then sat again as she took her place in a chair pulled up by the gate-legged table at which Philip ate.

Philip said, "You've all met my wife, Temperance?"

"She's been a very gracious hostess," said Israel Folsome.

"Did you all get enough to eat?" At their nods, she added, "If you gentlemen are finished, my husband will give you a glass of brandy before we retire."

"If you'll excuse me just for a moment, I'll speak to the men outside." To them, Philip said, "I'll be sending Captain Folsome outside in a few minutes. He'll set a watch. Stay alert. There may be trouble. I don't trust Fanning not to double back."

Philip's light horse regiment had spent the last ten days pursuing Colonel David Fanning, the infamous young Tory, whose raids on the Patriots were causing such panic and havoc. Most recently, less than ten days ago, Fanning and his band had captured Colonel Ambrose Ramsey and forty of the Chatham Militia at the Chatham Courthouse and was rumored to be marching them to Wilmington. Philip and his men had set off that way, hoping to catch up with Fanning and free the prisoners.

Back in the parlor, Temperance invited the men to seat themselves. When Philip returned, he filled four glasses with brandy from the decanter, smiling a little at Temperance's headshake, "No." She rarely indulged in spirits.

"You need to know this, so let me fill you in on what happened after you left me at Thomas Taylor's. Temperance," he turned to his wife, "a scout had brought us word that Fanning had paroled most of the men he'd captured, and that the rest were well on the way to the jail in Wilmington. I decided to turn back. It was a useless pursuit. I sent a few of the men on here, and the rest of us stopped at Taylor's plantation, and I was holding him at gunpoint in his house until all the horses had been watered, and the men had gotten a little something to eat. Taylor has kept the Loyalists well-supplied with food and goods, it seemed only fitting that we also should benefit from his generosity. He was taunting me with tales of Fanning's raids, and how he'd join with Fanning to make us pay for this. And then he said something insufferable. I cannot repeat his words in the presence of my wife."

Philip paused, avoiding Temperance's gaze. "A rage came over me. I could hear blood pounding in my ears. Before I realized what I was doing, I had pulled the trigger of my pistol, and he was lying dead, a ball through his head. I joined the other men in the yard. Taylor's slaves were beginning to gather, and I gave the order to ride."

He heard the intake of breath from Temperance. Her eyes had widened, and her mouth was open. "He's an enemy combatant, and was threatening my men. We've hanged men for less than that, Temperance."

"As we rode, we came across Kenneth Black, leading a crippled horse, near his place at Ray's Mill Creek. When he saw us, he tried to get on the mare and ride, but one of the men pulled him off. Young Isaac Martin, I think it was. They held him for me, and I rode back to question him. He said Fanning had spent the night at his place a couple of nights before, with fourteen prisoners, and that he'd ridden on with Fanning towards

Wilmington until Fanning's horse went lame. He'd swapped horses and had turned back leading Fanning's mare when we encountered him."

"I told him he could be shot for giving aid to Fanning, and he grabbed for his musket. Isaac was nearest to him, and he wrestled the gun away from him, and bashed him over the head. Blood was streaming down his face." He looked at his wife. "I'm sorry, Temperance." He thought he'd never seen her so pale.

"He was begging for his life, but Isaac just kept hitting him. I ordered the men to ride on, and we left him there dead. I told Isaac I'd deal with him later. I doubt we gained anything by killing Black. He was loyal to the King, but he was a kind man."

"Poor Kate." Temperance said, trying to control herself.

"I stopped by their house to tell her what had happened. I told her how sorry I was. I failed to control my men. She was going to send someone for his body. Perhaps you can ride over with me in a day or so, and we can offer our help."

"I parted company with the rest of the men a little ways down the road, and Dave and I came on home. I'm not sure where Fanning is, if he's gotten to Wilmington yet, but I can't imagine he'll let this go. I've told the men we'll muster here on Tuesday. This is war, and this isn't over."

And it wasn't over, indeed! In the half-light of early morning, Temperance, holding little Philip by the hand, hurried the shrieking Elizabeth and stoic Tempie into the bedroom, thinking how right Philip was. This *was* war, and it was happening in her house. Two of Philip's men pushed past her and headed for the windows on the rear of the room. Most of the shots seemed to be coming from that way. One shot flew through a window, shattering the glass.

"Nan, I want you to stay low, and push that bench into the fireplace as far it will go. Oh, do be careful with my mother's pitcher! Put it on the floor. Elizabeth, I want you and Tempie and Philip to go sit on the bench with Nan. Don't move. And for the dear Lord's sake, Elizabeth, stop that screaming. It won't help, and you're scaring your brother. Give me the baby, Nan." She sank down beside the bed and offered Winnie her breast. Winnie's wails subsided.

"Nan, crawl over and throw me some cloths from the cradle. She's soaking wet!" Musket balls flying, and the baby's needs still had to be met.

Time passed. Two of the young men were carried up the stairs and laid on the floor in the boys' room across the hall. Stephen Collins had a ball through his arm just above the wrist, and John Spears had taken a shot to the knee. Temperance crawled awkwardly into the hall, carrying Winnie clutched to her chest with one arm, and then ran quickly up the narrow stairs, and Nan's mother, Priss, who had been sleeping with the children when the shooting commenced, came in, shaking with fear, to help Temperance dress the wounds, tearing a sheet into strips.

Another young man made it to the top of the stairs, holding his crumpled shirt to his head. Will Smith had a scalp wound. A ball had grazed his top of his head, leaving his sandy hair thick with blood. Lucky boy, thought Temperance. Another inch lower, and I wouldn't be worrying about stopping the bleeding. "Tear up another sheet, Priss," she said with resignation and then chastised herself mentally for worrying about the loss of her linen.

The ball had gone cleanly through Stephen's right arm, and if it didn't fester, he should be all right. John's injury was worse. There seemed to be more damage, and he was unconscious. He'll be hurting when he wakes, Temperance thought. Poor boy. She knew from her conversations with him that he was Jem's age, sixteen.

She resisted the strong urge to go downstairs to check on Jem and her John. Philip had armed them and stationed them at one of the windows. He'd sent two more of the young men to keep watch at the windows upstairs. She hoped the little ones were minding Nan and staying sheltered in the fireplace. Oh, God, please keep them safe! Amazingly, Winnie had fallen asleep on a quilt on the floor beneath the bed her sisters slept in. She took a minute to pray for the safety of her children and for the slaves. She knew that Dave was downstairs with Philip, Nan was with the children in the huge fireplace, and Priss was here with her, and she hoped the rest were safely away in the cabins or sheltering in the woods, out of the range of the guns.

It was full daylight outside now. She heard a scream of pain, and Philip called up to her from downstairs. "Here's another one, Linnie." He and Dave were helping a very pale James Griffin up the stairs. James was bleeding badly from a couple of wounds, one on his forearm and another in his scalp.

"I'm afraid we'll have to get another mirror for the parlor, Linnie." Philip managed a smile as she took the slumping young man and laid him on the floor. He turned and ran back down the stairs, as another volley of shots rang out from the field behind.

"I'm sorry, Miss Linnie," an ashen James said. "I'm bleeding all over your carpet." Then he fainted.

Miss Linnie. Nobody calls me that. I guess he heard Philip call me Linnie. Temperance was ripping another sheet. "Bess, hold this wad of cloth on his arm and press hard while I get this bandage around it. That scalp wound's probably not as bad as it looks. I'll bandage it next after we get the bleeding stopped on this one."

"Look out! There's a man in British uniform leading a charge towards the fence!" came up the stairs from below.

"He's mine!" That was Duckworth's voice, Temperance thought. A shot. "That was the British officer that's been traveling with Fanning. Can't remember his name. McRae, maybe. That stopped him!"

"It's awfully quiet out there," Temperance said to the boy at the back window after a few minutes. "Aren't you Lowden? What's happening?"

"Yes, ma'am, Lowden. Nothin' right now. Wait. There's one of Fanning's men with a lit torch running towards the house!"

A single shot, and then Philip's triumphant, "I got him!"

Quiet reigned again. Temperance crawled over to the window where Lowden was crouched. "What are they doing?"

"I don't know, ma'am. There's a negro man over near that outbuilding doing something. Look, he's loading hay in an oxcart. Why's he doing that?"

"Oh, dear Lord! That's Rufus!" Forgetting herself, Temperance ran to the door and down the stairs. "Philip! Fanning's got Rufus setting fire to that hay and rolling it up to the house!" She looked quickly around. Oh, thank you, God! John and Jem were both there and both fine, and the children and Nan were still crouched in the fireplace. But whose was that still body pulled against the wall at the foot of the stairs?

"He's behind the cart. I can't get a clear shot," Duckworth yelled over his shoulder from the side window.

"Oh, don't shoot him, Captain. It's that free black man that lives at Dowd's Mill. He's simple. He's not got the sense of a puppy." This from Temperance.

"He's firing the hay, Colonel."

"The children, Philip!" Temperance was at this side. "We've got to surrender. Wait, not you, Philip!" Philip grimly and silently was pulling off his white neckerchief. "Fanning will shoot you on sight. I'll go. He won't shoot a woman."

"No, Temperance!" But she was already running towards the door at the front of the house. She took a deep breath, squared her shoulders and stepped out onto the porch waving the piece of sheet she was still holding.

"Colonel Fanning!"

"Hold your fire!" A man separated himself from the soldiers and walked towards her. She had never seen the infamous Tory. His head was covered in what looked like a silk scarf tied at the back.

"Come out! Are you Colonel Alston's lady?" He stopped.

"Yes, Colonel Fanning. I am." She walked to meet him. "Here are our terms. We will surrender, sir, on condition that no one shall be injured; otherwise we will make the best defense we can; and if need be, sell our lives as dearly as possible." Her voice was firm and calm.

They met eyes. Fanning thought, She's a remarkably beautiful woman. What bearing. Alston is a fortunate man.

Temperance thought, He's so young. And why does he wear that foolish-looking scarf?

"I accept your terms, lady. Bring out your husband and his officers."

Temperance turned to the house and nodded. She called, "Come out, Philip, with your officers."

It was all over by noon. Fanning left his dead to be buried, and carried off the wounded. Philip gave orders for the burials, including the young boy in the living room. Philip signed a parole written by David Fanning, acknowledging his condition as a prisoner of war and restricting his movement to a five-mile radius.

Temperance watched helplessly as Fanning's men went quickly through her house, slashing upholstery and feather beds, and smashing dishes. There wasn't a window left intact. She was grateful that it was summertime. They'd be weeks repairing all the damage, and there was nothing to be done about some of the bullet holes. She had taken a minute, when she walked upstairs to get Winnie, to push her mother's pitcher far under her bed, so it was safe, and she was glad of that.

It could have been worse, she supposed. The four injured young men, James, John, Stephen, and the other Stephen, who had somehow managed, right at the end of the skirmish, to trip over a chair and sprain his ankle, would all survive. Only that poor young boy, John, whose last name turned out to be Miller, who'd taken one of the first balls in the chest, and two men of Fanning's group, the British lieutenant, who had been identified off-handedly by Fanning as "McKay, McRay. I don't know. He's a Scot. Hard to understand him," and the man who'd tried to set fire to the house would be buried on the rise where William slept. Three new graves. Temperance would write John Miller's mother and tell her where he lay.

I imagine they knew we would surrender. No, I *hope* they knew we would surrender. Who would burn a house with women and children in it? *Her* children. And now Jem was full of himself. Over a pieced-together meal, brought in by Dinah, who had waited out the battle crouched in the kitchen house with Sall, he'd bragged about his shot that had wounded the soldier by the fence. His mother, short-tempered and exhausted, ordered his silence. There weren't enough unbroken chairs left in the parlor, so Philip stood to eat. Elizabeth was wan and quiet. Terror had drained her. She ate nothing. Tempie, too, sat quiet. Her dark eyes followed her father as he paced the room, still full of a nervous energy. Her mother wondered what thoughts were in that little head. Baby Philip was distressed only that he was not allowed down on the floor to play until the glass was swept up. He'd be fine.

THAT EVENING, Temperance and Philip sat in the ruins of the parlor. Blessedly, it was raining, which would cool the house. The wounded men were still upstairs in the boys' room. James Griffin was awake and much improved, and very grateful for Temperance's attention. She told him, "I just wanted to be sure you'd make it to Florida to see the alligators." His cousin Jesse was staying with him until he was ready to travel. The boys who had been shot were in a lot of pain, and she and Priss had done what they could for them, dosing them with willow bark tea. Stephen with the sprained ankle was anxious to know if he would be considered to have been wounded in battle, and she assured him solemnly that he would be.

It would be a while yet until John's knee would let him be moved, but Philip thought he could send him and the two Stephens home in a wagon in a week or so.

"Now, I think, I *will* have a glass of that brandy," Temperance said. Miraculously, the decanter had not been smashed. Philip found two glasses in the rubble. "Tell me," she said. "What went wrong on the way home?"

"You never miss a thing, do you?"

"Not with you."

"You remember Thomas Taylor. He came to dinner here once."

"Yes, an unpleasant man. I remember that he kept looking at my bodice. And he drank too much. Didn't someone have to carry him home in a wagon?"

"At Thomas Taylor's house, I did have my pistol aimed at him, and he did threaten me and my men, but then Dave came in the door to tell me the men were about ready to pull out, and Taylor looked at him and said, 'I see you didn't leave your good-looking slave home this time to take care of your wife while you're gone.' Those aren't the exact words he said, but I don't want your ears to hear them."

"And then he said something about 'Are you even sure all those children are yours?'

"And I said, 'I will not listen to this nonsense.' And then he said something about your breasts, and Dave grabbed my gun and said, 'If you're not going to kill him for that, I will,' and shot him. Just like that."

"I was horrified. They'd hang Dave for killing a white man, no questions asked, so I told him to run out the back door and come around and get on his horse and ride off. I heard people shouting and running towards the house, and I walked out the front door and gave the command to mount and ride. They can blame me for killing him if they want to. He was an enemy combatant and threatening me and my men."

"I didn't realize Dave wasn't with us until I dismissed the rest of the men. I waited a little in case he was behind me, and then rode back in the direction I'd come. It wasn't far back to old Hector MacNeill's place, and a woman stepped out of the cornfield as I got near and said, "Colonel Alston. They've got your Dave up to the house."

"I asked her why she was telling me this, and she said, 'Oh, your wife was good to me, sir. Tell her Maisie says 'Thank you.'"

Philip looked at Temperance, who was smiling. "I remember Maisie. I didn't do that much. I taught her boy to read."

"Hmm. I doubt Colonel MacNeill much appreciated that."

"His wife sent me the boy. She's a good woman. Hector's all bluster. Go on! I know you got Dave back, but how?"

"Well, as you say, his wife's a good woman. I'm not sure what Hector was planning to do. Maybe turn Dave over to Fanning. We had some words, MacNeill and I. I was beginning by then to think the day would never end. It's entirely possible I may have threatened him. Mrs. MacNeill intervened at that point and sent someone out to let Dave out of the shed they had him locked in. They gave him back his horse, and finally, finally, we were on the way home, only to have this happen today. Temperance, I am truly sorry you had to go through this."

"It's over for us now, isn't it? The war, I mean."

"Yes, I paroled myself. I won't fight anymore. At any rate, I think this won't last much longer. The news from other parts is good."

"Philip, what are you going to do about Dave?"

"I'll talk to him tomorrow. He needs to understand that I can fight my own battles. I have to say that I was shocked when he shot Taylor. He's the one who never could kill a rabbit or a deer, much less a man. And all he would say on the way home from MacNeill's was that nobody was going to talk about Miss Temp like that."

"Did you see that Colonel Fanning wears a scarf? It seems odd."

"Yes, he used to have a repulsive scalp disease called 'scald head,' they tell me. Oozing sores. It cost him his hair and left him scarred."

"Oh," Temperance said. "How sad. Poor man."

Philip looked at her in astonishment.

LINN: EIGHT
Late Wednesday night

THE HOUSE WAS QUIET WHEN LINN LET HERSELF IN. Mom had left the light on in the kitchen, and Linn turned it off. Moonshine roused himself from his spot in the living room and followed her slowly up the stairs.

Shiny's getting old, Linn realized. I can almost hear him creak. He padded into her room and sank down on the rug by her bed. Soon he'd be snoring. The little whuffling noise always made her smile.

Linn pulled her phone out of her pocket and read the text from Marcie again: "Call me. It's important." It's too late now, she thought. She'll be asleep. Marcie had stayed on for summer school. It's probably about a dorm room for fall. It can wait until tomorrow.

She and Gran had watched an old movie after supper. They both loved the black and white romantic comedies of the thirties. Especially the musicals. This one was a favorite: The Gay Divorcee. Fred Astaire and Ginger Rogers. Linn had turned her phone to vibrate. Gran was funny about cell phones. She hated their potential for interruptions. Not that anyone was likely to call me anyway, she thought. But she had noticed the blinking light when she dug in her purse for the car keys and found the phone first. There was a missed call from Marcie, followed by the text.

It was late, but Linn wasn't sleepy. She stepped out of her sandals and peeled off her jeans, shirt and underwear, tossing them on her desk chair. Where were the pajama bottoms and tee she'd worn to bed last night? Oh, on top of George Willcox's book on the floor. She'd been reading the section about Connor Dowd last night. She was amused by the total disregard for spelling back then, when he was listed as Conor, Coner, Conner, Connor or even Conrad once, and Dowd, Dowde, or Doud. She smiled, thinking of a clerk listening to him say his name and then just writing down whatever occurred to him. They probably didn't say "Whatever" back then, but they sure wrote whatever.

On the banks of the Deep River,
March, 1785

It had been A BLUSTERY WEEK, but today looked much more promising. Temperance pulled the curtains aside and looked out. Yellow! The sun caught glimmers of yellow against the drift of brown leaves near the fence. The daffodils were blooming. When baby Mary Drew woke from her nap, she'd wrap her up all nice and snug and take her and the little girls—and young Philip, if she could find him—outside to pick a few blossoms for the pitcher.

She read again the letter that had come yesterday. A mail carrier had ridden through bringing a letter from Florida. She was looking forward to sharing it with Philip and had already passed along the greetings to the children. Elizabeth had been insulted. "He didn't even remember my name."

She smiled as she read it:

Dere Miss Linney, I am riting this for James Griffin. He is hear with us in North Florada. He says to tell you that he has sene a big allagater. He told you they wer reel. His cusin Jesse Michel is in Georga now in Washinton Coutie. So is his cusin Michel Griffin. Tell the Curnal (there were two other attempts at this, marked out) ther is good land in Florada and Georga. Tell your little dawter hello. The brave one name Tempie that you put up the chimbly. Tell yor other chillin hello to. If you ever need any-thing, tell me or my cusins. You all was good to us. Your servent, James X Griffin Wrote by James Brown, Sen.

PERHAPS PHILIP AND THE BOYS would return soon. He had taken them, along with Dave, to New Bern for the General Assembly meeting. She'd have to stop calling them "boys." They were men. Jem was twenty now, and John eighteen. Jem preferred "James" now, and she was having a difficult time making that change, too. It was hard enough to remember that their part of Cumberland County was Moore County now, named for Alfred Moore, who'd been elected Attorney General by the North Carolina General Assembly. Alfred had come for a visit once, and she hadn't been terribly impressed, but Philip often brought visitors that he thought might help his career in politics.

The years since the war ended had been eventful. So much had changed. There'd been a general exodus of Loyalists, some heading to Europe, some to Canada, and some to the Caribbean. Most had lost property, seized by the state. There had been some unpleasantness between Connor Dowd, the mill owner, and Philip, soon after the war began. Philip had been charged with the duty of getting the local men to sign loyalty oaths to the new United States, and Connor had refused. Philip promptly had him locked up, demanding a huge sum as bond! When the war was ending, Connor had fled, heading first to Wilmington, and then when the British evacuated that city, he sailed to England in late 1781, leaving behind Mary and his ten children, some still at home. How could he? Philip would never have done that. She had helped Mary write several letters to him, asking for his return or his financial help, and over Philip's objections, she had advised Mary how to petition the state for relief.

Philip had been made a Justice of Peace and then elected Clerk of Court. He had been promised that James would be made Clerk of Court in his place when James turned twenty-one, and then just this last month, Philip had been elected to the State Senate. He was ambitious, and they were prosperous now. With the coming of spring, there would be parties again, as Philip schemed to garner favor with their wealthy neighbors. Truly, Temperance thought, I dread it. Smiling and making conversation with people I care nothing about.

She turned from the window and peeked into the cradle. Still sleeping. Near the fire, Nan sat on a low stool, mending Winnie's torn petticoat. "Nan, have you seen little Philip?"

"Yes, Miss Temp. He was headin' down to the stable to groom his pony. He sure loves that pony."

"If he's with Joe or Cesar, he's in good hands." Joe and Cesar between them managed the livestock on the plantation. "Come fetch me when Mary Drew wakes, Nan. I want to go see the progress on Elizabeth's new gown."

"Miss Lizbet is gonna outshine all the other young ladies!"

Elizabeth, Tempie and Winnie were gathered upstairs in the room they shared. Priss, called to duty as a seamstress, was carefully fitting a deep green dress to Elizabeth's slender body. Elizabeth at fifteen was a heart-stopping sight, with her grandmother's blonde curls and fair skin. She was scowling.

"Mama, Priss keeps sticking me," she complained.

"If you jes' keep still, Miss Lizbet." Priss muttered.

"You're an absolute marvel, Priss. The gown is lovely. Elizabeth, if you'd put a smile on that face, you might be a match for the gown," Temperance laughed. "What mischief are you two up to?" she asked Winnie and Tempie. They had their heads together over by the fire.

"Priss gave me the extra cloth from Sister's gown, so I'm making a gown for Winnie's doll." The doll had been Tempie's, but at nine she was endeavoring to be a young lady and had passed her doll on to her little sister. Tempie was learning to sew. She had begun her sampler under her mother's instruction and was faring much better than Elizabeth had at her age. Tempie was a serious child. Sometimes too serious, her mother thought. She could often be found tidying the books or dusting the mantels. She was the one to ask if something went missing in the household. She could always locate the misplaced comb or hairpin. Watchful. That was the word for her. Watchful. Her dark brown eyes in her thin face missed nothing.

And she was patient with Winnie. Temperance looked at the four-year-old by the fireplace, leaning close to Tempie as she sewed. She walked nearer. Tempie was frowning a little, deep in thought. She put her sewing down in her lap.

"Mama, I'm named for you, Philip is named for Papa, James is named for Uncle James, John is named for Papa's grandpapa and Uncle John," she put her fingers up, turning one down at a time as she named the family, "Elizabeth is named for Papa's mama *and* your mama. Baby Mary Drew is named for your grandmama *and* your papa. And baby William"—she knew about the little grave on the rise by the river; Temperance often walked there with the children—"was named for Papa's other brother. But who is Winnie named for? Do we have an Aunt Winifred?"

"Have I never told you about my friend Winifred McLeod? You probably don't remember her. She and her husband Duncan left the Deep River area when you were younger than Winnie is now. She was a dear friend, and I still miss her."

"Was she a Tory, Mama?" Tempie's eyes were wide. "Is that why she left?"

"Yes, but being a Tory doesn't always make you a bad person. She and her husband were from Scotland, and most of the Scots in North Carolina were loyal to the King. She and her husband came to the colonies before the war and acquired land near here. They were from Skye."

"From Sky?" Now Winnie's eyes were wide in wonder. "Is that like being from Heaven?"

Temperance laughed. "Well, to hear Winifred tell it, it was. No, sweet, Skye is the name of a Scottish island. There was fighting in Scotland, too, and Winifred and Duncan had to leave there because the army that Duncan fought with lost the war."

Tempie considered this. "Oh, did they have to leave America because they lost the war here, too?"

"Not exactly, but I think Duncan saw how things would go. They sold their land and went back to Europe just before the war. I haven't heard from them since. I don't know where they ended up. I pray for them often."

"Did they have any children?"

"No, God didn't give them children. That's one of the reasons I named Winifred for her, because she would never have children of her own to name. Oh, I wish she could have met you, Winnie."

"Would she like me?"

"Oh, yes, indeed. She surely would. Elizabeth, do you remember her?"

"Yes, Mama." Priss was helping Elizabeth out of the gown. "Ouch, Priss! I remember going with you to visit her. She let me try on her beautiful rings and necklaces. I imagine she took them all with her." There was a sorrowful note in her voice.

"Here's the story she told me about why she was named Winifred." Temperance settled down on the hearth.

"Once upon a time, long, long ago, there was a girl named Winifred whose father was going to make her marry a wicked man. She didn't want to do that, so the wicked man had her head cut off. Her head rolled away from her body, and where it landed, a spring of water gushed up from the earth. It was a special magic kind of healing water, and there's a well there to this day, in a country called Wales."

The girls were paying close attention. "Really, truly, Mama?" asked Winnie.

"That's the story they tell. Girls are named for St. Winifred even now. But my friend wasn't named for St. Winifred. She was named for a woman who was named for St. Winifred.

"This woman was Winifred Maxwell, and she was a countess. She was married to an earl." She saw Winnie's questioning eyes. "Countesses and earls are royalty. Like a King, only not as important. That's one of the ways we're different here in America." She was trying to make this simple for the girls. "Here we don't think you should be important and get to tell people what to do just because your father was important."

"But that's not the exciting part of the story. Winifred Maxwell's husband was fighting for a man who thought he should be king of Scotland, but the king of England was king of Scotland already. So there were battles about it, and Winifred's husband, who was called the Earl of Nithsdale, fought in the battles. Yes,

Nithsdale *is* a funny word, Winnie." Winnie was giggling, trying to repeat it.

"The Earl's army lost, and he got captured by the English soldiers and sent to the Tower of London. That was like a jail," this was for Winnie. "They were going to execute—kill—him. But the night before he was going to be exe—killed—Winifred took two friends and her maid and bribed the guards—that means she gave the guards some money, Winnie—to say farewell to him. Once they were inside, the other three women walked around talking to the guards and to the other prisoners while Winifred went in her husband's cell, helped him shave off his beard and dressed him up in a woman's cloak and smuggled him out of the Tower. The guards were so confused that they didn't notice there was an extra woman until it was too late. Winifred and the Earl escaped to France and then lived the rest of their lives in Italy."

"Our Winifred McLeod's mother was one of Winifred Maxwell's two friends. She went back to Scotland, and when she married, she named her daughter for the brave and clever woman who rescued her husband from the Tower of London."

"What a good story, Mama! So, our Winnie is named for a Winnie who was named for a Winnie who was named for a saint!" Tempie said triumphantly, ticking the Winnies off on her fingers.

"Exactly!" Nan appeared in the doorway holding a smiling baby girl. "Now, who wants to go out with me and look for daffodils?"

"I wish I were a Countess," said Elizabeth.

LINN: NINE

Late Thursday morning

IT WAS NEARLY TEN WHEN LINN WOKE. Downstairs, held onto the fridge by a magnet from the local exterminating company, there was a note from Mom.

Linn:
Unload dryer/fold towels.
Taco night. Thaw hburg.
Home by 2 PM.
It ended with a little heart with "Mom" written inside.

Linn poured a cup of cold coffee from the coffeemaker pot into a mug and zapped it in the microwave while she rummaged in the freezer for a package of ground beef.

She'd put her phone on the counter. Guess she'd better call Marcie and get it over with. She wasn't going back no matter what Dad said. Marcie would know if there was some kind of withdrawal form to be filled out. And she needed to figure out how to get the rest of her stuff home. She'd had to box up what she didn't bring with her on the plane to be stored in the basement until fall.

"Hi, Linn." Marcie answered on the second ring.

"You called me, Marcie? Before you say anything, I need to tell you I'm not coming back in the fall so I don't need a room."

"What? No, that's not why I called. Linn, it was Jake Munro you went out with, right? He's been arrested for rape. A girl that's here for summer session. I don't think you know her. He's saying it was consensual. He attacked you, didn't he?"

"Yes, but . . . "

"I talked to her parents. Their attorney wants you to come back and testify. If they can show a pattern, it'll help her case."

"Come back there? No."

"Yes. I don't know exactly when yet, but I can let you know in plenty of time. Linn, you've got to. He needs to be stopped. This girl, Courtney, he messed her up."

"Marcie, I don't know. I haven't told anybody about what happened. You're the only one who knows."

"You need to talk to your parents, Linn. Jake committed a crime. He raped Courtney. And he assaulted you, if nothing else. And what do you mean, you're not coming back?"

"I haven't talked to them about that either."

"Linn, you've got to talk to them. And call me tomorrow morning. This is a good time. I'm back from class. Call me at ten, or I'm calling you. I mean it."

"I will, Marcie.

"I'm serious."

"Bye, Marcie." But she had already hung up.

The microwave had dinged while she was on the phone. She splashed some milk in the mug and took it in the laundry room with her. She wasn't hungry anymore. Some folding and thinking helped Linn come up with a plan. She'd bake some brownies and ask if Gran could come over for dessert. With her there, maybe she could get out what she needed to say, and surely, Dad wouldn't yell at her in front of Gran. But the rape thing. What to do about that?

Her dad had a lot of respect for Gran. Susan Sullivan had been the wife of the senior partner of the law firm that still carried his name. Linn had heard the story many times as part of her dad's "I came up the hard way" saga. Sullivan and Drake had hired Bill McKinney fresh out of law school at the somewhat advanced age of twenty-nine. It had taken Bill quite a few years to make his way through college and law school, because he had to find jobs to support himself. No student loans for him, no sir! If you couldn't pay for it, you shouldn't have it.

When he'd applied at Sullivan and Drake, Granddad Sullivan had looked at his grades and the glowing recommendations from the faculty at Emory University, laughed at his resume, which included bartending, convenience store clerking, and playing Santa at a mall, and hired him on the spot. "You're just what we need, Bill. We can use you at the Christmas office party if you don't work out anywhere else."

Bill had made junior partner a few years later, and Susan Sullivan had brought her unmarried-school-teacher daughter Anne to the cocktail party held at the office to celebrate his promotion. Anne liked his down-to-earth qualities and invited him to dinner at her parents' house, but it took Bill nearly two years after that to summon the courage to ask her to marry him. "After all," he liked to say. "I grew up on a turkey farm in rural Georgia. I had nothing in common with this exotic swan of a woman."

Linn smiled now, thinking of her mother. Anne was an attractive middle-aged woman, and she'd certainly been attractive as a young woman, too. Linn had seen photos. But "exotic"? Hardly. Linn got her honey-brown hair from her, and her regular features. But Mom's nothing out of the ordinary. Love sees with different eyes, Linn thought.

It'll be about the money with Dad, she thought. Her first year of school had cost him a bundle. Will he think of it as wasted? And if she had to fly back for a court case, that'd cost. But Gran's got a little money. Maybe I can borrow from her and pay her back after I graduate. And I'm going to need a car even if they let me live at home and go to school here. She stopped folding, grabbed a pencil from the counter and an envelope from the recycling bin and calculated how much money she'd earn this summer at the Rec Center plus the amount in her savings account from last summer plus some money from Gran for transcribing the family tree. Oh. It won't be much of a car. Oh, well. That was okay.

Upstairs, in her room, she looked at GeeGee's notes again. Who was this George Glascock that Philip had Dave-the-slave kill? She turned on her laptop and googled "George Glascock" "North Carolina."

An hour later, she turned away from the computer, confused. Some of the accounts claimed Glascock's mother was first cousin to George Washington; others said no, the relationship was more distant. Some said he was a surgeon in the Revolutionary Army at the Battle of Guilford Courthouse; others said no, he billed the government for one pound, a shilling, and sixpence for medicine three years after the battle.

Linn didn't really care. All the accounts agreed that he died in 1787, at the hands of Philip Alston's slave. Who was named Dave.

On the banks of the Deep River,
August 18, 1787

"Linnet, WHERE IS DAVE?" Philip's voice was quiet in her ear. He had come up behind her, as she stood on the porch watching the dancing in the yard. The gathering was in honor of Elizabeth's birthday, and neighbors from the neighboring plantations had ridden in. "He should be here passing drinks."

"I haven't seen him all evening. Not since he helped clear away the dinner. I'll go ask in the kitchen."

"No, I'll send someone to do that. There's Philip," he said, spotting the nine-year-old sitting in the shadows, his legs dangling through the porch railings. "Come here, son."

"Yes, Papa. But I'm not bothering anyone."

"Go to the kitchen and ask if anyone has seen Dave. Come tell me, and then go up to bed."

"Yes, sir." There was a deep sigh, and the boy slipped out the back door to head to the kitchen house.

"Lindy can manage the drinks. There's Lindy now." She beckoned Lindy to her side. "Lindy, make sure everyone gets something to drink until Dave comes back."

"Yes, Miss Temp."

"Dinah will be bringing in some late supper soon, and Sall

can help serve. I wonder where Dave has taken himself. It's not like him. I'll need to slip away for a few minutes to feed Drew." The newest member of the family was six weeks old now, little Drew Smith Alston. Mary Drew had become simply "Mady" to everyone but Temperance, so she and Philip had decided to name this baby for Temperance's beloved father, too. Little Mady's attempt at his name sounded like "Drew-rie," and the other children were already calling him that, so Temperance was careful to say "Drew," in referring to him.

Drew was a small baby, the smallest of her babies, Temperance thought, except the ones who didn't live. She worried about Drew. Nursing seemed to tire him, and his tiny nails had a blueish tinge. Perhaps it's just the heat. It had been a draining summer. When the cool weather comes, we'll all feel stronger.

Elizabeth was dancing in the yard, her fair face flushed. She was certainly the prettiest at the party, in a sapphire blue gown that matched the color of her excited eyes. Her seventeenth birthday gift had been her mother's string of pearls, and they bobbed now against her young breasts as she bounced down the length of the couples. A fiddler sitting on a bench under a tree was playing the tunes, and all the young people were dancing, including James and John. The Willcoxes had come over from Gulf, bringing their daughters Betsy and Polly, and Polly and James were leading the dance now. Temperance thought it was kind of James to dance with twelve-year-old Polly, who was promising to be a beauty. John was just behind him with Tempie.

There was Dinah speaking to Philip. Temperance eased over to hear her.

"I ain't seen him, Mister Philip."

"Can you and Sall manage?" Temperance asked. "I'll send Nan from inside. I'm going in now. She can help you bring in the food." She turned and walked quickly through the open door. Philip followed, saying, "You're right. It's not like Dave to shirk his duty. Where do you think he can be?"

Temperance shrugged and shook her head. "Do you think people will stay much longer? I'm so tired."

"I can make your excuses, little Linnet. You have a new baby bird to care for."

"Oh, Philip, I *do* love you. I don't think anyone will even notice if I leave. Everyone's watching Elizabeth."

"She's not as lovely as her mother. Go on to bed. I'll be in as soon as they all go home." He leaned to kiss her. As she turned into their room, he gave her bottom an approving pat. "You're a beautiful woman, my sweet. Get some sleep."

The night was short for everyone in the house. The next morning, a Sunday, started early, with a banging at the big front door. "Colonel Alston, Colonel Alston!"

John was the first one at the door. He and James had slept in the parlor. There had been a general reshuffling of sleeping arrangements to accommodate the Willcoxes so they wouldn't have to make the trip across the river and back to Gulf. Some of the other guests had elected to sleep in their wagon beds, and there were even some young men bedded down on the porch. John could see heads emerging from blankets.

"Son, get your father." There were two solemn-faced men standing there.

"Why? What's happened?" James was behind John now, elbowing him aside, as Philip came out of the bedroom.

"Yes?" said Philip.

"Colonel Alston, we've arrested one of your slaves for shooting George Glascock. He tried to escape, but one of George's sons caught him when he was trying to ride away."

"Glascock? One of my slaves? I don't understand."

"That light-skinned man you take everywhere with you. Dave, is it?"

"Dave shot George Glascock?"

Temperance was in the hall, pulling a wrapper around herself, capless, with her hair tousled and tumbling in her shocked eyes.

"He very nearly got away. He's not talking, but folks are saying you sent him."

"I sent him?" Philip was shaking his head in disbelief. "Come in. Wait in the parlor. I'll be back. Give me a few minutes to dress. James, see if these gentlemen need anything."

Temperance followed Philip back into their room, picking up Drew from the cradle by the bed. He was shrieking in fury at being awakened. She tugged her shift aside and settled back onto the bed, giving him her breast.

"What are you going to do, Philip?"

"Do? I'm going to go bail him out and insist on a trial. They'll hang him, you know, if I don't intervene."

Philip was dressing hurriedly, but with his usual care. He ran his hand across his face. He'd shaved just before the party. It would have to do. He slipped into the office and brought in the lock box, opened it and added a thick wad of bills to his purse, which went into his pocket.

"I'll be back as soon as I can. Send James to have Cesar get two horses ready for a trip. Without anyone noticing, if possible. And get Dinah to go to Dave's cabin and pack his things. Quietly. Oh, and tell her to get some provisions ready."

"Philip, you're not going to run off with Dave!" Temperance was pale. "What do you think possessed him to go shoot Mr. Glascock?"

"I don't know. I'll find out." Philip answered her last question first, then, "No, Linnie, I'm going to send James with him to Georgia. Don't argue with me," he added as her mouth opened.

"Wait. Not James. Send John."

Philip studied her face.

"Everyone will notice if James is missing." There was resignation and acceptance in her voice. She was right. John lived in James's shadow. "If anyone should ask, we can just say that John has gone back to Charleston to William's house to continue his studies."

"John it is. Talk to him and James, and tell John to be ready. If James gives you an argument, tell him I need him here. I have no idea how long this will take."

And he was gone, shutting the door behind him.

Temperance wondered briefly if she'd ever see the land Philip had bought in Washington County, in Georgia. A year or so ago, he and the two older boys, with Dave, had ridden off to look at some land. He'd come home pleased with himself. He'd struck a good bargain for a property on the Oconee River that included some islands. "There's even a little cabin on the river bank," he told her on his return.

"But why, Philip?" she asked him. "Why do we need land in Georgia?"

"Land is always a good investment. More and more people are going to Georgia. We can hold on to it for a few years and then sell it at a profit. Oh, remember the Griffin boy who wrote you?" Temperance's face was already lighting up as she nodded. "Some of his kin are there in Washington County. I met a young man, Benjamin Mitchell Griffin—calls himself 'Mitchell'—who was carrying chains for the surveyor. He knew all about our family. You must have made quite an impression on James Griffin. Mitchell asked about you specifically. Called you 'Miss Linnie.' He knew the story of how you put the children in the chimney. I liked him. He's a good-looking young man. Tall, blond, strong. Very capable. Elizabeth's age, I'd guess. Younger than James and John. James didn't much like him, but I don't know why."

"I can guess. Did you offer him much praise? James likes to be the only star in your eyes."

Philip had nodded. She was right. James was never gracious about being outshone, by anyone. John had always had to be second-best. James would have it no other way.

Drew was soaking wet, of course. She called Nan in to tend him and went to talk to her older sons.

It had been such an unsettling few years, politically. The Glascock family had relocated from Chatham County to the Deep River area, buying land from James Muse over on Killet Creek. When Philip had been elected Clerk of Court in Moore County in 1784, he had named George his deputy. Henry Lightfoot had been elected first senator from Moore County to the new General Assembly that same year, with William Seal and John Cox elected as representatives. Then the next year, George Glascock, as a justice, had cast the deciding vote for the office of Sheriff, electing Richardson Feagin, who promptly appointed George's son, John Milton Glascock as his deputy. Philip came home raging about that.

An alliance formed—Philip called it the Unholy Trinity—among Henry Lightfoot, Glascock, and John Cox. The three lived in settlements that were mainly populated by Scots, and there were still some hard feelings among the Scots towards Philip. Philip was elected to the Senate in 1785, defeating Henry Lightfoot. In December of that year, an indictment was read in the General Assembly charging Philip with the murder of Thomas Taylor. Several testified that Taylor at the time was an enemy of the State. Philip applied for and received a pardon from Governor Richard Caswell, but there still remained the formality of a trial in Wilmington, at which the charges would be dismissed.

Philip won a Senate seat again in 1786, defeating Thomas Tyson and Thomas Mathews. At the November session in Cross Creek, now renamed Fayetteville after the Marquis, Lightfoot filed a memorial and Glascock, a petition saying that Philip should be removed, because he was still under indictment for Taylor's murder, the case not yet having come to court. Glascock, added that Philip was an atheist and had threatened him. (Philip, in recounting this to Temperance at dinner, said darkly, "Not yet, I haven't.")

Philip lost his seat temporarily, but Lightfoot, who had offered himself as a replacement, lost to Thomas Tyson. Philip's arrest followed, and his bail set at one thousand pounds. Temperance scrambled to come up with that sum. In court on December 11th, the governor's pardon was accepted, and the charges were dropped.

And then in May, George Glascock triumphed, and Philip lost his seat permanently, because of his avowed atheism. There had been a swirl of suits, accusations, and petitions passing back and forth between George and Philip in the summer months. Temperance had lost track. Philip's life was consumed by the controversy, and he and James, along with Dave, were frequently away from the House in the Horseshoe. John was continuing his studies in Charleston, staying at his Uncle William's house.

On his rare days at home, Philip and James plotted and planned, seated in the parlor, with Dave in attendance, ready at the decanter. In late July, Temperance had interrupted one of the evening strategy sessions, which centered on causing as much political and financial damage as possible to the Trinity, but most especially George Glascock.

"Philip, enough is enough. George will be your enemy as long as he lives. I don't really understand the hatred he seems to bear you, nor you him, but I do not want this house and my family poisoned any longer by this." She stood straight and unsmiling.

Philip looked at her in surprise. It was unlike Temperance to intervene in his political affairs.

Before he could speak, James was on his feet. "Mama, this is no concern of yours."

"I think it is, son." Temperance turned and addressed him. "I've made many concessions to your father. There are women I'm not permitted to invite into my home any longer for tea or for Bible study, simply because their sons or husbands have had disagreements with your father. George Glascock is unlikely to change, even if you defeat him temporarily. As long as he lives in this county, and you treat him as an enemy, nothing will be different. You cannot win. I want you two to leave all this behind when you come into your home. Have you two even noticed that the rest of the family avoids being with you?" She was flushed, but her voice was steady and quiet.

"She's right, James." Philip saw that his son was clenching his fists. "This house belongs to all of us. Linnie, my love, you have my promise. James and I will keep this business out of the house, but I can't promise you it won't go on when we are away from here. And you are equally right in saying that George Glascock will never let go of his vengeful behavior against my family as long as he's alive."

No one noticed Dave, standing by the sideboard, decanter in hand. He squared his shoulders and bit his bottom lip, his eyes narrowed in thought.

LINN: TEN
Thursday afternoon

THE BROWNIES WERE COOLING IN THEIR PAN, and the bowl of chocolate frosting was ready to spread on top. Linn filed the recipes back in the recipe box. She smiled, noticing how stained and frayed the two cards were. She could almost hear her mother, "Wish I had a dollar for every time I've made a batch of these."

Time to clean up a little after she browned the beef and chopped the lettuce and tomatoes. She cut up some onions. Dad liked onions on his tacos, she and Mom didn't. She put the lettuce, tomatoes and onions in serving dishes, covered them with plastic wrap, and stashed them in the fridge next to the sour cream, grated cheese and picante sauce. Anything else? Black olives. She found a can on the shelf.

Upstairs she changed her t-shirt to a yellow blouse—Dad's favorite color—and brushed her hair out of its ponytail. Sandals on her feet. Dad didn't like bare feet at the dinner table. She could never figure out why. It wasn't like you put your feet on the table.

There was still an hour before she needed to be back in the kitchen. She moved a stack of folders to her desk, pulled out Philip Alston's family chart and opened her laptop. Pulling up what she'd entered on Family Tree Maker, she studied the dates. She hadn't noticed that Philip had lost a daughter, Elizabeth, about the same time his wife died. Elizabeth was about my age, she thought. Nineteen. I guess she never married.

Turning, she reached to the bed behind for George Willcox's book and found the chapter on Philip's descendants. Apparently nineteen was just a guess for Elizabeth. It was all based on when Philip sold some property of hers in May of 1789. She flipped back a few pages to re-read a section about Temperance. Same thing. She was alive in March of 1788 when she signed a deed, and dead by April of the next year when Philip sold some of her property. It seemed a little sad to think these two had left so little mark on the world that nobody knew exactly when they were born or when they died. Or how they died, she realized.

How MANY TIMES HAVE I WATCHED for Philip to come home? Temperance turned from the window overlooking the drive leading from the gate, letting the curtain fall back into place. The house was very quiet. She had forbidden the younger children to come upstairs or to make noise, and Nan was keeping them in the parlor, with a subdued ten-year-old Philip taking his "man of the house" position to heart. She had sent John riding to fetch Philip and James home from their pursuit of yet another law suit against—oh, who remembered who now? And did it even matter?

Elizabeth lay dying just behind her in the room she'd shared with her sisters. Sall was bringing clean bedding from the wash house, and she had sent Tempie for hot water. The terrible flux and the vomiting had drained away Elizabeth's life. She had lapsed into a dreadful stillness from which they could not rouse her just a few hours ago at dawn.

Temperance squared her shoulders and turned from the window. The room was oppressively hot. They'd kept the fire going constantly, because Elizabeth had complained of the cold when they first carried her upstairs. Temperance wished she could hear the fretful voice just once more. Behind her, carrying a steaming basin, Tempie slipped quietly into the room. She put it down on the washstand and dipped a cloth into the water. Wringing it out, she brought it to her mother. Temperance gently washed the last dribble of vomit from Elizabeth's chin and smoothed a sweat-stiffened blonde curl back from her daughter's ashen face. Elizabeth's breathing was shallow and labored.

"I don't think it will be long now. Perhaps you should tell Nan to bring the others one at a time, if they'd like to say a farewell." Temperance choked on the last word.

Her daughter, taller at thirteen than her mother, hugged her silently and left the room.

Temperance, waiting alone, opened the curtains to the morning. Elizabeth's trunk stood against the wall, still unpacked. Two days ago, late afternoon, the carriage had arrived, and John had jumped down and run quickly up the steps, calling for his mother. He and Elizabeth had gone, with Priss, to Chatham County to visit the aunts and uncles. Since their grandfather's death in 1781, there had been a time of reconciliation in the family. Once Elizabeth had learned that Grandfather Alston's youngest son, Jack, was buying land and setting up house in Chatham County, she had talked incessantly about making a visit. Jack was the same age as her brother John, twenty-two. Nearby, Philip's brother John's widow, Ann Hunt, was living with a whole houseful of Elizabeth's cousins, including three young men in their twenties. What fun that would be!

Her parents had finally agreed. Perhaps it would be good to have Elizabeth meet some young men. She was close to nineteen now, and so far, no one had captured her fancy, or, more importantly, asked for permission to court her. Letters had been exchanged with the family in Chatham County, and in early March, after a flurry of dressmaking and packing, Elizabeth, chaperoned by John, had left in the carriage, an unhappy Priss accompanying Elizabeth as lady's maid.

Philip's brother William was not in residence in Chatham County during the visit. He had just left to travel to Virginia to take the waters at the sulfur springs. For years he had been in poor health, but it had been his wife who had died, unexpectedly, three years earlier. He had piled his five children in on his sister-in-law, Ann Hunt, so her household when Elizabeth and John arrived consisted of eight children under twelve, in addition to her grown sons.

Elizabeth did not find the visit at all pleasing. Jack gave parties, but she didn't receive the attention she thought she deserved. Other young women were there, and they seemed to have more conversation than she did, even though she knew she was by far the prettiest. Elizabeth was glad of an excuse when she found herself feeling suddenly unwell. She thanked her aunt for her hospitality and had Priss pack her trunk in the room she'd been forced to share with four silly, giggling little girl cousins who annoyed her by begging to try on her finery.

Temperance had been surprised at their unexpected return, but her surprise turned quickly to dismay, as Elizabeth was carried from the carriage. John told Temperance, "We had to stop often along the way for her to vomit, Mama." He lowered his voice. "And she has the flux."

Elizabeth said only, "I'm home, Mama," and "I'm cold."

The doctor, sent for from Carthage, shook his head. "See if you can get her to hold down some broth. Keep her warm. There's nothing I can do."

The end came quickly. Elizabeth gagged and choked on the broth and vomited again. Temperance, with Sall and Tempie, changed linens and wiped her face, but it was only a matter of hours before the sunken eyes, gray skin, and labored breathing told Temperance that she was losing her oldest daughter. Temperance held back a sob. She wanted to run screaming from the house, but that wouldn't do. She wanted to tear her hair out and rip her clothes. How did people bear this? Beautiful Elizabeth. Where was Philip? How could she do this alone?

Tempie was watching her anxiously. "Mama?"

"This is going to be very hard, sweet."

"What's going to happen now, Mama?"

"Elizabeth will die, and we'll bury her, and we'll grieve for the life that's lost. And then, someday soon, we'll remember some of the silly things she did, and we'll laugh and miss her."

"Will she go to heaven, Mama?"

"Yes, surely. God loves her even more than we do."

Philip didn't get there in time. He didn't get there in time to say farewell to his wife, either. The next day, when Elizabeth was buried, Temperance felt as though the life had drained out of her, too. There was a bone-deep exhaustion that she had never felt before. She had dressed that morning in the darkest gown she had, a deep gray gown that Philip had never liked.

On the way back to the house from the little burial plot, she had felt a sudden cramping in her midsection, and had a moment to wonder if cholera was striking her, too, before a gush of fluid told her that she was losing the baby she hadn't yet told Philip was coming. Her courses had been irregular in the last year, and she was not sure about the baby until she felt the familiar faint flutter in her middle.

Back at the house, she called for Dinah and laid an old quilt on the bed before climbing onto it. The baby, a little girl, was delivered quickly. She was the size of Temperance's hand. The bleeding wouldn't stop. Dinah massaged her womb through her belly, but nothing helped. "Get Tempie." The request was barely audible.

A pale-faced and shocked young girl was led to her mother's side. The metallic stench of blood was overpowering. Temperance managed to raise herself on one elbow to say, "I need you to be strong. Hold this family together." There was a pause for breath. "I love you all so much. Look after your papa."

"Mama! No!"

"Look after Papa. Promise me."

"I promise, Mama."

And that was all. Temperance lowered her head to the pillow and closed her eyes. Dinah held the sobbing child as the rest of the children and the slaves gathered, stunned, in the room and in the hall. The House in the Horseshoe without the mistress they all adored. It was unthinkable.

Sall and Dinah laid her out on the bed, washing her tenderly. They brushed out the brown curls, touched now with gray. The tiny baby was wrapped in a piece of white linen and placed in her arms.

Nan kept Mady and Drew in the parlor. Winnie and Philip went down to the gate to watch for their father and their big brothers. Tempie sat with her mother for a long time. Then she looked at the empty white pitcher on the mantel and jumped up and grabbed it and ran out the back door. Yes, she was right. Coming back from burying Elizabeth she had noticed yellow blossoms. She picked a pitcherful of daffodils and took them back to the house.

Philip and Winnie were still keeping watch at the gate when Philip rode up with James and John. Philip reined in his horse when he saw them, and swung off. "Is Elizabeth all right? Where's your mother?"

"Oh, Papa!" Winnie wailed and threw herself at him, sobbing. "Elizabeth's dead. The baby's dead. And Mama's dead. They've all gone to heaven."

James and John had dismounted, too, and were running to the house. Philip followed more slowly, carrying Winnie, with young Philip close beside him. As they entered, Tempie was walking into her mother's room, carrying a pitcher full of bright daffodils. For a heart-stopping moment, Philip saw Linnet, but then Tempie turned. "Papa," she said. "She's in here with the baby."

"Give me a moment," he said, and walked into the parlor. James and John were already there, questioning a weeping Dinah. He listened silently to her answers. Dead. All dead.

A crackling fire was burning in the fireplace. "Is there anything I can get you, Mr. Philip?" she asked. Nan and Sall were waiting in the hall, and he saw Joe and Cesar there, along with Toby. I'll have to write to Georgia and let Dave know, he thought. He should be here. He killed for her twice. What was he calling himself now? He couldn't think. Dinah took his headshake as a "No," and started to turn away, but Philip said, "Wait, Dinah. Whiskey. James, John?"

Dinah nodded to Toby, who had taken Dave's place. He came in and filled three glasses. John said "No, Toby. Thank you, though," to his silent offer of the third glass. Philip drank his down in one swallow, took the glass John had refused and downed that, too.

Tempie had come into the parlor. Philip took her hand and followed his daughter, his oldest daughter now, he thought, into the room he shared for so many years with his wife. Five, no, seven children had been born in that room. From nowhere came the thought: I wonder if Linnet named this one.

"Can you leave us, child?" Tempie slipped her hand from his and left the room, closing the door softly behind her.

Linnet was different somehow. Her face, that he had seen so often in laughter, was still. Her deep brown eyes were closed. I've done this to you, he thought. I left you to deal with the real things, the everyday things, while I chased after justice, and my reputation. He moved the linen cloth aside that covered the tiny body lying in her arms. I didn't even know. The little creature seemed barely human; white, tiny, and wizened. A girl, Dinah had said. I'll ask Tempie about a name for her. Names were important to Linnie. We'll bury her tomorrow with a name. Oh, dear God-that-I-don't-believe-in. How can I bury her? You were so real to her, God. Why can't I believe that she's happy to be with you, happy to be at peace?

Philip lay that night, not sleeping, wrapped in a blanket on the floor by the bed, after James and John had said their goodbyes to their mother. James was silent; John wept. On the mantel, a white pitcher full of daffodils kept watch.

In the morning, Philip asked Tempie about a name for the baby. Her reply was prompt: "Dinah." Philip was silent, thinking. And then, "Yes. Dinah was with her through all your births. She was there through the joyous times and the sorrowful times. Your mother would like that. We'll call the baby Dinah."

On the rise above the river, another grave was dug. Temperance Smith Alston and her daughter Dinah joined the others buried there; Elizabeth in her fresh grave; baby William; the boy who had died at the foot of the stairs that hot July day, John

Miller; the Scotsman, McCrae, if that indeed was what he was called; and the nameless man who tried to set fire to the house. A little way off was the slave graveyard, with six mounds marked with wooden slabs. Temperance's visits on Sunday afternoons had ensured that both little cemeteries were well-kept. Who would tend them now? Philip wondered. I can't stay here without her. I can't.

John led the mourners in prayer, neighbors, slaves and family; reading the burial service from his mother's well-worn leather-bound prayer book, while Dinah, for whom the baby was named, wept quietly. Philip stood behind the group, silent, staring past everyone to the river.

LINN: ELEVEN
Thursday evening

Linn put her frosted brownies on a plate, grabbed a few napkins from the basket on the counter, and headed back into the dining room. Mom had been more than willing to have Gran come for dessert when Linn asked, and had suggested that Linn extend the invitation to cover supper. "Your Gran's not crazy about tacos, but I know she gets tired of cooking for herself. I'll make some guacamole when I get home. There are some corn chips in the pantry. That'll stretch things a little."

The coffee maker proudly announced its production of a pot of decaf with a shrill series of beeps, and Linn and her mom brought in mugs and cream and sugar.

When they were all settled at the table, Gran said, "I think Linn has something to tell you."

Both of her parents looked at Linn with alarm.

"No, wait, don't panic. I'm not getting married or having a baby or anything. It's just that I've decided not to go back to school in Massachusetts. There's no point, because I'm really not cut out to be a lawyer. Wait, Dad." She could see that his mouth was open, ready to jump in. "Let me talk first. I know that this is something you've always wanted for me. But it's not anything I want for myself."

Bill McKinney's face was grim. "Really, Linn? Not everyone gets the opportunities you've had. I would have given anything to have had your advantages."

Oh, no, he's going to launch into his coming-up-the-hard-way spiel. "But there's something else I have to tell you. Gran, you don't even know this yet. Last spring, well, right before spring break, I went on a blind date with this guy. He attacked me, tried to rape me."

Linn's mom was on her feet now. "He did what? Oh, Linn."

"Nothing actually happened. I guess the muscles from all that swimming helped. I was able to fight him off. I kneed him and punched him and scratched, until he gave up. But then today I heard from Marcie—the R.A. on my floor. Turns out he actually *did* rape someone this summer. Marcie says I should come back there and testify at a hearing. I don't want to. Do you think I have to, Dad? Can they make me?"

Her dad said, "I'm not a criminal attorney, Linn. I'll have to check Massachusetts law. Can you get me the number of—does the girl have an attorney? This boy needs to pay for what he's done."

"Marcie says Courtney—that's the girl—that her family does have a lawyer. The lawyer is the one who told Marcie to call me. See, Jake is saying that what happened was consensual. But it wasn't, any more than it was for me."

"Get the facts for me. The girl's name, her attorney, a phone number, and I'll see what I can do. Are you positive he didn't, you know, physically," there was a pause, and Bill looked down at his coffee cup as though the answer lay there, "penetrate you?"

"Yes, Dad. I'm really sure. But if I go back, I'll have to tell them that I was drunk from all the punch I drank at the party. That was the first time I've ever done that. Gotten drunk, I mean. I'm sorry, Mom. Dad." And then the tears came.

"No, it's okay, honey," Anne was crouched on the floor by Linn's chair now, holding her. "Nothing gives a man the right to force you to have sex. I'm just furious that this happened to you. I wish you had told us. Why didn't you tell us?"

"I should have. I know I should have. I just felt so ashamed. I felt like it was partly my fault. If I hadn't drunk all that nasty punch. She shuddered now, remembering. "And then GeeGee died."

Gran had been silent. The evening was certainly not going according to plan. She had rehearsed her part in her mind as she drove to the McKinneys' house. If she needed to, she was going to remind Bill that he'd had to buck his own parents to become what he wanted to be. Well, that could wait.

But still...

"Bill, are you going to be all right with Linn not working for you this summer? She wants to go back and lifeguard at the Rec Center. They want her to teach swimming to the beginners."

"Please don't be mad with me, Dad."

"I'm not angry, Linn. It's not that. I just want you to be sure before you make any rash decisions."

"I am sure, Dad. I knew before I even went off to school that I didn't want to go. But you were so proud of my being accepted there. I've thought about it a lot this year. I want to go into nursing, maybe end up in pediatric nursing."

"Have you thought about medical school? Maybe you could change your major to pre-med?"

"And what's wrong with pediatric nursing, Bill?" her mother said. "Here, sweetheart, blow your nose." She was on her way back to her chair. "That's something you'd be perfect doing. You've always been so good with children. Bill, think about the babysitting she's done the last couple of years for the Grahams. You know, Mom, the family with the little boy with cerebral palsy," she turned to her mother.

"Well, first things first," Bill said. "Get me that number tomorrow morning and call me at the office. Honey, it's okay. Stop crying. And pass the brownies. You know you're still my next-to-favorite child."

Linn managed a smile. This was a longtime tease from Dad.

It's not over, she thought. He's not going to give in this easily. But it went better than I imagined it would.

Linn excused herself after Gran left and went up to her bedroom. It was still pretty much the room she'd moved into as an eleven-year-old. Twin beds so she could have a friend for sleepovers. She slept in the one under the window, and she looked now at the other bed, piled high with dirty clothes and stacks of folders. Mom was pretty good about not hassling her about her messy room, but it did look as though an eleven-year-old still lived here. She gathered up an armload of the slightly smelly clothes she'd dumped from her suitcase on Sunday and piled them in the laundry basket on her floor. I'll deal with them tomorrow, and then I'll call Marcie. I guess I could text her, but she said to call.

If Dad and Mom will let me stay on here and go to school, I could be a little neater. Wonder if they'd let me paint. She looked speculatively at the lavender walls and the rainbow curtains and matching spreads that she'd insisted on eight years ago when they'd moved into the house.

Clearing a spot on her desk and transferring the folders, she saw a loose piece of paper that must have fallen from one of them. It was a copy of an item from a newspaper, the North Carolina Chronicle: "Broke gaol on the 5th inst., Philip Alston, late of Moore county, committed as accessory to the murder of George Glascock. All persons are required to be aiding and assisting in apprehending, so that he be again committed to gaol, and any expenses thereon will be paid by the subscribers. Thomas Wright, Sheriff, Wilmington, January 8th, 1790."

What does "5th inst." mean? She googled "inst." It meant "within this present month." So Philip escaped "gaol"—she knew that was "jail'—on January 5th. Amazing! First a British prison ship, then jail. Wonder how he managed this one?

On the banks of the Deep River,
January 5, 1790

A BANGING ON THE HEAVY DOOR of the brick jail in Wilmington brought the jailer to the little barred window. A tall handsome blond man, dressed against the cold, looked back at him.

"Is this where you're holding Colonel Alston? I'm his attorney, Milton Gresham. How about letting me in? It's cold out here."

"The sheriff's not here, but I guess that would be all right, Mister...?"

"Gresham."

The jailer, a stocky red-faced man in his fifties, opened the door and admitted the visitor, who was followed by a graying mulatto man, burdened down with a stack of papers and a leather satchel.

"Can't leave my man Joe out there. If he freezes, he won't be much good to me. I have some papers the Colonel has to sign. We need to sell off some of his land to pay off some debts. His daughter and son will be along soon. They need to sign, too, and perhaps you can witness the signatures."

"Yes, sir. Have a seat, sir. Take that bench near the fire."

"What's your name, fellow?"

"Francis O'Neill, sir."

"Well, Francis, how about joining me in a warming beverage? Where's that bottle, Joe?"

"Here, Mister Milton." Joe rummaged in the satchel and brought out a bottle of rum.

"Well, hand it over, then. Here, you first, Francis."

Three-quarters of an hour later, Francis's face was even redder, and tears were running down his cheeks. He was laughing at yet another crude joke told by the attorney. There was a knock at the door, which brought a slurred, "Well, open it, boy!" from the jailer. The man called Joe opened it to a girl in a serviceable brown hooded cloak, followed by a slightly-built young man.

The blond man introduced them to the jailer, who swayed slightly as he got to his feet. "This is John Alston and his sister Temperance. Mr. O'Neill, the jailer. He's been very helpful."

"Thank you for your kindness, Mr. O'Neill. Which way is Papa's cell?" The girl saw O'Neill looking at a door on the opposite side of the room. "This way? Is he all right?" Temperance had opened the inner door and was headed down the narrow passageway, calling, "Papa? Papa?"

They heard her voice, "Oh, you look sickly, Papa. We're here with some papers for you to sign. Mr. Gresham, John, please come," she called back. "Hurry. Papa doesn't look well."

As they followed, the attorney's man Joe held out the bottle again to O'Neill. "It is mighty cold down that hall. They don't need us yet. Let's us stay here by the fire."

Very shortly, a figure cloaked and hooded in brown came into the front room, led by John and followed by the tall blond man. "That's done. Here, boy. Take these papers. We need to get on the road. It's getting dark. Thank you again, Francis. You can keep the rest of that bottle."

There was a burst of cold air as the three left by the heavy door. And then a girl's shout from the passageway. "Jailer! Hurry! Something is wrong with Papa!"

Francis struggled to his feet, confused. Didn't she just leave? He headed through the door and staggered down the hall, bumping the wall as he went. Temperance was beckoning him on, and leaning into her father's cell. "Hurry. Do!"

As he came in and went past her to what seemed to be a blanketed figure on the cot, Temperance swung the iron barred door shut and ran, cloakless, through the hall towards the front door. Outside, a mounted Mitchell Griffin waited, holding the reins of Temperance's horse. He threw a cloak around her as she swung quickly into the saddle, and they were off, headed to Georgia.

Mitchell looked over at the fourteen-year-old galloping next to him, her hair blown back as she rode. He remembered his cousin James's description of her: "Skinny little brown-haired thang, but brave as you could imagine. Bullets flyin' everwhar, and she wuz jest as steady as could be, holdin' on to her little brother's hand, sittin' up on a little bench in the chimbley, with her big sister squallin' away lak a banshee beside 'er."

That would have been what? Eight years ago, about. James had talked about that day often. From what Mitchell could figure, it hadn't been much of a battle, not many casualties, but the Alston family had certainly found a place in James's heart and imagination. The kind woman he called "Miss Linnie." The aristocratic Colonel. The brave little girl, Tempie. Mitchell had been glad to put faces to some of them when Colonel Alston, along with his older sons and a slave, had come to Washington County to buy some property. When the Colonel had found out Mitchell was kin to the Mitchells and the Griffins, he'd paid him to survey the land. And then, a year or so later, someone had come to the house where he was staying to say that John Alston was looking for him.

He was happy to be able to help him out. Alston was hiding a fugitive slave, the one that Mitchell had met, who looked to Mitchell like there was some white blood mixed in with the black. He settled John and the slave into the rough little cabin on the Alston property and helped them lay in some provisions. John had a document of manumission—Mitchell couldn't read it, but it looked impressive. John told him the names on it were false, not realizing that Mitchell couldn't have read them. It said that someone named James Stanton of Richmond, Virginia, was freeing his slave, Jonah. That was the name Dave had chosen to be called. That document was in the satchel Jonah was carrying now, in case they were stopped.

Temperance and Mitchell caught up with the others at the crossroads. They'd ride inland a day or so, then make their way into South Carolina, then down into Georgia by way of the ferry at Augusta. All the men were familiar with the route, but for Temperance, it would be her first trip out of North Carolina. They rode silently in the moonlight for another two hours, then turned off the road and led the horses deep into the woods, where they made camp for the night by a stream. Mitchell helped Temperance unbuckle her saddle bag. "Oh, do be careful," she said. "There's something breakable in there."

They talked in low voices, as Temperance filled her father in on the scheme she'd hatched after he was imprisoned.

"I wrote to Mitchell to ride up from Georgia and pretend to be your attorney. I'm not sure why he brought Dave—he's Jonah now, I keep forgetting—and I said I'd come with John from Chatham County and meet him in Wilmington. I figured if he could get the jailer drunk enough, my plan would work. And it did." She was smiling broadly now, leaning nearer the fire, a deep dimple showing in her cheek. Mitchell realized she was not as plain as he'd thought. A wee bit gawky still, but she'd fill out.

"I brought Jonah because he wouldn't stay behind." Mitchell didn't tell them that he'd had to ask Jonah to read the letter to him, and once he had, there was no leaving Jonah in Georgia.

"I'm going to stay with you in Georgia, Papa. We can manage. I can learn to cook, and Jonah's been getting work as a cabinet maker. People send for him from as far away as Savannah and Augusta. Jonah Stanton is getting famous!"

"That's no life for you, Tempie," Philip said. "I thank you, more than I can ever say, for rescuing me. You're a clever, brave girl, just as you've always been. But you should be with your brothers and sisters in Chatham County. James can provide a good home for you. Selling off the land in Moore County has given him enough to start on. You need to be together now." His voice lowered, and he stopped talking.

"We can decide all this later, Papa," said John. "We should try to sleep. We need to ride on as soon as it's light enough. I think old Francis is probably still scratching his head trying to figure out what happened, but soon enough *someone* will. I doubt they'll chase us past the border, but we need to put some miles between us and Wilmington tomorrow.

Temperance settled herself close to Philip and reached out for his hand. "It's going to be fine, Papa," she whispered. "You'll see."

1789. The worst year of my life. I'm so glad it's over. 1790 can only be better, she thought.

LINN: TWELVE
Friday morning

L INN WOKE, HAVING SLEPT THROUGH THE NIGHT, feeling rested. She sat up, swung her legs off the side of the bed and looked around her. The basket of dirty clothes was waiting. I'll get a wash started, then I'll call Marcie. Moonshine must have already made his way downstairs to go out into the back yard before his breakfast.

She closed George Willcox's book, reading once again a letter written to Edward Telfair, the governor of Georgia on October 28th of 1791:

Sir,
We just received a Letter from Capt. Benj. Harrison who lives on the Oconey River below the mouth of Buckeye informing us that This morning about Break of day Col Alston who lived near him was killed by a gun that was fired through the house as he lay in bed though known person was Discovered to do it. The Capt. Is of the opinion that it was some white person that has ill against Alston. This letter was requested to be sent with Speed, in consequence we got the Bearer Mr. Nelly to come with it and hopes he may have some compensation for his trouble. We are Sir your Humblst Servts
Jared Irwin, John Watts

PS I parted with Col. Alston Sumtime after night last Evening near Col. Irwin's he informed me that his life was Threatened, though he was Groggy. I am, Sir, Yours, John Watts

A QUICK SHOWER LATER, she headed down to the laundry room, humming. Mom's last day of class is today, and then Monday I start at the Rec Center. I'm going to need a new swimsuit, maybe two. Maybe tomorrow I can go to the mall.

Coffee with lots of milk, some cereal with a sliced banana, while she read the comics and Dear Abby in the paper, standing up at the kitchen counter. She looked at the clock on the microwave. Too soon to call Marcie.

For the first time in months, there was no knot in her stomach. If I have to go back and testify, I will. But I'm not going to give in on going back there to school. I need to start checking on nursing schools and what I have to do to apply. Gran said she'd help me with that, if I needed her to.

She cleaned up the kitchen, washing the coffee pot and putting some dishes in the dishwasher. I could be a big help to Mom if they'll let me live here this fall. She tucked that idea into her growing arsenal of weapons to use. The money weapons were for Dad. "It'll be cheaper. No trips to Massachusetts. No dorm fees or meal plans. If I do well at the Rec this summer, maybe they'd hire me for one of the after-school programs. I can help pay my way." For Mom: "I can clean, cook, grocery shop, and help with Moonshine."

As if he'd heard her thoughts, Shiny plodded into the kitchen through the dog door and stuck his long nose into his empty water bowl. He looked at her sadly, then back at the bowl. "No problem, boy. I'm all over it!"

His noisy slurping over the next couple of minutes made her smile. How could anybody enjoy water that much? "Want to go around the block?" "Block" was a word in Moonshine's vocabulary, and he thumped his tail while she hooked his leash on. By the time they got back, it'd be ten and she could call Marcie.

She was lost in thought as Moonshine made his slow processional around the block, nose to the ground as he snuffled each bush and fireplug they passed. She had read last night just before she went to sleep of Philip Alston's murder. Wonder what that was about? Did "groggy" mean he was drunk?

Just as they rounded the last corner, her cell rang. It was Dad. "Linn, I've been asking around. I think it's remotely possible that a deposition would be enough. I hope so. I really don't want you having to go through a cross-examination about that night. I'll still need the girl's attorney's name and number, though."

"Okay. I'm walking Shiny. When I get home I'll call Marcie, and I'll get back to you."

Marcie answered on the first ring. "Linn, did you talk to your folks?"

"Yes. My dad's a lawyer. He says can you get—it's Courtney, right?—anyway, can you get her lawyer's name and number?"

"Courtney Sheffield. Yes, I can do that. I'll text it to you. Now what's this about not coming back?"

"I'm going to transfer to a nursing program here."

"Seriously? If you are, you need to talk to someone in admissions and withdraw."

"I know. And I've got some boxes in the basement there. I've got to figure that out."

"They're labeled, right? We can FedEx them to you."

"I'll let you know. I'll talk to you later, Marcie. Thanks."

"Bye, Linn."

The doorbell rang as Linn was transferring clothes to the dryer. She had already called her father with the information Marcie sent.

Her Uncle Jack was on the doorstep, all six-feet-four of him, a big grin on his face. "How about this one?" he said. "Want to test-drive her?"

"Her" was a gray Honda with a few years on her.

"I had her checked out. She's good to go. A little over ninety thousand miles on her. Almost new tires, good battery. Only a couple of minor dents. Come on, let's take a ride."

"Sure. Let me get my license. Come on in."

Shiny greeted Jack, tail wagging. Jack was a favorite of his. Jack leaned over and scratched Shiny behind his long ears. "Hey, old buddy. How's it goin'?" The tail wagged harder.

"Have you talked to my dad?" Linn asked, as they headed for the car.

"Yes. He said to bring her on over for you to look at. He also said something about having to work out the finances with you. You're going to be working for him this summer, right?" He tossed Linn the keys.

"Actually, no. But I *do* have a job. I'm going to be lifeguarding and teaching swimming at the Rec Center."

"Hadn't heard that. How does Bill feel about that? I thought the whole point was to get you some experience at the firm."

"It was. But if I'm not going to go to law school . . ."

"You're not?" She could feel his eyes on her as she pulled out into the street.

"No, I told Mom and Dad last night. I want to go into nursing."

Her Uncle Jack laughed. "I never did see you as a lawyer, Linn."

"Really? Why?"

" Maybe you're too nice?" Jack laughed again. "I don't know. You just don't seem the type. Sue and I have talked about it."

"What do you think about me and nursing? I've been considering pediatric nursing."

"I can see that. Linn, you've got one of the kindest hearts I know, and you're very capable. So how does the car feel to you? I know she's not flashy, but she'll give you great mileage."

"I like it a lot. I'm going to have to have a car to get to work this summer, and to school—wherever I end up—come fall. How much?"

"I guarantee it'll fit your budget. Bill told me how much you've got in savings, and that'll make a substantial amount down. We can work out the monthly payment details later, but she's yours right now, if you want her. Drop me by the dealership, and we'll fill out the paperwork."

142

On the way, Linn told him about the unsolved murder in the family history. Uncle Jack was interested. "Buckeye Creek? I know right where that is. You know my family's from Laurens County. Buckeye is near Dublin. It runs into the Oconee River."

On the banks of the Oconee River,

October 28, 1791

A gunshot WOKE TEMPERANCE from troubled dreams. She screamed, "Papa!"

"Missie? Is that you? Stay down!" Jonah shouted from outside the cabin. She could see him silhouetted by the moonlight streaming through the unshuttered window over her father's bed. Jonah hesitated, then headed towards the road, a pistol in his hand.

Tempie dropped to her hands and knees. "Papa!" She crawled across the rough floor. Her father lay still on his cot. She reached out a hand to rouse him. "Oh, God, no!" Her fingers, touching his chest, found a hot wetness, black in the moonlight. She shook him. "Papa!"

Jonah was inside now. "He got away. I heard him riding off. Mr. Philip? Mr. Philip! Get a light, child!"

Fumbling on the mantelpiece, Tempie's shaky fingers found a candle, which she lit from the embers in the fireplace. In a matter of three steps in the small cabin, she was back at Philip's bed.

"He's not breathing, Missie." Jonah was shaking his head. "He's not breathing. Your papa's dead."

"What happened? I heard you bring him in during the night. He was drunk again, wasn't he? Oh, Papa!" Temperance was sobbing. She squared her shoulders and took a shuddering breath. She sank to her knees by the bed, holding her father's warm hand.

"He had been drinking, yes. I brought him home. I found him at the tavern near Jared Irwin's place, talking to John Watts. He was telling Mr. Watts that he'd been threatened. He said he found an unsigned letter in his saddlebag."

"Did you see the letter? Did Papa know who sent it?"

"If he knew, he didn't say. I saw him throw a wad of paper on the fire in the tavern."

"Did you see who shot Papa?"

"Not to recognize, no. He had his back to me, and he was galloping fast by the time I got outside. I didn't recognize the horse, either."

"It's nearly daybreak. Dave, I mean, Jonah." It was the first time she erred on his name in months. "I'll stay here with Papa. Ride over to the Harrisons' and tell them what happened. See if Captain Harrison will come. And then go get Mitchell."

"Why are you here, Missie? I thought you were staying over at the Harrisons' tonight, helping out."

"I asked Captain Harrison to bring me on home. Charity was feeling much improved, and they didn't need me any longer."

"Then latch the door behind me, and if you hear anyone outside, get under your bed. I'll be back as soon as I can."

THE NEXT TWO DAYS WERE WORSE than Temperance's worst nightmares. That first day, Saturday, feeling numb, and with the help of Charity Harrison, she washed and laid out her father on the table in the cabin. Seeing her father's slim naked body, with the ugly wound nestling among the curly black hairs close to his left nipple, shocked her past tears. Someone, but who? had leaned into the cabin through the open window above the bed and shot him as he lay in an alcohol-induced stupor. Jonah, on her instructions, burned the blood-soaked bedding and the narrow bed. Mitchell and Jonah together built a coffin, and on the second day, on a Sunday morning, they buried Philip beside the Oconee. As her father would have wished, her prayers were silent. It grieved Temperance that she wasn't able to take him home to North Carolina to sleep by his wife. The House in the Horseshoe had been sold to someone called Thomas Perkins, and likely she'd never see it again.

Captain Harrison had suggested that Jared Irwin and John Watts write the governor, informing him of Philip's death. They sent John Nelly with the letter to Augusta, and Edward Telfair promptly offered a reward of fifty pounds for information leading to the capture of the assailant. The reward went unclaimed.

And then the argument with Jonah began. Temperance wanted to stay in Washington County. She'd been there with her Papa and Jonah for nearly two years, and while it had been a difficult time, she'd learned so much. At sixteen she was the woman of the house. Going back to North Carolina to live as a dependent in her brother James's household with her brothers and sisters was unthinkable, although seeing them all again was tempting. How the little ones would have grown! She added in her head. Philip was almost thirteen now, Winnie was ten, Mady was seven, and Drew would soon be six. She had been in correspondence with her older brothers, and John had come once to visit, in late spring, bringing the news that James had married Polly Willcox. Temperance had been glad of that, but startled by the realization that Polly was only a few months older than she was. If she went to Chatham County, how would it feel being the spinster aunt in the household when James and Polly began having children? Would Polly give her any responsibilities at all?

She tried to explain her reservations to Jonah the evening after they buried Philip. "I've made this into a home. I've learned to cook and to sew. I've managed the washing. I grew a kitchen garden. A nice one, too. I've kept the cabin clean and neat." She looked at the mantel, with the white pitcher precisely in the center, and then at the table where Philip had lain, now covered with a white cloth. "I don't want to go to live in a house where someone does everything for me."

Jonah said, "Don't you think it's time you lived like a lady again? You were raised to be a lady like your mama. Ladies sew and paint."

"They don't sew; they embroider. And paint? I don't want to paint little flowers."

"You could *grow* little flowers. Your mama did. She had some beautiful roses, remember? It's just not right for you to stay here alone."

"But who'll cook your meals if I'm not here?"

"Missie, I got along fine those years I lived here by myself before you and your papa came. I like being by myself. You made a good home for your father, and he appreciated that, but you know he never got over missing your mother. Most men your father's age who lost a wife would have found another. When Miss Temperance died, it was as though the life went out of him, too."

That was true. Papa hadn't even seemed to care when he was arrested and taken off to Wilmington to face trial for being an accessory to George Glascock's murder.

"Think what your father would want you to do."

Temperance knew how difficult it had been for Philip to agree to allow her to stay in Washington County after the five of them had made their way to Georgia from Wilmington that cold January, but she had been determined not to leave her father alone. What had finally swayed him was her recounting the solemn promise she'd made to her mother to look after him. So John had returned alone to join his brothers and sisters in Chatham County.

Mitchell was living nearby with some of his kin, and he rode over often to see them. Temperance looked forward to those days, when Mitchell would join them for the simple suppers she had learned to cook—stews, soups, greens, cornbread—and sit by the fire afterwards, talking to her and to Papa, while Papa drank from a bottle of brandy. He and Papa were both storytellers, and she loved to listen to them. Mitchell was making his living carrying chains for surveyors, and he kept them informed of the newcomers to the county. Many had been given land grants based on their service in the war with England, including some of Mitchell's extended family. There were even Glascocks now in Washington County. Mitchell had been too young to serve, but liked hearing Philip's war memories and had a few tales of his own involving his North Carolina kinfolks.

Philip allowed some of the settlers to farm the land on the Sister Islands in the Oconee, in return for some of the harvest or some of the profits. Requests from Temperance to build a bigger house, or at least enlarge the little cabin, had been ignored. Philip's ambitious days were behind him now, and he whiled away his time sitting on the porch, or by the fire, depending on the season, waiting for evening, when he'd ride off to the tavern, to drink and play cards with the other landowners.

Temperance's days were full during those months, and at night, she usually fell asleep quickly, if often to dream of shootings and deaths and to wake trembling and dry-mouthed. Their lives fell into a simple pattern, and if Temperance occasionally wondered what the future held for her, she pushed the thoughts aside.

The years changed her. Her sixteenth birthday only a few days before her father's murder had passed almost unnoticed. Jonah remembered, and brought her a pair of hand-carved candlesticks. The pattern on the base matched the embossed daisies on her mother's pitcher.

"They're lovely, Jonah. Thank you." She put two of their candles in them and placed them on the mantel, flanking the pitcher, stood back, and moved them a little farther apart.

"I'm sorry, my dear. I hadn't noticed what day it is," her father said. "Sixteen years. Can it really be that long ago? You have your mother's eyes, you know." He was quiet then, remembering the day she'd been born, and how struck he had been by her eyes. They were Linnet's deep, deep brown, and set in her face at the same angle as her mother's, but Tempie's face was narrower, and she was taller, with broader shoulders. When she smiled, her face showed some of her mother's beauty, but she lacked Linnie's charm, her infectious joy.

Two weeks since Papa died, and this was one of the longest conversations she'd ever had with Jonah. He spent most of his days working in the cabinet shop that he'd built near the cabin, or sitting outside his shop, reading one of his precious books. He slept in the shop, too, but most nights lately, he had followed Philip when he rode over to the tavern, to make sure he got home safely.

There was a knock at the door then, and Jonah opened it to Mitchell. Jonah shook his head and left. "*You* talk to her," he said.

Mitchell came in and took the empty chair by the fire. "I had somebody send word to your brothers to come get you."

"You did *what?* I'm not going anywhere." Temperance looked at Mitchell. His blond hair caught the red glow of the fire. She felt the familiar jolt in the pit of her stomach. At twenty-one, his muscular thighs swelled the dark wool trousers he was wearing, and his broad shoulders strained the buckskin jacket. Did he have any idea that she daydreamed of those rough hands touching her? She watched his lips as he prepared to respond, and wished she could put a finger in the deep cleft in his chin.

"Tempie, you can't stay here. A girl your age can't live alone." He looked at her appraisingly and surprised them both by saying, "I'd marry you myself and keep you here if I had the money."

Temperance's dark eyes widened, and her hand flew to her mouth in shock.

"You're a hard-working girl, and not bad to look at. You'll make someone a fine wife, and I'd be content to be that someone, but I can barely feed myself yet."

"I have some money," Temperance rushed to speak. "Or I will have. I'm one of Papa's heirs. I think there's still some land in North Carolina, and there's this property. I could sell some of it." She wished Papa had been willing to talk about their finances with her, but he had always turned away her questions.

"No, we don't do it that way in my family. A man supports his wife."

"Oh, Mitchell, I can wait. Why can't I wait here?"

"You need to go on back to your family. When I can buy up some land and build a house, I'll come for you."

"Do you promise, Mitchell?" Temperance launched herself across the hearth to his lap. She wound her arms around his neck and pressed herself against him.

Mitchell put his hands on either side of her waist and set her on the floor, standing up himself. He kissed her, pulling her body against him. Damn, she felt good. He ran his hands down her hips. Wide enough for easy child-bearing.

The door opened, and Jonah came in. His eyes narrowed when he saw their embrace.

"Jonah!" Temperance said, "Mitchell asked me to marry him! He's going to come for me in North Carolina!"

"Is that so, Missie?" He was looking at Mitchell. "I need to have a word with Mr. Griffin outside."

With Mitchell following, Jonah walked until he felt sure Temperance wouldn't overhear them.

"What's all this about marriage?" he said to Mitchell.

"You wanted me to talk her into going back to North Carolina." Mitchell was grinning broadly.

"If you hurt that little girl, I'll kill you. I'll hunt you down, and I'll kill you. I will, you know."

Mitchell looked speculatively at the man glaring at him in the dusk. There were rumors, but he'd never been sure they were true. John Alston had turned up that day with a fugitive slave, and no real explanation of what was going on. "Jonah, I'll have to marry someday, and it might as well be Temperance. I figure three years at the most I'll have enough put by to get married. I'll keep my promise, if she'll wait for me."

"She'll wait for you, Griffin," Jonah had dropped the "Mister." "I've seen how she watches you when she thinks you're not looking. She's her mother's daughter. Raised right. She'll be true to you and stand by you. But she's better than you deserve. She comes from a good family, an educated family. Have you even told her you never learned to read and write?"

"That won't matter to her. If one of us can read, that's enough. And I'm good at figuring."

"I meant what I said. Nobody is going to hurt that child and not get hurt himself. You have my word on that."

"Let's go in. I want you to witness the promise I make to her."

LINN: THIRTEEN
Friday evening

L INN AND HER MOTHER WERE IN THE KITCHEN putting the finishing touches on what Anne was calling a "School's Out" celebration meal. Anne had stopped at the fish market on the way home to pick up a couple of pounds of shrimp, and while Linn peeled shrimp, she was at the stove putting a gumbo together. Rice was simmering, and there were rolls ready to go in the oven.

Bill, home for the weekend, had swapped his business suit for shorts and a T-shirt, and joined them in the kitchen, grabbing a beer from the refrigerator. Linn, impulsively, hugged him as he passed.

"What's that for?" They weren't much of a hugging family.

"The car, Dad. I love it already!" Anne had already admired the small gray car parked in the driveway.

"Oh, that. Well, you're going to have to figure out a way to make the payments."

"I know. I will. Guess what I'm going to name it, Dad!"

The naming of cars was something she and her mother did. Bill pretended to think it was silly, but he was always amused at the intensity of the arguments over the years. Currently he drove "Black Beauty," a Lincoln, and Anne's hybrid was called "Ralph."

"I'm not even going to guess," he said.

"Punch!"

"Punch? As in "Punch and Judy'? Or 'Knockout'?" Bill asked.

"No, as in 'My gray horse called Punch.' Remember, I told you about Drew Smith's will?"

"Oh, yes," Anne said. "The horse he wanted sold. Dinner in fifteen minutes," she told her husband's back, as he retreated to the family room with the newspaper.

"I should still be able to transcribe GeeGee's research, even with the job this summer and school this fall. Gran said if I did, she'd help with the car payments. Mom, it's really interesting. I was looking through the file GeeGee had on Mitchell Griffin and found a copy of a marriage bond between him and Temperance Alston. I looked it up. In those days, a man had to put up money—five thousand pounds on that one—if he planned to get married, and then if he didn't go through with it, he forfeited the money. People co-signed with you. I guess it was kind of like bail. If you skipped town without marrying the girl, they lost their money, too."

"Times have changed. It was hard for women then. They had no financial standing of their own. Their property belonged to their husbands. You know, Linn, it's changed just since I was a girl. Your Gran never worked outside the home. It was considered a reflection on the husband if he couldn't support his family. It took some convincing when your dad and I married for him to let me go on teaching. The compromise was that I'd stay at home with any children until they started school. It turned out to be just you, so I was only away from teaching for the five or so years."

"Were you ever sorry you only had just me?"

"We wanted other children, but if there was only to be one, I'm so glad it was you, Linn." She smiled at her daughter's earnest face.

"Is Dad going to be okay with my quitting pre-law?"

"I think he'll be fine. It just takes him a little while to get used to new ideas."

154

"I need to start looking into school for the fall. Will you help me?"

"Of course, honey. Do you know your work schedule yet?"

"Yes, I'll have Tuesdays and Thursdays off, and I work half-days on most Fridays. All day Saturday."

"Tuesday it is, then. We'll make a list and hit some admission offices. You know, I was thinking. What about Emory? It may be too late to go there this year, but you could probably transfer there as a junior. That would thrill your dad, to have you at his alma mater. Hand me that potholder."

"I wonder who got the money if someone skipped out on a marriage bond? The girl's family?" Linn mused as she reached for the potholder.

*F*our YEARS. TEMPERANCE LEANED INTO THE MIRROR over the dressing table and smoothed her hair back, tucking a loose wave into the neat coil of light brown hair on her neck. He would be here soon. She tugged the drawstring neck of her blue-gray silk gown a little lower and wondered if he would notice that her breasts had grown. With trembling fingers, she clasped a string of pearls around her neck. The pearls had been Elizabeth's, and their mother's before that, and James had passed them on to her when she'd returned to North Carolina.

Several times—no, more than several—she had despaired of seeing Mitchell again. Then, when nearly all hope was lost, another letter would come from Jonah with a message from Mitchell: he was well, he was busy, he hoped she was well. She wrote Jonah with messages for Mitchell in return, but she could only say that she was thinking of him and hoped to see him soon. Imagining Jonah reading anything more than that aloud to Mitchell made her blush, and what she longed to say to Mitchell, she could only whisper into her pillow at night: I love you, I want your kisses, I am waiting for you.

A few of the young men from the neighboring plantations

had spoken to James about courting her, but she had refused to consider them, in spite of James's arguments, and with each passing year she grew less eligible. She had spent most of the four years with James and Polly. They were kind to her, and she tried to make herself as useful as possible. Her sewing skills improved, but she refused to embroider with Polly. Under the guidance of Dinah and Sall, who had come with James to Chatham County, she had mastered bread-making and could make tasty soups and stews using a variety of meats. Polly had questioned the need for acquiring these skills, but Temperance felt sure that her new life in Georgia with Mitchell would not have the ease of the life that Polly lived.

Polly was not a gardener, so Temperance took on the herb and flower beds. In this she was helped by Cesar, now a white-haired old man. His days of hard labor were behind him, but he enjoyed working with the quiet daughter of his beloved Miss Temp, and he liked passing on what he'd learned about the herbs they grew.

Polly was a settling influence on James. Temperance knew that during the last year of her mother's life, James's temper had caused legal difficulties, including an arrest for assault. At thirty-three now, he devoted most of his time to his plantation. He was beginning to talk about a move to Georgia, where land was plentiful. Polly was resistant. Her widowed mother Rebecca Willcox was in nearby Gulf, living with Polly's brothers and her sister Jane, and if James insisted on removing to another state, she might never see her again. After the loss of a baby a year ago, Polly was now awaiting the birth of a child with great excitement. This would be the first grandchild for her mother, and Polly hoped to have her mother close as her child grew up.

A commotion downstairs alerted her to Mitchell's arrival. James had told her he intended to have a few words with Mitchell before sending for her. A gentle tap at the door, and Mary Drew entered the room she shared with her sisters. "He's here, Sister." At twelve, she was on the threshold of young womanhood. Like John, she had her father's dark hair and blue eyes. She and John shared similar features, a short straight nose and their mother's singularly sweet smile.

Mady and Tempie had grown close these last years. Mady liked spending time with Temperance as she went about her daily tasks, but the lazy summer afternoons spent fishing down at the river with Drewry tagging along were the times Mady looked forward to. Mady had hazy memories of digging earthworms with their mother, and the smell of the worms as she threaded them onto fishhooks conjured up a picture of a smiling face with curls tumbling from a bonnet and soft hands that guided her small hands as she struggled with a pole and a fishing line.

Mady knew that upriver stood the house she'd left as a child when her mother died. Twice James had let Tempie take the carriage and call on the Perkins family to ask permission to visit the little graveyard on the rise up from the river. It was disheartening to Tempie to see how quickly it had become overgrown. She knew where the stones were that marked her mother's grave, as well as her sister Elizabeth's grave and those of the babies, William and Dinah. A little apart from these were the graves of the young man who had died at the foot of their staircase, the Scotsman, and the man who tried to set fire to their house. Farther still was the burial place of several of their slaves, marked with wooden markers, now rotting. John, who was visiting from Charleston, and Mady went with her the first time, soon after Tempie's return from Georgia, and helped her clear away some of the vines and briars that covered the stones.

The Perkins family was not hospitable. On the first visit, a servant had come to the door and shut it in their faces, leaving them standing on the broad porch while he carried Tempie's polite request to visit the cemetery to his master. The three had not been invited in for refreshment, nor offered water for the horses. James was reluctant to let Tempie return to the House in the Horseshoe, and refused to let Mady go at all, after hearing how they had been treated. He had insisted on accompanying her on the second trip, along with Polly. This time they were met at the gate by Thomas Perkins himself, who told James they were not receiving company. Tempie, from her seat in the carriage, said, "Oh, please, sir. I just want to visit my mother's grave."

"Well, be quick about it, and then leave my property."

James swung down from his horse and approached Perkins. "I fail to understand your rudeness to my sister, sir."

"You're Alstons, aren't you? I don't want you on my land. Your father was a murdering bastard. He got what was coming to him."

"No, James!" Polly cried, hastening down from the carriage, as James balled up his fists and lunged towards Perkins. She had seen what James had not, an armed man coming from the house. Another stepped from behind a tree.

"We'll go, but I wish you no joy, sir." James saw that tears were running down his sister's face. "You have no call to be unkind to my sister." After that, Tempie made no further request to visit the graves, but she often walked to the river bank to send silent prayers upstream.

From time to time Temperance was invited by one of the cousins to visit during a confinement. Uncle John and Aunt Ann Hunt's oldest son, another Joseph John, who was called Joe, had sent for her when his wife Esther's time grew near, and she was there for the birth of yet another Joseph John in 1793 and for the birth of that Joseph John's sister Mary the following year. The strong personality of Philip's father continued, even after his death, to influence the family. Temperance never met any of her grandparents, and it was a sorrow to her that her papa and mama would never know any of their grandchildren.

And now Mitchell was here in Chatham County, staying with some cousins. He had sent word two days before that he had signed the marriage bond, along with Archibald McBryde and William Thompson, and that he was coming to marry her. She should be ready at noon on Saturday with her bags packed. He would bring a preacher.

James and Polly were deeply shocked at the haste and practicality of the wedding. There was no time to invite guests or prepare a proper celebration. Temperance, shaking with anticipation, had spent the morning gathering her few belongings, including the white pitcher, still boxed from its last trip north from Georgia. She had vowed to herself that she would unpack it only when she had a home of her own.

James, acting hastily, had transferred ownership of Phoebe, a widow about Temperance's age, and her seven-year-old son Sampson, to Temperance. "He's young, but he's going to be strong. His father was. You will need help, wherever you end up in Georgia. I need to talk to this Mitchell of yours. I can't say I like this. I don't know him. I thought he'd come and court you before marrying you and taking you away from your family."

Mady, now, was clinging to her sister. "I don't want you to go."

"I promise you that I will send for you as soon as I am settled. Drewry, too, if he wants to come." This had been much discussed in the family. James, considering it, felt that having family already settled in Georgia would help him persuade Polly to relocate. Winnie had been included in Tempie's invitation and was not interested in the move. She and Philip had made their place in the society of the younger residents of Chatham County. She had her eye on William Waddell, and if she had her way about it, there'd be a wedding when she was sixteen.

Tempie cast a final look at the mirror as a knock came at the door. From the hall, Phoebe said, "Miss Tempie, your fellow is here."

Temperance opened the door. Her pale face alarmed Phoebe, who said, "Now, don't you worry. He's a fine-looking man. Tall, ain't he? And you look mighty nice."

Temperance picked up the rose-patterned shawl from the bed as she and Mady left, and Phoebe followed them down the stairs, whispering, "Me and Sampson, we're all ready to go. We'll bring your bags and boxes down. You go get married."

Solemnly, Temperance entered the parlor with Mady. He was there, just as she remembered him. She noticed, without really seeing, the small man at his elbow, prayer book in hand. James, frowning, was at one side of the fireplace, and Polly stood next to him, a cautionary hand on his arm. Philip, Drew, Winnie, and William Carroll were there. John had left unexpectedly the day before for Charleston on business, leaving behind his good friend William, who was visiting.

"I said I'd come, didn't I?" Mitchell looked appraisingly at the young woman facing him. She'd filled out a little. That shiny hair was a sign of health. A broad smile brought light to his hazel eyes, and she answered the smile with one of her own. Good teeth, too.

"I knew you would," she said. "You promised."

LINN: FOURTEEN
Saturday morning

LINN WOKE EARLY, IN SPITE OF A LATE NIGHT the night before. She had called one of her friends from swim team, Kaylie, after supper to see if she wanted to hang out. Okay, truthfully, to show off Punch. Kaylie had suggested going to McGonigle's, the ice cream shop near the high school, so she had picked Kaylie up, and the two headed there. Linn and her friends had spent a lot of afternoons at Mickey Gee's after swim practice.

Linn was happy to learn that Kaylie was going to be working at the Rec Department, too, assisting with the summer camps that provided child care for so many working parents.

"So, tell me about school." Kaylie said, sliding into a booth with her mocha fudge sundae. "How was Massachusetts?"

"You wouldn't believe the snow in the winter. I never thought I'd get tired of it, but I did! I mean, it's beautiful and all, but getting around is a pain. Even just between the dorm and classes. If you're not wearing boots, it gets all down in your shoes and melts, and you have to sit there in class with soggy cold feet. I decided not to go back. Not because of the weather," she stopped and smiled. "Oh, I'd forgotten how good McGonigle's pistachio is!"

"Why? I thought you were planning on law school."

"It was more that my *dad* was planning on law school. I'm going to transfer to a school here in Atlanta and study nursing."

"Really? It'll be great having you in town. Seems like everybody took off. So where are you going?"

"I'm not sure yet. Tuesday Mom and I will start figuring it out. You'll still be at Agnes Scott, right?"

"Definitely. I love it. My roommate this year is from Caracas. She's gone home for the summer. We're going to room together again next year. Elena. You'll like her. She's a lot of fun. She was a huge help to me with my Spanish."

"I'm probably going to live at home and save a little money. You know my dad and money."

They laughed. Linn's friends knew about her father's reputation for being "cautious" with his money.

"Did you hear that Lindsay and Dwayne broke up?"

"Are you for real? After all this time? What happened?"

"Well, do you want to hear what Lindsay said or Dwayne's version?"

The two girls settled happily into the booth for a gossip session. Linn had noticed that Kaylie looked up each time the door swung open, so she was not all that surprised when Eddie English, who had graduated a year ahead of them, came in with a guy she didn't know and walked over to their booth.

"Okay if we join you? Hi, Linn," he said as he slid in the booth next to Kaylie. Linn scooted over to make room for the tall young man with glasses. She smiled at him.

"Hi, Eddie."

"Linn, this is Phil Manning. Linn McKinney."

"Linn. Hi." They shook hands awkwardly, side by side, and Linn looked into the bluest eyes she'd ever seen. The tips of his ears were pink. Wonder if he's shy? she thought.

"Nice to meet you."

"Phil's at Tech with me. Another engineer type."

"Are you from here?"

"No, just down 75. Macon."

"Was this your first year at Georgia Tech?"

"Yep. Wasn't sure I'd make it, but I did."

Eddie laughed. "Don't let him kid you, Linn. He's a lot smarter than he looks."

"Thanks, Eddie. I appreciate that," Phil said. "I'm going to get a coke or something. Can I get anyone anything?"

"I'll go with you," Eddie stood up. "That pistachio brings back happy memories. Be right back, Kaylie. Don't go away."

Kaylie smiled at Linn across the table. "Well, what do you think?"

"About what? You're a sneaky one, Kaylie. That's what I think."

"I should have said Eddie was going to meet us here, but he wasn't sure if Phil would be free. He's really a nice guy, Linn. Phil, I mean. A little geeky, maybe. I've been going out with Eddie since Christmas, and, seriously, when I met Phil for the first time, I thought of you. I had planned to get the four of us together this summer, so when you called, I thought, perfect, so I called Eddie, and taDA!" She looked expectantly at Linn. "So, what do you think?"

"Jeez, Kaylie, I've barely met him." She looked across the room at the young man standing next to Eddie at the counter.

Nice build. The auburn hair was a plus. She'd always liked red hair. "He seems okay. But what does he think about me?"

"Guess we'll see." The guys were heading back to the booth.

Eddie had not outgrown his class clown persona, and soon had them laughing at his stories of people he met working out at the gym. Phil noticed the dimple in Linn's cheek. She's really cute when she smiles, he thought.

The conversation turned to Atlanta and what Phil had seen of the city since he'd been in school. "Not much, really. I spent most of the time studying. When I had a free weekend, I'd usually head home. I won't be doing that this summer. My folks are in Oregon. My dad's an architect, and he's got some big project going on, and my step-mom decided to go with him.

"So you're in school this summer?" Linn asked.

"Right. Seemed like a good idea, with my folks gone. I'm working at the library and living in the dorm."

"You should take the time and see some of Atlanta. Have you been to the zoo yet?"

"No, but I've heard it's a good one. Why don't we all go? Maybe Sunday afternoon?"

"Wish I could, but we're going to my grandmother's for dinner," Kaylie shook her head. "I can't get out of that."

"And I've got to work," Eddie said. "You two should go."

"Would you like to do that, Linn?" Phil's ears were turning pink again. "You can be my guide."

"Sure, that would be great."

Phil pulled out his phone. "Give me your number, and I'll call you tomorrow and get your address."

"Here, I'll enter it." He handed her the phone and leaned close, watching the screen.

"L-I-N-N. I would have misspelled it."

"It's a family name. 'Philip' is a name in my family, too. I have an ancestor called Philip. "

"I'm named for my grandfather. I'll give you a call on my lunch break, if that's okay."

"Sure."

Eddie was getting up. "We should go. Good seeing you, Linn. See you tomorrow night, Kaylie." He leaned over and kissed her quickly. "Bye, babe."

"Good night, Eddie. Talk to you tomorrow, Phil," Linn waved as they left. *Such nice eyes.*

"I guess that answers the question," Kaylie was smiling.

"What question?"

"Whether he likes you."

We'll see, Linn had thought as she climbed the stairs to bed as quietly as she could, sandals in hand. *But I think I like him.* She remembered those blue eyes. That was the last thought she had before she fell asleep.

Now Linn swung her legs over the side of the bed and looked around her room in the morning light. *Okay, the purple paint's* gotta go, and so do the curtains and bedspread. I can do the painting. Wonder if Gran would help me make some curtains? Or would it be cheaper to buy?

Later, down in the kitchen, she poured a cup of coffee. Her mom was making a grocery list.

"Want me to go to the store for you?"

"No, honey, I'm actually looking forward to it. I'm going to run by the Farmers Market and check out the veggies. Do you still want to go to the mall this afternoon and look for a swim suit?"

"Sure. And I wanted to ask you. Do you think it would be okay if I painted my room and got some new curtains and bed linens?"

"Have you finally outgrown the purple, Linn? I'd say it's about time! Do you have a color in mind?"

"Maybe like a pale blue for the walls, with a darker blue for the spread, and white curtains. Sort of beach-y."

"Sounds lovely. If we have time, we could look at curtains and linens, and go by a paint store and pick up some color chips. Have you thought about painting those dark wood headboards? A coat of white paint would change them completely."

"Good thought. I'm going to work on genealogy this morning. I'll be ready after lunch. I'll clean up the kitchen, Mom. You go on."

Linn was busy entering the Griffin line. Weird. Here was a deed that Benjamin Mitchell Griffin signed with an X. He couldn't sign his name, but he still got elected coroner for Telfair County, and then state senator. Couldn't happen now. But his wife was literate. And, oh, wow. They had a daughter named Linney. Is that where my name came from? But, she figured in her head, 1797 to 1808, there was an eleven year gap between the first child and the second. Wonder what happened?

Beside her, her phone played a few notes from "Shiny, Happy People."

"Hi, Phil."

On the banks of the Ocmulgee,
May 9, 1808

A LONG NIGHT, STEAMY AND STILL. Phoebe had opened the shutters to admit any breeze coming from the river, but only mosquitoes drifted in. She swatted one now on her neck and turned back to the bed. The woman writhing there in the last throes of labor attempted a smile. "Almost over, Missie," Phoebe told her. "Here come anoth'un. Now, push."

With a final mighty grunt, Temperance expelled a slippery baby that Phoebe caught deftly and wrapped in a waiting blanket. "It's a little girl. A pretty un, too!"

"Is she breathing?" Temperance's anxious question brought a laugh from Phoebe as the baby burst into hearty squall.

"Oh, she breathin' all right!"

Mitchell came home towards morning. He shrugged when Phoebe told him he had another daughter. But as he told Temperance, "At least it's alive." Temperance named her Mary Catherine and then added "Alston" for her father. Eleven-year-old Betsy was thrilled to have a baby sister, and carried her around the house like a doll.

Mitchell had first taken Tempie, along with Phoebe and Sampson, back to Washington County, Georgia, after a three-day stay in a little cabin that belonged to a member of his extended family near a creek in Chatham County. Phoebe and Sampson had stayed behind at James and Polly's house, to be picked up when the trek to Georgia began.

Tempie thought she knew what to expect. Polly had talked with her, blushing and whispering, and Tempie understood that the marriage act might involve a little pain at first. It certainly did. Mitchell ushered her into the cabin in the late afternoon, after four hours of a bumpy, cold ride on the wooden seat of an open wagon. She had attempted to keep up a conversation, but her husband's responses were brief, and, discouraged, she fell into a silence.

Once she had to ask him to stop so that she could creep behind some bushes on the roadside to relieve herself. From where she crouched she saw Mitchell unbutton the fly on his wool trousers. He didn't bother to turn his back. Perhaps he didn't realize he was visible to her. She smiled ruefully. Her mother had always insisted on what she called "decent behavior." Tempie's brothers had been taught to go beyond eyesight if they were outdoors and felt the need. But not everyone was raised that way. She knew that. But still...

At dusk, he stopped the wagon beside a small cabin and unhitched the two horses. In the cabin, he lit the fire that was already laid, and Tempie looked around. The cabin was tidy. Quilts were piled on the bed to the right of the door, and a small table with rough benches held two wooden bowls and two pewter spoons and cups.

"Wait here," he said, and went back to the wagon to fetch a bottle of whisky and some cornbread wrapped in a napkin. Then he brought in a kettle which was filled with what appeared to be a venison stew with beans. Mitchell hooked the bail on the kettle onto the crane and swung it nearer the fire.

"We'll eat when that's hot. Would you like some whisky? It will warm you." For the first time, he seemed to notice that she was trembling. "Here, drink this."

Temperance gagged down the whisky from the cup he handed her. A warmth spread through her belly.

"Are you still cold? Get nearer the fire. Or," he smiled, "we could get into the bed."

Temperance's eyes widened as Mitchell approached her. He loosened her one-handed grip on the thick wool shawl and unwrapped it, tossing it onto the nearer bench, taking the cup from her other hand. Then he untied the bodice of her dress, pulled it over her head, and unhooked the skirt, which fell to the floor in a puddle around her feet. She stood there in her chemise and stays, her stockings and shoes, with the string of pearls around her throat glimmering in the firelight.

"Don't be afraid. I'll be gentle. Step out of your shoes." She was still wearing her black pumps. "Don't you have any shoes sturdier than these?"

"Yes, in my satchel." She spoke, finally. Her husband—husband! I'm married—untied her garters and rolled the wool stockings down her legs, smoothing her calves with rough hands. He unlaced her stays and laid them aside.

"Take off those pearls and get under the covers." As she did, still shaking, although the small cabin was warming fast, Mitchell quickly shed his clothes and joined her.

Beneath the quilts, as he kissed her, his fingers probed her. She stiffened. What was he doing? Then he pushed up on an elbow, spat on his fingers and quickly, after a brief transfer of wetness, shoved himself into her. She cried out, "Oh, don't!" But a few thrusts later, he rolled away, breathing hard. He swung off the bed and stepped into his trousers, pulling his shirt over his head.

"Let's get some supper. Those beans should be hot enough, and I'm hungry. We'll try again in a while. Come on, wife. It'll be better next time."

He looked back at the woman in the bed, who was still trembling. She had rolled onto her side and drawn her knees up to her chest. "I'll go slower. Don't be afraid." He threw her his handkerchief. "Wipe yourself."

Mitchell dished up some stew into one of the bowls and balanced a piece of cornbread on top. He took it to her in the bed. "Sit up and eat this. You'll feel better. And how about some more whisky?"

He busied himself, adding a log to the fire, eating a bowl of stew, drinking some whisky. Temperance shook her head no to the whisky offer, but Mitchell refilled her cup and stood by until she drank it.

She did feel better after eating. The shaking had stopped, and she managed a smile when Mitchell offered more of the food. *The worst is over,* she told herself. *All wives must go through this on their wedding night.* The thought was comforting, and when Mitchell came back to bed, she welcomed him, and he did go slower. His kisses and the whisky sent warmth coursing throughout her body.

THE NEXT DAY WAS SUNNY and much warmer, and Mitchell produced poles so they could fish in the creek after a breakfast of bacon cooked over the fire and cold cornbread. Tempie fried their catch in the bacon grease from breakfast, and they ate the fish along with some hoecakes Tempie made after finding cornmeal in the little cupboard. "Get some rest. I'm going hunting." With little to do, Tempie tidied the cabin and added a log to the fire before deciding to lie down for just a bit. The bed was tempting, and she pulled a quilt over herself and fell into a deep sleep. She woke when Mitchell came home just before dark with two rabbits. He laughed. "You're smart to sleep. I have plans for you tonight!" They roasted the rabbits on the spit over the fire.

Tuesday, after another day of love-making and preparing meals together, they climbed back into the wagon. Tempie snuggled against Mitchell's broad shoulder, and they picked up Phoebe and her son and headed for Georgia. Mitchell had not offered to take her to meet his family. "No time, and besides, some of them are moving to Georgia anyway."

Their destination proved to be the cabin on the banks of the Oconee where Philip had died. Temperance had hoped for a home that carried no sad memories, but someone had cleaned it carefully, and there was a new bedstead and table. A shed room had been built on the back, and Phoebe and Sampson slept there. She unpacked the pitcher and placed it on the mantle with the candlesticks that had been Jonah's gift.

Soon after their arrival in Washington County, the vomiting started. Phoebe tried all the remedies she knew for the nausea that wracked Temperance, but it continued throughout the months of a difficult pregnancy that produced a small baby girl whose wails sent Mitchell from the house. "Name her Temperance," he said. "She looks like you, all drawn-up and complaining. We'll have a boy next time."

Tempie was hurt by that. She seldom complained. But she named the child Temperance Elizabeth, for her mother and her sister. Phoebe was the one who first called her Betsy to distinguish her from her mother, and after a hard few sleepless months for Tempie and Phoebe, little Betsy learned night from day and became an alert baby who walked early and soon had the run of the cabin. Sampson proved his worth by watching her carefully and keeping her out of danger.

She saw Jonah from time to time. He was nearly fifty now, gray-haired, but slender as ever. His needs were few, and he had bought the piece of land on which his shop stood. He only accepted work that challenged him these days. Tempie had sent word to him when they arrived in Washington County, and he rode over to see her not long after, bringing a small carved bird. "It's a linnet," he told her. "I found a picture in one of my books." He had painted this carving, and the bird's shiny dark eyes brought a smile to Temperance.

"I never was sure what a linnet looked like. I can see now why Papa called Mama 'Linnet'".

"And why they named you for her," Jonah said. "I see you still have her pitcher."

"Yes, and the candlesticks you gave me on my sixteenth birthday. Jonah, are you the one who made the improvements on the cabin?"

He ducked his head in acknowledgement. "I didn't want you to see it the way it was, all bare and dirty."

Mitchell was often gone, surveying in Washington and Montgomery counties. Tempie said to him one day when Betsy was nearing her second birthday, laughing so Mitchell wouldn't think she was complaining, "If you truly want to have a son, you're going to have to stay home at night."

She didn't see his expression, but he made a point of coming home by dark until she told him she thought they would be having a second child. Her nausea wasn't as severe this time, and the little girl who was born to them didn't cry, even once. She was stillborn. Tempie tried to hide her grief because it seemed to annoy Mitchell. He told her the first time he found her weeping, "There will be other children. Maybe you'll have a son next time."

Tempie had contracted a recurring illness that plagued some of the other Georgia settlers. The first bout left her exhausted. She burned with fever, throwing off the bed covers, then shook with chills and huddled under blankets, unable to get warm. Her headache was almost blinding. Soon after that she had lost the baby.

Several months passed before she fell sick again. The bouts were unpredictable, and she learned that when they came, she would have a few days of misery, and then slowly regain her strength. Mitchell had little patience when she was bedridden, but Phoebe was there to help out with Betsy and make sure there was food prepared when Mitchell came home.

One day not long after the burial of the stillborn child, named Ann for Tempie's aunt, Phoebe had come to her. "Around the county, they're saying that Mr. Mitchell has been visiting Bradshaw's widow. Sometimes he spends half the night there."

Tempie said, "Why are you telling me this? You must be mistaken. Mitchell wouldn't do that. I'm sure he's just trying to be kind to her."

Phoebe shrugged. "I didn't want you to hear it from someone else. You should talk to him, Missie."

That night, as they were preparing for bed, Tempie, her back to Mitchell, said, "How is the Widow Bradshaw?" She tried to keep her voice calm.

"What are you talking about? How should I know?"

"I just thought maybe you'd seen her."

"Why would I have seen her?"

"Someone just said . . . "

"Someone? What someone?"

"It's not important. You haven't seen her?"

"I told you I hadn't."

She turned and looked at him in the candlelight. He was holding one boot in his hands, studying the sole.

"My boots need new heels. I'll take them in to the cobbler tomorrow."

And that was that. Temperance breathed a sigh of relief. He wasn't seeing young Prudence Bradshaw. Phoebe was wrong.

Another year went by. Two. There were occasional bouts of chills and fever, followed two more early miscarriages, both girls. Betsy was nearly six when Temperance miscarried a tiny boy. Mitchell was angry. "What's wrong with you? By now, I should have had sons." He stormed out of the house, leaving a weeping Temperance with Phoebe, who was shocked into silence, briefly.

Her silence didn't last. "He ain't got no call to talk to you like that. It ain't your fault. Maybe if he would stop that cattin' around . . . " her voice trailed off.

"What do you mean?"

"Ain't none of my business, Missie. You jus' deserve better."

"Please leave me alone now, Phoebe." She named the tiny boy Philip, and he joined the row of small graves by her father.

BY THE TIME MARY WAS BORN in May of 1808, the family had settled in Telfair County, on land backing up on the Ocmulgee River, having moved there from a two years' residence in Montgomery County. Brother James and his family had also made the move to Montgomery County bringing brother Drew, along with three sons, John Drew, James, and Philip Henry, and two daughters, Elizabeth and Rebecca. Another son, William, was born in Georgia after their move, before Temperance and Mitchell's Mary was born, and Mitchell ticked the boys off on his fingers to Temperance when he looked at his new daughter. "John, James, Philip and William. Four sons, and all I've got to show is two girls. Next time, wife, it needs to be a boy."

JONAH MADE A RARE TRIP TO VISIT after the move to Telfair County, bringing the mantelpiece for the parlor of their new house. He caught Temperance in the throes of a bout of malaria. Phoebe was with her. "Why did she never tell me she gets sick like this? Does it happen often?"

"Ever' few months, but you know she don't like to talk about her troubles."

"I still have my hearing, you know," Temperance said, shaking uncontrollably in the bed.

"I have something that will help you," Jonah said. "I read about this sickness in a book by a French doctor. They call it malaria. I bought some Jesuit bark the last time I was in Savannah. Ned Bailey, a man I built some cabinets for, used to get the fevers just like you do. I have some of the bark in my herb box in the wagon. Phoebe, I need some boiling water."

Soon Phoebe was holding a cup of steaming water up to Tempie's lips. "What is it?" Phoebe asked Jonah.

"Tea from a bark that comes from a tree that grows in South America," Jonah said.

Tempie took a tentative sip. "Oh, it's bitter!" She turned her head away.

"Drink it anyway, Missie. I'm standing right here until you do."

She made a face at him and choked down the drink, her mouth puckering.

Jonah left a supply of the bark with her. "When you feel a spell of fever coming on, make a batch of the tea and drink it. Mrs. Bailey says her husband is much better. He doesn't get the bad fevers anymore."

The Telfair County house was an improvement on their previous homes. Mitchell was gaining prominence and wanted his house to reflect that. His brother William had adjoining property on the river. Mitchell built a four room frame house. A wide open hallway ran through the center, from the deep front porch to the back, and the four rooms opened onto the hallway, two on either side. The kitchen was in a small separate outbuilding, Phoebe's domain, and other buildings soon sprouted. There was a cabin for Phoebe and Sampson, a smokehouse, a barn with stalls for the horses, a spring house, and a corncrib. Farther on beyond the privy there was a pigpen.

At a meeting to discuss a name for the settlement, Mitchell had suggested "Griffin."

Another man had called out "Willcox."

"Mizell," said someone else.

"Burch!"

"Coffee!"

"Graham!" By then there was widespread laughter, as each man called out his own name.

A voice from the back of the room said, "We'll never settle it this way. Let's name it for the quality we'd most like to see here in Telfair County, and for the kindest woman in the community. Let's call it 'Temperance.'" Men nodded. Mitchell's wife had earned a reputation for loyalty to her family and for open-hearted generosity. Some there knew that Mitchell often gave her cause to be less than loyal, but no one spoke of it, certainly not to Temperance.

There was general agreement, and soon after a sign proclaimed the post office on the River Road to be "Temperance."

Tempie's days were filled. Sampson had met a young woman called Portia who belonged to the owner from a neighboring farm. Tempie had campaigned successfully for her purchase, pointing out that a strong young couple like Portia and Sampson would produce offspring. They were married in 1806, and a boy, Darius, was born the following year. Among them, the three women managed the household chores. There seemed to be no end to those chores. There was always laundry to be done, clothes to be made or mended, meals to be cooked, and pots and dishes to be washed, crops to be planted, tended, harvested and preserved, children to be minded and taught, livestock to be fed, eggs to be gathered. The list went on.

Mitchell entered into the lumber business. Logs were cut and sent on rafts downriver, eventually ending up on the coast in Darien. Jacksonville was the center of the political life of Telfair County, and Mitchell often found reasons to ride there. He was elected first coroner of the new county, which filled him with pride.

LINN: FIFTEEN
Saturday evening

LINN LEANED BACK IN HER DESK CHAIR and stretched. Wow! That was an interesting bit of information. What a scumbag!

Wonder if Gran knew about that? She reached behind her for her phone. She'd tossed it on her bed after a text exchange with Phil, who wanted to know if she would like to get lunch before going to the zoo tomorrow. She'd suggested a picnic and said she'd bring sandwiches and cookies if he'd bring soft drinks. It turned out he liked tuna salad, so she'd make some after church. She had stashed the leftover brownies in the freezer, so she'd bring those along.

She called Gran, who picked up on the second ring. "Gran, I was working on James Griffin's family. He's my sixth-great-grandfather, so your fourth, I guess. Do you know what he did to his family, the jerk? He went off to Alabama and started a whole new family there! He left his wife Susan and six kids behind in Georgia!"

Gran said, "Yes, I remember Mother telling me that story. Her cousin—well, our cousin—Clifford Dwyer discovered all that. The family story was that he'd been killed by Indians, but Cliff found him on deeds and censuses in Alabama, with another woman and ten more children! Cliff got in touch with your GeeGee through their genealogy research, and they became close friends."

"I guessed that. There are several letters from Cliff in the file, with copies of land plats and deeds. There's even a map showing exactly where James's land in Alabama was. Oh, guess what, Gran? I have a date tomorrow afternoon to go to the zoo!"

"Really? Who's the guy?"

"His name is Phil. I thought that was kind of a coincidence, since I've been learning about Philip Alston. Anyway, remember Kaylie, from swim team? Her boyfriend is at Tech, and it's a friend of his. I met him last night. He seems really nice. Kind of quiet. Oh, do you want me to pick you up tomorrow for early church? You can meet my gray car, Punch."

Gran laughed. "Yes, your mom called me about the car. I'd love to meet Punch. Why don't you come about ten after eight. I'll be watching for you. That'll give us plenty of time. Did you say you're going to the zoo? I'll bring my family pass along to give you. That'll give you a discount on the admission. It's not cheap, but it's such a great zoo."

"Oh, thanks. Phil offered to take me to lunch, but I'm not sure what his wallet's like, so I said I'd bring a picnic."

"Tell me more about this Phil. Where's he from?"

"I don't know a whole lot yet. He's at Tech. He works in the library there part-time. His dad's an architect. They're from Macon. He did call me right when he said he would, and he texted me tonight."

"What does he look like?"

"Tall, dark red hair, beautiful blue eyes, glasses. Nice-looking. Great smile. He's just finished his first year at Tech. So he's probably nineteen, like me. I'll find out more tomorrow."

"Sounds promising. I hope you have fun with him! See you in the morning, honey. Good night. Don't stay up too late!"

"I've got a couple more of James the Jerk's kids to enter, and then I'm going to bed. Oh, Mom's going to let me redecorate this room. I'll tell you about it on the way to church."

"It's about time you painted over the purple! Night, Linn!"

"Night, Gran."

It had been a good day. The trip to the mall with Mom was fun. They laughed a lot and made plans for painting and shopping for new curtains and bed linens. Now Linn had two new swimsuits for work and a really cute coral-colored sundress with spaghetti straps. She thought about wearing the dress to the zoo, but decided that shorts and sneakers would be more practical for picnicking and walking around Grant Park. She could save the dress for another time. She hoped there'd be another time!

At dinner, Dad had said only that he hoped she wouldn't put the idea of medical school completely out of her head. She agreed to consider it, but her thought was no, I really like the thought of nursing. But Dad had made so many concessions. It was kind of amazing how calm he was about this all. He did call her into the family room after she helped Mom clean up the kitchen to ask her one more time if she was sure she hadn't been, umm . . .

"Raped?" she prompted.

She saw her father's grim face and hastened to reassure him. "I'm very sure, Dad. It's a good thing I'm tall and strong. It really helped."

"I'm just glad you're okay. If you'd been hurt . . . I'm sorry about the other girl. Her attorney said there was medical evidence." He was having a hard time with this. He turned away from her. "Vaginal tearing and bruising. They did a rape kit, too. So the DNA evidence will help when it comes in, and with the physical damage on record, they'll have a hard time proving it was consensual."

Linn turned back to the computer and the file on James, Sr. He fathered at least seventeen children, because GeeGee listed a daughter Harriet who only lived a year and a half. Wonder if they had child support in those days for the kids he abandoned in Georgia? Not likely!

On the banks of the Ocmulgee,
April, 1810

"**D**ON'T WORRY, SUSAN. I'LL TALK TO MITCHELL. We'll figure something out." Tempie hugged the red-eyed woman awkwardly. Susan had her youngest, Isaac, a sturdy eighteen-month-old child, perched on her hip. Isaac, in response to his mother's tears, was yowling and burrowing his face into the front of Susan's faded calico dress. The profuse discharge from his nose and mouth had left slimy trails. Mary was clinging to Tempie's legs, distressed by the emotional upheaval above her.

"Betsy." A head of blonde curls appeared too quickly around the doorframe of the door leading into the hall. Tempie frowned at her. As she had guessed, Betsy had been hovering nearby, listening. There would have to be a conversation later about eavesdropping, but more importantly, about discretion.

"Is Martha there with you? Martha, run out to the kitchen house and get your brothers. Tell Phoebe to wrap up the rest of the tea-cakes for you to take home." While she and Susan had talked, she had sent the girls and Susan Griffin's James, Will and Lenn to the kitchen house for refreshment, primarily to get them out of the way. Etheldred—why had James named him such a pre-posterous name?—at nearly fifteen was already working with the men cutting logs and loading them on rafts. James, Jr. would be put to work soon, she knew.

Susan's husband James, one of Mitchell's cousins, had relocated his family to the Temperance community from the Tensaw district in Alabama only two years ago. Mitchell had helped him, a pregnant Susan, and the six children get settled in a cabin on a piece of their land just down the River Road from them and found James work in the logging business. Tempie barely remembered James from the battle at the house in Moore County when she was five, but recalled that her mother had treasured the letter he had sent from Florida. James, in his mid-forties now, was still a charmer. His frank admiration of her family could not help but endear him to her, especially when he talked about his fond recollection of her mother's kindness.

"I named Marthy for your mama. She's Martha Linnie, after Miss Linnie." James was a teller of tales, and Betsy always stayed at table with the grown-ups, enthralled, when the other Griffin family joined her family occasionally for Sunday dinner after church. Betsy and Martha were nearly of an age and became friends, but James kept Martha close to home much of the time, to help Susan in the fields, along with her little brothers as they became old enough.

Susan was a small woman, worn down from pregnancies and hard work. Once she might have been pretty. She seldom spoke at the infrequent family gatherings, but Tempie had learned from the times she visited Susan when James was away that she had a quick mind and a wry sense of humor.

Tempie found out from table talk on occasional Sundays that after the war and a stay in Florida seeing the sights and the alligators, James had married young Susan Brown and brought her north to Burke County, Georgia, where he had joined his father Samuel, his mother, and his younger brothers and sisters. His brother, Samuel Junior, had served in the Revolution, too, and had married Elizabeth Bruner, whose parents were German settlers in the region. Hearing about the free land in the Florida Territory, several of the family groups had migrated west to the

Tensaw Settlement in the late 1790's, including both Samuels, James, and two more brothers, William and George. James acquired acreage along Smith's Creek, which ran into the Tombigbee River, simply by occupying it.

And now James and his brood were back in Georgia. Tempie, asking, got only a vague reason from Susan as to why they left. "Oh, James never can stay put for long. He likes to see new places." Tempie translated that to a "Grass is greener" philosophy on James's part and let it go.

In late December of the previous year, a letter had come for James. He brought it to Tempie to read.

"Oh, I'm so sorry, James. It says your brother Samuel has died, and that you are executor of his estate. You'll need to go back to the Tensaw settlement as soon as you can." She looked up from the letter at James and was surprised to see a smile on his lips. His eyes were shining with excitement. He saw her look and rearranged his face into an approximation of grief.

"Soon" proved to be the very next morning. James consulted with Mitchell, and left Dred to go on with the logging. Susan and the older children could manage the house and fields. And off he rode, on the only horse they owned, to make the four hundred mile journey to the Tombigbee River.

Four months had gone by, and today Susan had brought another letter. Tempie's services were called for again.

When she unsealed it, there was money. A bank note, promising the bearer one hundred dollars. She handed the bank note to Susan, puzzled, and read the letter aloud.

"Dear Susan, I am writing this for James. He wants you to know that he is needed here, so he will not be coming back to Georgia. He will send you and the children money when he can. Your friend, Clarinda Griffin."

"Whatever does this mean, Susan?"

"Clarinda is his brother George's widow woman. Her and her young'uns was living in a cabin on our place. She had a little girl and a little boy. Rebecca and Riley. Read it again, please." Susan's voice was shaky, and her face was pale.

That was when Tempie had sent the children, all but the babies, out to the kitchen house.

"What will people say?" was what Susan kept repeating, shaking with sobs. "It's that Clarinda done this. I know it's that Clarinda."

Mitchell, that night, was not as shocked as Tempie expected him to be. "Oh, I reckon he'll change his mind and come on home soon. He's just acting the fool."

"Mitchell, Susan is heartbroken. Can she manage by herself? Why does James think his brother's family needs him more than she does? Samuel has grown sons. They can look after their mother." Tempie paced the floor. "What can we do? Can you go talk to him and bring him back?"

"No point in that. He'll come back if he wants to come back."

"He might listen to you, Mitchell. He's always respected you."

Mitchell thought a minute. It might be worth the trip to see some of the land in Alabama. People were relocating there, and a settlement was growing up along Mobile Bay. It might be a good investment.

"If he's not back here by the time I get home from Milledgeville, I'll take Dred and go to Alabama." Mitchell's recent election as state senator would take him away from home to the capital from time to time. Tempie knew he relished his new-found status.

It was early fall before Mitchell found the time to lend James's firstborn son a horse and set out with him on the long trek to the Tensaw Community on the Tombigbee. Tempie swallowed her misgivings for Susan's sake. There'd been tales of Indian uprisings along the river. Most of the Creeks had settled into a peaceful co-existence with the white settlers, and some of the traders had married Creek and Choctaw women, but there was a growing resentment among some of the young Creek men over what they saw as a loss of the old ways.

It was a bemused Mitchell who returned near dark one night weeks later from the Alabama trip. He stopped by the house only long enough to get Tempie and leave the horses with Sampson to feed and water. Phoebe came in to watch the children, and with a quiet Dred trailing behind them, he and Tempie walked the quarter mile to Susan's cabin.

"I don't know how to tell you, Susan," he said. "James is living with that Clarinda. They've got a boy they're calling James, and those young'uns of hers call him 'Paw.' He sent a little money for you. He's been doing some fur trading at Fort St. Stephen with the Choctaws. He says he hopes you'll forgive him, but he's not coming back."

A white-faced Susan turned to Dred. "Did you talk to him? What are we going to do? Did you tell him we need him here?"

"No, ma'am. I didn't. If he don't need us, we don't need him, Ma. He's got him a whole new family. He don't want us no more. He can rot in hell in Alabama. I don't care. He's as good as dead to me. In fact, I'm gone tell people he IS dead."

Marthy and James were holding hands. Marthy said, with resentment in her voice, "He named another boy of his 'James'? He already has a "James.'" She squeezed her brother's hand.

"Not no more, he don't. And don't call me 'James' no more neither. Call me 'Jim.' We'll look after you, Ma," he said. He pulled himself up to his full eleven-year-old height. "I reckon the Indians shot him. That's what we'll say. Paw went off to Alabama and got himself shot."

Linn: Sixteen
Sunday morning

On the way home from the early service at St. Margaret's, Linn, who had been quiet for a few minutes, said to her grandmother, "I think the worst part of dealing with all of GeeGee's research is not knowing what happened to some of those people. I mean, for instance, well, take Temperance and Philip Alston's children, nobody seems to know what happened to the sons named John and Drew. James we know about, and Philip, Winifred and Mary Drew. And, of course, Temperance the daughter—I call her 'Temp Two' to myself—we know about her, since we're descended from her. And we know Elizabeth died young. But John and Drew—they just seemed to have vanished. It's kind of sad."

Gran smiled at the serious young woman at the wheel. "Some new information may turn up some day about them. We have better access now to records, and there's more and more online. People are cataloging cemeteries and indexing censuses. Your GeeGee did some of that when her eyes were still good, remember? She put in many hours at the library transcribing microfilms of censuses. Sounds like you're enjoying going through all those folders."

"It's fascinating. I have to make myself stop and go to bed."

"Take your time. There's no hurry on this."

"Well, I'm taking the whole day off today! It'll be fun at the zoo. I haven't been there in a couple of years. And I'm sure I'll be able to tell you more about Phil after today."

They were at Gran's parking lot. "I can't come in, Gran. I've got to go make sandwiches and change."

"Promise you'll let me know how it goes!" Linn's grandmother waved as Linn drove off.

At home, Linn stuck her head in the family room, where her father sat reading the sports page, a cup of coffee beside him. "Hi. Where's Mom? Hi, Moonshine." The old basset lifted his head, thumped his tail once and went back to sleep at her dad's feet.

"Upstairs getting dressed, probably. You look mighty happy about something."

Linn blushed. Was her excitement that obvious? "It's such a beautiful day."

"Oh, right. You have a date with some boy just you met. Be careful."

"Dad, we're going to the zoo in broad daylight. And Eddie's known him for a while. I'll be fine."

"Make sure there's no alcohol involved. And call if you need us."

"Oh, that reminds me." Linn pulled her phone from her purse. "I turned it to vibrate for church."

There was a text from Phil: "See you at noon."

She texted back: "I'll be ready."

"Talk to you later, Dad. I've got stuff to do." She headed upstairs.

Downstairs a little later, in white shorts and sneakers, and as a compromise, a lime green sleeveless blouse with a ruffled collar instead of her usual tee-shirt, and with her hair neatly brushed into a ponytail, she gathered the makings for tuna salad. Three sandwiches in baggies went into a little cooler, and she added the brownies and two apples. Chips? No, there weren't any in the pantry. Maybe they could buy some at the zoo if they were still hungry. What else? Carrot strips. She peeled a couple of carrots and cut them up.

Mom came into the kitchen as she was bagging up the carrots. "You look nice. When are you leaving? And when will you be home?"

"Soon—ten or fifteen minutes, maybe—and I don't know, but early. I start work tomorrow, and Phil has class."

"Let me know if you're not going to be home by seven or so. I'll save you some supper. And, honey, be careful."

"Not you, too! But I will. I'm going to run up and get Gran's zoo pass. I left it in my room."

As she reached the top of the stairs, the doorbell rang. "I'll get that," her father yelled from the family room.

He's early. Oh, poor Phil. I hope Dad doesn't say anything embarrassing, she thought, as she grabbed the zoo pass from her desk and ran down the stairs, slowing as she reached the last steps.

"Hi, Phil." She smiled at him. He was even taller than she remembered. And his ear tips were pink.

"Dad, this is Phil Manning. Phil, my dad, Bill McKinney."

Phil put his hand out, and the two men shook. "So you're going to the zoo?"

"Yes, sir. We have a nice day for it."

"Drive carefully. Atlanta traffic can be rough."

"I will. I've gotten used to it, though."

"Manning. Where are you from?"

"Macon."

"Any relation to Deke Manning? I went to school with him."

"Yes, sir. Deke's my dad's first cousin."

"How's he doing? I haven't seen him in years."

"Doing fine. Still practicing law in Bibb County."

That's so Southern, Linn thought. Who's your family? It's good, though. Dad's made a connection. Maybe he won't worry about me so much.

Mom came from the kitchen carrying the little cooler, which she handed to Linn. Linn made the introductions.

"We should go," Linn said.

"Nice to have met you," Phil said to her parents.

Linn's mother said, "Be careful, and call if you need us."

On the way to Phil's car, which turned out to be a red Honda, Linn said, "Sorry about that."

"No, it's fine. They care about you. Are you an only child?"

"Is it that obvious?" Linn laughed.

Phil opened the door for her and took the cooler from her hand and put it on the back seat, next to a folded up blanket and another small cooler.

"I didn't know what you'd like to drink, so I brought lemonade and water."

"That's perfect. Do you have brothers or sisters?"

"One of each. Both older, both married. I'm the baby. And a step-sister, also older. My dad married again after my mother died."

"Oh, I'm sorry. Not that your father married again. About your mother."

"That was seven, no, eight, years ago. Cancer."

"That must have been hard."

"It was. But I'm glad Dad met Jean. That's my stepmother. She's good for him."

"Did you have any trouble finding my house?"

"No. And I've figured out how to get to Grant Park. Would you mind if we eat before we go to the zoo? I'm hungry."

"No, that would be fine."

"So what did you do yesterday? You said something about some shopping."

"Mom and I went to the mall. I needed a new swimsuit for work. I ended up with two! We picked up some paint chips, too. I'm going to paint my room. It hasn't been painted since I started sixth grade!"

Phil stole a quick look at the girl seated next to him. Pretty hair. And nice legs. They were crossed neatly at the ankles. She turned toward him and caught his eye. His ears turned pink again. Linn smiled.

Phil looked quickly back at the road. "So you're going to be teaching swimming?"

"Yes, and lifeguarding. Do you like to swim?"

"Oh, sure. I'm probably not as good at it as you are. Maybe you could give me some pointers some time. Is the pool where you'll be working open to the public?"

"Oh, definitely. It's part of the county rec department. You could come. But it's always jam-packed with kids. There's a pool at my Gran's condo that I'm allowed to use. It's pretty quiet."

Sounds like he plans on seeing me again. Her heart thumped. Change the subject. Don't push it. I don't want to seem too eager.

"Did I tell you that my Gran's hired me to transcribe some family records? I've been working on some of my people that ended up in Telfair County. I had to look that one up. It's in south central Georgia. They were in a community called Temperance, which is coincidental, because that was the name of the wife in the family."

On the banks of the Ocmulgee,
December 1, 1811

Temperance TAPPED AT THE BEDROOM DOOR. "It's time, Mady." "Come in, Sister. I'm nearly ready."

Mary Drew Alston Carroll was folding an embroidered night dress into a small satchel which sat open on the bed. The rest of her belongings had already been taken down the road to William Harris's house to await her arrival as his wife. All that remained to complete this transition was a simple ceremony at Concord Methodist Church that would take place as part of the regular Sunday service.

"You look lovely, Mady." Tempie studied the young woman standing before her wearing a dove-gray woolen dress. Mady was twenty-seven now, but bore the years well. Not having children keeps you young and slim, Tempie thought, with a brief flash of envy. Oh, God, please let this marriage be a happy one for her.

She had been shocked the afternoon before, as she and Mady folded and packed the last of Mady's clothes into a trunk. Mady seemed unusually quiet, so her sister had attempted a small joke. "Well, if you call out your last husband's name in the throes of marital bliss, your new husband will never know!"

Mady had burst into tears. Tempie dropped the shawl she

was holding and embraced her sister. "What is it, Mady? Do you miss William so much?"

William Carroll had married Mady in 1799, when she was fifteen. Temperance, hearing the news in Georgia, had misgivings. *She's still so young. I wish we'd been able to send for her sooner.* But the letter from James had only praise for William Carroll. He was well-educated, his finances were stable, he'd never been married, he'd been a very close friend of John's. William had plans to relocate to Georgia, so perhaps Tempie would see her soon. James said he thought his wife Polly was considering the idea of a move to Georgia more seriously, knowing that Mady and Tempie would both be there, and that Drew would come, too. John still spent most of his time in Charleston, but his business sent him traveling throughout the southern states.

Mady and her husband William Carroll were a part of a general exodus from North Carolina, claiming land in Georgia. Winnie, however, had married William Waddell in 1800 and stayed behind with him and their growing family of two daughters and a son. Brother Philip married Ann Ramsey the following year and was already the father of three daughters and a son, living on land that he bought near Gulf, by the time Tempie's Mary was born.

James had given ownership of Sall, who was a widow now, and two of her children, along with Bet and Jacob, to Mady when she married William Carroll, as her marriage settlement from her father's estate. The settlement also included a payment of 326 pounds. One of Sall's children was a young woman called Sarie; the other was Marcus, who had been serving as house boy to James.

Mitchell was rising in local politics. When he had been elected to the State Senate from Telfair County in 1810, William Carroll had been chosen as a state representative. Mitchell was also active in the local militia, helping to build forts to protect the residents in the event of a Creek uprising. There had been incidents from time to time with the Indians of the area. He was often gone, to Jacksonville on business or to the capital in Milledgeville.

Susan Griffin and her children were managing well enough without their husband and father. Dred was a muscular sixteen-year-old now, working hard as a logger. Marthy and Jim worked alongside their mother in the fields. Gus was nine now, and able to keep an eye on Lenn and Zack. What most pleased Tempie, though, was that Susan had come to her soon after Clarinda's letter to say that she wanted her children to be able to read. Lesson times were a little hit or miss, because of work, but rainy days found all available Griffin children clustered around the dining table at Tempie's house or on the porch on pleasant days learning to write and figure. Even Dred came when he could.

One chilly fall day saw an unexpected visitor to the Temperance community. Mitchell was away in Milledgeville when the dogs alerted Tempie to an approaching wagon. She'd come out onto the porch with little Mary, squinting against the sun, to see who this might be. Jonah! Tempie was shocked by how frail he'd grown. His hair was completely gray, and his shoulders were stooped. She came down the porch steps, calling for Betsy to fetch Sampson. "Hush, you two!" she said to the hounds who were still barking. "It's Jonah!"

"Come in, Jonah. Sampson will take the horse. You must be worn out. Phoebe! Oh, there you are."

The commotion had brought Phoebe and Portia from the kitchen house, where they were paring apples to slice and dry. "Here's Jonah! Portia, help him down from the wagon, and Phoebe, bring him some coffee and something to eat."

Phoebe and Portia looked at each other. What brought the old man here? There were no secrets between Portia and Sampson, and Portia knew exactly who this was. Jonah, half-brother to Miss Tempie's father. The one who used to be called Dave. Who killed that white man back in North Carolina. He didn't look much like a killer to Portia, but it looked like something was bad wrong with him now.

The old man nodded to Phoebe and handed Sampson the reins to his horse. "Thank you, Sampson. Is this Portia? And these are your children?" Portia had one baby on her hip and a toddler by the hand.

Sampson beamed. "Yes, Mr. Jonah. Darius and Dick. And we got another one coming."

"Jonah, come in and warm up," Tempie interrupted. Jonah had begun coughing. "It's cold out here. No, I'm not going to have an argument about this. Come in."

With Portia supporting him on one side and Tempie on the other, Jonah, who was doubled over in the spasm of a severe bout of coughing, was taken into the parlor, where Tempie had been mending clothes. Mary resumed her castle-building by the hearth. "Do you recognize those blocks?" Tempie said. "They're the ones you sent when Betsy was a baby."

Phoebe came in with a tray. "I made you some tea, Jonah, and I put some honey in it for that cough. It don't sound so good. How long you been coughing like that?"

Jonah looked to Tempie, who said, "We'll be fine, Phoebe. Thank you. You can get back to the apples now. Mary, put your blocks in the basket and go with Phoebe."

Settled onto a chair by the fire, with a cup of tea in his hand and a piece of apple pie on the table beside him, Jonah got right to the point. "Shut the door, Missy. There are some things I need to say. I'm not going to live much longer. Hush, now. It's all right," he said as Tempie opened her mouth to protest. "Just listen."

"I've sold off my land and cabinet shop to a cabinetmaker. They're going to build a new house on the property. I can stay on in the cabin. The family that bought the shop have agreed to let me do that and to look after me. That was part of the bargain."

"But, Jonah—"

"No, pay attention. I want to talk to you about what happened back home. I'm not going to apologize about Thomas Taylor." He saw the confusion in Tempie's eyes. "Mr. Philip didn't kill that man. I did. But I'm not sorry about killing him. I'm just sorry that your papa took the blame for that. Maybe if he'd told the truth and let them hang me, the rest of it wouldn't have happened.'

"I was younger then and arrogant. I thought I had the power to fix things for your mama, make everything the way it was when she and your papa were first married and so peaceful together, just by killing George Glascock. But I got caught, and it turned out I made things worse. They came after Mr. Philip for the killing after he sent me off to Georgia. I tried to talk him out of sending me away, before Mr. John and I rode off, to just go ahead and let them have me, but you never could tell that man anything. You couldn't tell me anything either back then." There was a wry smile on his face.

"There was nobody in the world like your mama, for your papa or for me. It broke my heart when I got word that she and your sister had died. I would have done anything for her. I just wish your papa could have been happy without her, but you saw that he couldn't be. I like to think that they're together now. I know Mr. Philip never believed in all that heaven business, but just because he didn't believe it doesn't mean it isn't so."

Tempie was crying quietly now, tears rolling unchecked down her cheeks.

"Here, child." Jonah reached in his jacket pocket and brought out a clean handkerchief. "I don't mean to make you cry. I don't know if you're happy with Mitchell. I do know he's not the man you thought he was."

Tempie didn't look up. She dried her eyes and blew her nose. "I think he loves me as much as he can. He doesn't mistreat me or the girls. He's never hit me. And he always comes back."

There was a rueful smile on Jonah's mouth. "I told Mitchell when he asked you to marry him that I'd kill him if he hurt you. I guess I'm not much good at killing any more. But I want you to be able to take care of yourself if he doesn't come back some day." Jonah pulled a cloth sack from his other jacket pocket. "This is for you. It's gold from the sale of my property."

Tempie was shaking her head. "I can't take that."

"And why not? You're the only family I've got. You're the only person I care anything about. Who else would I give it to? None of the others in your family have ever bothered about me. And none of them are likely to need it someday. Keep it in a safe place for you and the girls. Just promise me you won't tell Mitchell. I mean it, Missie. Promise."

Tempie was nodding. She was thinking about Mitchell's cousin James and how he'd left Susan without so much as a warning that he might not come home. Could Mitchell do that? He'd promised her after the last horrible time, when Mrs. O'Keefe, furious, had marched her sobbing daughter Abby up to their door and demanded that Mitchell stay away from her, that it would never happen again. They'd given Mrs. O'Keefe enough money to send Abby to live with her aunt in Athens.

"I'll take it, then, with thanks, and I'll keep it safe for the girls. But, Jonah, why don't you stay here? I can look after you."

He smiled. "I don't think your husband and I could get along living in the same county, much less the same town. I'll be fine. The people who bought my land—Sanders is their name—are decent people. I told them how to reach you, and they've promised me they'll let you know when I'm gone. Now, stop that. I don't have another clean handkerchief."

Jonah left before dawn the next morning, before anyone else was up, after refusing a bed in the house. He'd eaten a little soup and gone off to sleep in the barn. Tempie cried again when she found he had left, because she didn't get to say goodbye. Then she realized he'd wanted it that way. During the day she gave some thought to hiding the money before Mitchell got home. That night, alone in front of the fireplace, with a sharp knife, she hollowed out the pages of a book of Plato's philosophy that had been her father's and returned it to its place on the shelf, after stashing the gold inside. She felt a little twinge of regret burning the mutilated pages in the fire, but she knew there was no chance Mitchell would ever open the book.

And then later that fall, William Carroll had sickened. Malaria was common in the area, but most people survived bouts of it. Tempie found that the extract of tree bark kept her attacks under control. William had a severe headache and an extremely high fever, and the tea she gave him seemed to make no difference at all. There was blood in his urine when Marcus brought him the chamber pot. He lapsed soon after into convulsions. Mady and

Tempie, watching at his bedside, knew the end was coming. Mitchell rode off to Montgomery County to tell the Alstons of William's illness, and John, who was visiting James and Polly, rode back with him. He had just arrived when William regained consciousness briefly after a strong convulsion. William's eyes fixed on John standing at the foot of the bed. "Johnny," he said, "I'm so sorry. Forgive me." And he was gone.

"What did he mean?" Tempie asked as she closed his eyes and pulled the sheet up over his face. Mady had run weeping from the room.

"I suppose he was sorry to die." John's mouth was a thin line in his face. He turned away from his sister.

"Why did he say it to you and not Mady? Why did he ask forgiveness?"

"I suppose he was delirious. How should I know? Go see to your sister."

Temperance narrowed her eyes at her brother before she left the room. There was more to this. They'd talk later.

Mady had grieved quietly and with dignity, living alone and wearing black for the full year. After church on Sundays, William Harris, whose third wife, Sally Coffee, had died three years earlier, stopped often to talk to her. He had been left with a son and a daughter, who tagged along after him in the church yard, young Peter clinging to his hand. Mady's kind heart went out to the children. Julia was six, and Peter had his fourth birthday in May. She knew the children would not even remember Sally, whom she had known and liked.

It was no surprise to Mitchell when William Harris came to talk to him in mid-October, asking for Mady's hand. He gave his approval, and Mady had accepted his suit, agreeing to marry him quietly, as soon as possible. There need be no fuss. She would put her house and land on the market and sell what furniture she wouldn't need and move into William's house. They settled on December first as a wedding date. She would be in the house and well settled by Christmas time. Sally's family, the Coffees, were happy with William's choice. Even if Mady proved to be barren, and there was every indication she was, since there were no children from her nine year marriage, they had seen how their grandchildren had taken to Mady. She'd be a good mother to them. Mady would bring a little money into the marriage, too, and five slaves.

But on the eve of her wedding, here was Mady weeping. Temperance patted the bed. "Sit down. Tell me what's wrong."

"William and I never—he couldn't, in bed. I mean, he tried, but nothing ever happened. He said it was his fault, not mine, and he offered to set me free.

"Sister, what are you saying? Do you mean you're still virgin!" Her conversation with John following William's death had opened her eyes, but she really didn't expect this.

Mady cried harder. "He said we could get an annulment, but I said no. What would people think? What would happen to me? He said he loved me, but not in the way a man should love a woman. Sister, I didn't know what to do. I was ashamed. He never even tried again after those first few times."

"Oh, Mady. I'm so sorry. Why didn't you tell me?"

"I thought it was my fault; that he didn't find me—I don't know—pretty enough to be able to—you know. So what should I do now?"

"Do you love William Harris?"

"I do. I know he'll be a good husband. He says he loves me. Last night, when we went for a walk by the river, he kissed me and held me tight, and I felt his—you know—through my skirt, pressing against my leg. He was breathing hard, and he said he could hardly wait for our wedding night. He's arranged for the children to stay at the Coffees' house for a few days. We'll be by ourselves. And it felt really good when he kissed me. I didn't want him to stop. Sister, he said I was beautiful." She was smiling now.

"You are indeed, Mady. But you need to tell him you're still a virgin. He'll know what to do."

"Won't he be disappointed in me?"

Tempie smiled, "No, I hardly think so. Dry your eyes. He'll be honored to be your first real husband. Do you want me to tell him?"

"No, I think I can. I really do care for him, and I am so proud that he's chosen me to be the mother of his children. Should I tell him before the service, in case he wants to change his mind?"

"I can promise you he won't. Smile, little one. I think you're going to be very happy."

THAT NIGHT, LYING AWAKE next to Mitchell, who was snoring softly, Tempie remembered her conversation with her brother John. It had been after William Carroll's burial. The neighbors had finally left Mady's house. Mitchell had taken the children and Betsy back to their house to turn them over to Phoebe and Portia. Tempie and John would be staying at Mady's for a day or two. Tempie had persuaded Mady to go and lie down in the spare room. Mady had refused to sleep in the bedroom she had shared with William, sending Tempie in to fetch night clothes.

John had gone into the parlor. Someone had brought a bottle of brandy, and he offered Tempie a glass.

"Thanks. I could use it. I'm exhausted." She tossed the brandy down in a couple of quick swallows and held the glass out for a refill. "Talk to me, John. What was all that about—the night William died?"

John looked into his glass. He didn't pretend not to understand her this time. "He didn't love Mady. He loved me. He should never have married her. I don't know what he was thinking."

"You and he? What do you mean? Oh, John." She didn't know how to think about this.

"I don't think I ever really loved him, Tempie, and I couldn't face what life would be like if we'd tried to be together. Do you remember that I left James's house just before your wedding?"

"Yes, you left so fast. I never understood that. Why you weren't there. William said you'd been called away on business to Charleston."

"Charleston was where we met, while I was studying there and living at my uncle's house. William had a room above a tavern, and we spent time together. I didn't mean for him to fall in love with me. I think I had not realized he had done so until he came after me when I went to Chatham County to visit all of you."

Temperance studied her brother. John was standing near the fireplace, half-turned from her, not meeting her eyes as he talked. He was forty-four now, still a handsome man, slim, well-formed. Mitchell had often wondered aloud why John had not married, and she had always replied that he must not have met a woman good enough for him. Did I always know he wasn't interested in women? she thought.

"We rode out to hunt, and he tried to press the issue," John went on. "He had a plan that we could sell everything we owned and live in France. We argued. I finally convinced him that I couldn't–wouldn't–do that. I told him to be realistic, that our families would cut us off, that there'd be no money to speak of. We both liked our little luxuries. Nice clothes, good food and wine. I asked him how he'd feel when the money ran out, and we were starving and shivering in an attic in Paris. I told him he should go home, but he said he wouldn't; that he just wanted to be near me. I said I'd be the one to leave, then. And I did. That very day. You know, I never saw him again until night before last. I always managed to be elsewhere. I was horrified when I heard he and Mady were married, but I suppose I thought he'd worked things out. In the back of my mind, I always wondered if he'd fallen in love with her because she looks so much like me."

Tempie managed a smile. "A trifle vain of you, brother."

"There are names for men like William and me. None flattering. And all else aside, a relationship like ours is illegal. Most men like us marry and raise families, in spite of how we feel about other men. I couldn't do that. It seemed unfair to pretend to love a woman just to have a place in society. But Mary Drew and William seem to have had a happy marriage. I'm just sorry there were no children. Thank God Mady's young. There's still time for her to meet someone else."

"Did James know about you and William?" Tempie was having difficulties in thinking all this through. If James knew and let Mary Drew marry a man who couldn't love her....

"I'm sure he didn't. We were very careful in Charleston, and certainly at James's house. There was so much at stake. I've always been cautious in my..." he seemed to search for a word... "dealings with men. The shame it would bring to my family, if I were discovered. And the thought of imprisonment. Prison just wouldn't suit me." There was a wry smile.

John turned to face her, squaring his shoulders. His face was drawn, and she noticed the silver in the stubble on his chin. "I'll understand if you choose to turn me out now."

His sister was quiet. She shook her head. "Don't be a dolt, John. You're still the same man you always were. I just didn't know who that was. And you're my brother. I do think it might not be wise to tell anyone else in the family. Especially Mitchell and James." She smiled suddenly, looking very much as she had when they conspired against James as children, a dimple denting her cheek. "Your secret is safe with me."

They talked on well into the night. John had always been her favorite brother. He told her about his thriving business in Charleston, importing furniture from the continent for the wealthy plantation owners along the coast. "There's someone in my life now," he said. "Someone I met in London. George Crawford. He's my business partner, and lives in his own establishment in Charleston. We're received in society. We're thought of as two very eligible bachelors. I think you'd like him. I know he'd like you. He's the practical one. Keeps me from spending all my money on clothes and horses."

Tempie climbed into bed beside her sister close to dawn, her head spinning from the brandy she and John had shared, and with the new understanding she had of her brother. Love was love, she supposed. Some people never found it. She wondered if what she and Mitchell had could be called love.

AND NOW, ON A SUNDAY MORNING a little over a year later, Mady looked radiant. Her eyes that were her father's blue eyes were glowing. Temperance had lent her Elizabeth's pearls, and her neat little kid boots were shiny. Sampson had seen to that. She had pulled her dark hair back into a small bun and wore a bonnet that matched her gown. Temperance handed her the shawl from the bed and picked up the little satchel. William Harris was a fortunate man.

LINN: SEVENTEEN
Sunday night

LINN, SMILING, SAT DOWN ON THE EDGE OF HER BED and untied her sneakers. One at a time, thoughtfully, she launched them towards her closet floor, laughing as they landed side by side, the toe of the right shoe lovingly overlapping the toe of the left. She stretched her arms over her head and plopped backward on the bed. Still smiling, she gazed at the white stars on her ceiling. Some of the points were peeling away now, and they no longer glowed as they once had.

So many nights as a young teen, she had stared at them in the dark, thinking about the day that had passed or the day that lay ahead, until her eyelids grew heavy, and she rolled onto her side and fell asleep. It was a good day today, she thought now, and tomorrow will be exciting. I start work, and I'm meeting Phil for ice cream at Mickey Gee's tomorrow night.

A really good day today. Conversation was easy, and they could make each other laugh. The picnic had been fun, and the leisurely walk around the zoo perfect. A good start. "A start." And that was wonderful, too, because as he walked her to her door in time for supper, as promised, he'd asked if she wanted to get together the next night. She'd thought fast. Too soon to ask him to come hang out here. "What's your schedule like?" she'd asked.

"Classes all morning, and I'm working a two to six shift at the library. What about you?"

"I get off at five-thirty. We usually eat around six-thirty."

"How about meeting at that ice cream place at seven-thirty? Will that give you enough time for dinner?"

"Micky Gee's? I mean, McGonigle's? Sure, that'd be great. Wait'll you taste their pistachio!"

They were at the door, and the quick kiss he gave her was awkward, landing alongside her mouth. They both laughed. "I'll do better next time," Phil said, his ear tips pink.

"I hope so!" There was that dimple again. "See you tomorrow! I'll text you when I leave home."

"Do you want me to pick you up?"

"No, that's okay. Mickey Gee's is about halfway between here and Tech."

"Okay. I had a great time, Linn."

"Me, too."

She'd been quiet during supper, lost in her thoughts, after telling her inquisitive mother that yes, she'd had a good time, and her inquisitive father that yes, Phil had been a gentleman.

Her phone alerted her to a text. She sat up, fished it out of her pocket, and read, "Sweet dreams."

"You, too," she answered Phil. Another text right on top of the one she'd just sent. This one was from Kaylie: "WELL???" all caps.

She smiled and typed back, "Tks for the fix-up. Nice guy."

"Will U C him again?"

"2morrow."

"Wow. Tell me more."

"Later. Work 2morrow. Nite."

"OK. CU soon."

Linn got up and finished undressing, putting on an old pair of gym shorts and a tank top. Wonder what Phil sleeps in? she thought as she tossed her shorts, blouse, socks and underwear in the laundry basket on the closet floor. I *am* doing better about my slobbiness. Yay, me. If he's in a dorm, he probably sleeps in *something*. I didn't find out about his roommate. If he even has one. He *did* say he was moving into an apartment this fall with two other guys.

Tomorrow morning. I have to be out the door by eight at the latest. She pulled open drawers and laid out shorts, a tee, and underwear on the other bed, adding sandals on top. Pushed to the back on the shelf of her closet she found the gym bag she'd used last year at the Rec. It still smelled faintly of chlorine. What will I need? They have towels. She threw in one of the new swimsuits and a hairbrush, then headed across the hall for shampoo and deodorant. She'd be assigned a locker, and she could leave shampoo and stuff there, so she wouldn't have to bring it every time. Sunscreen? Check. Oh, flip flops for the shower. What else? Extra rubber bands for a ponytail. Makeup? Probably not, unless I have a date after work. That could happen now, came the sudden thought. Chapstick, for sure. Change for the vending machine. She opened her desk drawer and found some quarters to add to her purse. I'll need to get organized and start packing a lunch. You can't live on crackers from the machine. Well, you could, but who would want to? Oh, right, there was still some tuna salad. I'll make a sandwich in the morning to take tomorrow. There was a fridge in the break room, and she'd learned last year to label her lunch, or it would go missing. Oh, and I need to take a plastic bag to put my wet suit in.

She looked at the alarm clock by her bed. Old, but still functioning. It had waked her for school all those years. She smiled at the memory. The clock would go off, she'd hit the snooze button, and before the alarm sounded again, Dad would be knocking at the door. "Up and at 'em, princess." He'd stand there knocking until she'd put her feet on the floor and said, "I'm up, Daddy." Invariable routine. As sure as sun up.

Time for her to take over making sure she was up and at 'em. She set the alarm for seven-fifteen. Enough time for a shower and breakfast. She thought again and reset it to seven. A little extra time tomorrow, since it's the first day.

It was only nine-thirty. She'd told Gran she was taking the day off, but . . . She grabbed the folder on James Griffin, Senior, from the top of the stack and settled back with it. How did people deal with all the grief and uncertainty? She looked at GeeGee's cramped writing on the family chart. She'd entered all the kids he had by Susan Brown, but how sad. A little girl first that had lived eighteen months. Harriet. But in the meantime, almost exactly a year after Harriet's birth, there'd been a boy, with that weird name. Etheldred. She'd googled that one. Pronounced with the accent on the middle syllable, thel. Uh THEL dred. And it wasn't even a boy's name. It was a *girl's* name. Seriously. What were they thinking? She'd have to tell Phil about that. Followed by five more kids, one every couple of years, all boys, but Martha, the second-born.

And, then, bam. James the Jerk heads off to Alabama and leaves Susan to raise them all. How did people get through such misery? Time helped, she knew that. She didn't think about what happened with that guy back in Massachusetts *all* the time now, the way she had at first. And somehow, although she hadn't thought it would, talking about it had helped. Dad, Mom and Gran knew now, and they didn't hate her for it. Or blame her. She'd been so ashamed, especially about the drinking part of it. Life Lesson Learned, she thought. I won't let alcohol sneak up on me like that again. But drunk or not, he still didn't have the right to try to force me into sex. That poor girl, Courtney. I hope she's got family that care about her.

I wonder if I should ever tell Phil? Maybe after I know him better. He's been through a lot, losing his mom. I wonder what that was like for him. He was probably eleven or twelve. I can't even imagine. Is it a choice to give in to what happens or to decide to fight your way through it?

That cousin of Dad's that he and Mom talked about last year at Christmas. Her husband and son were killed in a car wreck, and she started drinking and taking pills and ended up killing herself. No one seemed to know if it was a deliberate overdose or not. She'd been up in Massachusetts when cousin Dottie died in November, so she'd missed the funeral. She's never known the family all that well. She did remember the son. Zach. He was maybe three years younger than she was. She'd met him at the annual McKinney reunion, up in north Georgia where Dad's family was from. Part of a whole passel of cousins. Dad was the youngest of a large family who grew up on a farm. He was the one who was expected to stay home and take over as his parents got older. Didn't happen. Which might explain why he didn't make nearly as big a deal about law school as she thought he might. Did Mom talk to him? Or Gran? Then both his parents died within a year of each other, and the land got sold off. She never knew that set of grandparents.

Linn put the folder back on the desk and climbed into bed. Thoughts chased around in her head, and she took a deep breath and turned off the light. Her last thought before sleep caught up with her was "I wonder how hard it will be to get those stars off the ceiling?"

It was A DELIGHT TO TEMPIE to have the Harrises living nearby. Mady and William were expecting their first child around Christmas time, and Mady was overjoyed. She had taken to motherhood, and the two Harris children were thriving under her gentle care. She brought them to the impromptu school at the Griffin house on the River Road and helped with the lessons. There were plans in the community to build a schoolhouse to accommodate the growing number of children, and Mitchell had offered to give the land. Privately, Tempie thought a schoolhouse would be of more value to the settlement than the stockades that had already been built.

The year before, Tempie had given birth to a red-faced screaming baby boy. Mitchell, looking down at him, said decisively, "Junior. He'll be Benjamin Mitchell, Junior. He's a fine-looking boy." Benjy had dark fuzz on his head and Mitchell's hazel eyes.

In the next county over, James and Polly's family continued to grow, but, sadly, brother Drew who had lived with them for most of his life, succumbed to a bout of the weakness that plagued him since childhood. In January, Tempie had gotten a letter from James telling her that Drew was failing, and she had taken Mady, leaving her children in Portia's care and Mady's step-children with Sall in charge and made the day-long—and cold—journey to Montgomery County.

They arrived in time to take their leave of Drew, and both were with him when he died. His sisters were tearful, but comforted by the quiet way in which he left them. There had been no pain, just breaths which became farther and farther apart until Mady said, "I think he's gone now, Sister." And he was.

"He never had a strong heart," James said.

"No, but it was always such a kind one," Mady responded, bursting into tears.

Polly made her sisters-in-law welcome, and the day before the funeral was spent catching up. James and Polly promised to bring their children over in the spring to visit with the cousins. "You have two wagonloads of Alstons now!" Tempie smiled.

There were troubles all over the young United States. Mitchell, as a militia officer, set off in 1812, heading upriver to Fort Hawkins with some of the men from Telfair to train to do battle with the Red Sticks, the Creek warriors who were fighting against the loss of their land and culture. Poor planning and a lack of supplies sent them home again without being deployed. Mitchell and the other officers continued drilling their men at the stockades in the county.

The trees were beginning to drop their leaves, and night was coming earlier in mid-September when a mule wagon driven by a grizzled man clip-clopped down the road, raising a cloud of dust. Tempie happened to be on the porch, bringing in an armload of the firewood that Sampson kept stacked there. Was that . . .? "James? James Griffin? Is that you?"

James pulled back on the reins. "Whoa. Howdy, Tempie. I was heading to the house."

"Does Susan know you're coming?"

"Naw, I don't reckon she does. I was coming to fetch a couple of the children back to Alabama with me. He shook the reins. "Giddyup."

"James, wait! You're doing what?"

"Fetchin' some of the young 'uns. I could use some help. That Clarinda done died and left me with a bunch of babies to raise."

Tempie stared at him in amazement. "Wait. I'm coming with you." She ran back into the house for a shawl, calling over her shoulder, "Betsy, I'm riding over to Susan's house. Tell Phoebe I'll be back soon."

She clambered up onto the wagon seat next to James. "It's been more than three years, James. Why are you here now? What do you mean, you're fetching some of the children?"

Tempie was used to the general lack of personal cleanliness among the settlers, but James's odor was particularly rank. She scooted as near the outside edge of the wagon seat as she could. He'd have been traveling for days, she knew. She stole a sideways glance. Dirt was embedded in the deep creases on his face and neck.

"Well, I got two little ones of my own back on the Tombigbee and them two of my brother George's to look after. I need a woman to come take keer of 'em. I figger Marthy's old enough. And I thought maybe I'd take James, Jr. to holp me out with the farmin' and the trappin'. I kin leave Dred here with Susan—he don't much like me, anyways—and she kin have the little 'uns. I don't hardly know 'em, nohow."

"Clarinda's the mother of your two babies?"

"Yep. I kinda thought she was carryin' my baby when we come back to Georgia, and sure enough, when I went to Alabama after Sam died, she'd done had a boy and named him James. So I jes' stayed. She was a pretty little thing, Clarinda, and right smart. I named the new baby after her, but then the woman died on me anyways."

Tempie was at a loss. How did one respond to such a tale? I'm sorry the woman you left your wife for died? I'm sorry you haven't got anybody to look after your new set of children?

Her silence carried them to Susan's little cabin. It looked tidy. The yard was freshly swept, and there was a big pile of wood in the shed. Cheerful yellow gingham curtains hung at the two front windows, sewn by Martha. She jumped down and ran ahead while James looped the reins over a post.

"Susan? Are you home?"

Martha came to the door, with Dred behind her. Dred was just back from a trip down river to Darien with a raftload of logs. Susan, hearing her, came from beside the cabin, where she'd been boiling a washtub of laundry, drying her hands on her apron as she came.

"Here's James, come from Alabama." She walked towards Susan, whose face had gone pale. "Susan, don't worry; he's not here to stay."

Dred came down the steps. "What are you here for, Pa?" There was a belligerent tone to his voice.

James smiled at his son. "You're 'bout grown, aincha?"

"What are you here for?" Dred walked to his mother's side, Martha following quickly behind him.

"I'm thinkin' to take a couple of y'all back to Alabama with me."

Dred put a protective arm around his mother. "I'm thinkin' you ain't."

"I wasn't plannin' on takin' you, nohow. You kin stay with your ma. Where's James, Junior?"

"You're crazy, old man, if you think any of us are going back with you."

James turned to Susan with an ingratiating smile. "I been sendin' you money, woman. Now I got babies to raise, and I kin use some help. I want Marthy and James, Junior."

Tempie spoke quickly, "Susan, he's had another child with George's widow, but she died."

Susan's stunned face grew paler, and she slumped against her sturdy son. "Sit down, Ma," Marthy said. With Dred's help, she steered Susan to the rough bench on the porch.

"I knew it. I knew it was that Clarinda." Her voice was faint. Beside her, Dred's fists were clenched.

"Well, she's dead now, ain't she, and I need me a girl to raise them babies. And where's James?"

"I'm right here." Fourteen-year-old Jim came into the yard from the field, carrying a bushel basket of potatoes. He was trailed by his little brothers, Lenn and Zack, toting shovels and hoes.

"Paw wants us to go to Alabama with him, Jim, but I'm not going," Martha said.

"Me, neither. I'm staying right here."

"I been sendin' money. I got some rights," blustered James.

It was true. Money had come from time to time, but never more than a few dollars, and not that often.

"We don't need no more of your money." This from Dred, as he took a step forward. "You just get on back to where you came from. We're doing fine here without you. I get paid pretty good for lumbering. Everybody around here thinks you're dead anyway."

"James, you can't stay here where you're not wanted. Come on back to my house for the night," Tempie said. "We'll send you on your way back to Alabama first thing tomorrow morning. I think you've lost your rights to this family."

James scowled at Tempie. "I never thought you'd turn against me. You ain't as much like your ma as I thought. Well, Mitchell will fix this." He looked at Jim and Martha. "I'll come back in the morning for y'all."

"James, Mitchell's in Milledgeville, but I know he'll side with Susan and the children on this one. He knows how she's struggled and how hard she's worked to keep her family going. This community thinks you're dead, killed by Indians. You have another family now. Go on back to them. Martha, why don't you take your mama inside and make her some tea? I'll come over tomorrow after James leaves, and we'll talk, Susan."

Tempie climbed on the wagon seat. "Let's go, James. I'll give you some supper and then you can bed down in the barn." She looked back over her shoulder to see Dred and the other children helping Susan into the little cabin. She couldn't hear his words, but something Jim said brought a smile to his mother's face. She'd be fine, with those children at her side.

LINN: EIGHTEEN
Monday morning

THE ALARM WENT OFF, and Linn woke from a muddled dream of Phil coming to dinner, with an enormous tiger on a leash padding docilely behind him. She switched off the alarm, stood up, stretching, and noticed her phone flashing a message signal.

The text was from Marcie. "Too late to call. Call me when u wake up. Very important."

Really? At seven? But she said "Important."

Marcie answered on the second ring. "Linn. You'll never believe what happened last night. Jake was in a bad wreck. Speeding. He left a party, drunk, they say. He took a curve too fast. Hit a light pole. He didn't make it. I guess the good thing is that he was by himself."

"What do you mean: he didn't make it? Is he . . . ?"

"They're saying he died instantly."

Linn sank down onto her bed.

"Linn?"

"I'm here. I just don't know what to say."

"You should be glad."

"I don't think I'm glad, Marcie. I mean it's sad to die so young. And I'm sorry for his parents."

"Well, at least they won't have to see him in court and going to prison. I just thought you and your dad would want to know."

"Oh, I'm glad you let me know. It's, I guess, a kind of relief for me, and for Courtney, too, I guess. Does she know?"

"Yes. I talked to her last night when I got the news. She was still up. She says she doesn't sleep all that well."

"Maybe she will now. I still don't know exactly how to feel about this. Marcie, I've got to go. I start work this morning. Thanks."

"Call me later if you want to talk, Linn. Bye."

"Bye."

Linn showered and got dressed in a flurry of thoughts. His poor parents. Did Jake have brothers or sisters? She didn't know much at all about him. Only the bad parts. She hoped his parents would have some good memories of him. She was glad now she'd laid out her clothes and packed her bag already. No decisions to make. She shook her head to clear it. Got to tell Mom and Dad. And Gran. Maybe Mom can call Gran.

She headed down the stairs. Kids died all the time in wrecks. Those two boys who had wrecked that pickup her junior year in high school. They both died. Ejected from the car. No seat belts. But they were nice guys, not like Jake. Just going too fast. Reckless. She'd never thought about it before, but if you were reckless, sometimes you weren't wreckless. She shook her head again. Stupid thought. What's wrong with me?

She smelled the coffee as she headed down to the kitchen. Good, Mom was up.

Temperance PUSHED HER HAIR OUT OF HER FACE and listened. Was that Linney up from her nap already? She'd hoped to have a little longer to get the mending done. Yes, that was Linney's preparatory whimper. Soon she'd go into full wail. "Mary, can you get Linney?"

Mary looked up from the book she was reading. "Yes, Mama. I'm going."

Temperance smiled as Mary brought the baby in. Mary was a good child, biddable. Not like her wild little brothers. And Linney was a winsome thing, with Temperance's mother's dark eyes and Mitchell's blond hair. "Here, put her down over here by me. She can play with the blocks while I finish darning these stockings." Linney giggled when Temperance leaned over and kissed her neck, blowing against the soft skin.

"Go on back to your book, honey. It'll soon be dark, and time to get the boys in from the yard."

The children were under strict orders to play near the house. There'd been some trouble with the Indians lately. The treaty had pushed them back across the Ocmulgee, but Indians in full war paint had been seen in the county, and cows and hogs were being stolen. Although it had been five or six years since there'd been any violence, the families along the River Road still remembered when young Peggy Willis and her baby had been killed and butchered near Ashburn in retaliation for an Indian who had been shot thirty miles away for stealing a hog.

Temperance decided to feed the children and called them in. No telling when Mitchell would be home. She sent Mary to bring a pot of stew in from the cookhouse. The little boys were tired. Richard almost fell asleep eating his stew, and Temperance sent them off to bed, after walking them down the path to the privy. Mary sat up a little later on the bench in front of the fire, talking with Temperance about the book she was reading, while Linney got her last nursing of the day. Temperance thanked John Willcox silently again, for being so sharing with his precious books. Mary was a good reader—there really wasn't anything she couldn't read these days. It wasn't as easy teaching Benjie and Richard. They were more like their father who still couldn't sound out words. Mitchell could recognize only a few words, his name among them, although he was good with numbers and figuring.

Vixen lay at their feet. There was a muffled snoring, and Mary giggled. "Guess she's worn out, too. The boys were trying to get her to pull their wagon this afternoon. She didn't like it much."

Where *was* Mitchell? It was well past dark. Thoughts chased themselves around in her head.

"Mary, honey, I think you'd better go on to bed. Tomorrow I want you to help me cut out some quilt pieces. I'd like to get another quilt made for Betsy."

Mary kissed her mother on the cheek and hugged her and the sleeping Linney, wrapping her thin arms around them both. "Good night!"

She went across the hall into the room she shared with her baby sister. Temperance followed and carefully slid Linney into her little high-sided bed in the back bedroom, and tucked a little quilt around her.

Back in the parlor, she dished herself up a bowl of the lukewarm stew and crumbled a cold piece of cornbread into it. She'd been hungrier earlier but she'd wanted to wait for Mitchell. Venison stew was his favorite. Somehow it was hard to swallow, and she scraped most of it into Vixen's dish.

She took the empty bowl out to the kitchen house. There was enough hot water left in the kettle to wash the bowl and spoon in the dishpan. That done, she slung the dishwater off the porch onto the azaleas. They were budding and would be in full bloom soon.

Funny thing about flowers, she thought as she walked back to the house. You just can't have it all. She looked at her mother's white pitcher, holding pride of place on the mantelpiece. The children had brought in fistfuls of daffodils this morning, and she'd taken a few minutes to fill the pitcher with water and arrange the cheerful yellow flowers in it. The daffodils looked like sunshine, and smelled like spring, but it was a sharp, almost bitter odor. Azaleas were beautiful, too, but had no fragrance at all. If you cut a branch and brought it into the house, it dropped its flowers right away. Roses were lovely and fragrant, but so hard to keep alive. The junebugs could chew a whole bush into lacy leaves overnight, and you ripped your hands on the thorns when you tried to pick the wild pink roses that grew along the banks by the roadside. The dogwoods at the edge of the woods were breathtaking in early spring when the sunlight caught them, but the flowers were gone before the trees came into leaf. Somewhere, in another, better, world, there was surely a blossom that was lovely and fragrant—and endured.

Weary, she banked the coals in the fireplace and went into the bedroom. There was a pain in her heart as she climbed into the cold and empty bed.

Sometime towards midnight, Temperance heard the creak of the floorboards. She lay very still, her back turned towards the door. Boots bumped as they hit the floor, and she felt cold air along her back as the covers were lifted. Mitchell slid into bed. Without turning over, Temperance spoke to the wall. "I know where you've been." Her voice was flat.

Silence. She could hear Mitchell breathing.

"Billy and I sat up late, talking and drinking after we got his wagon fixed. Sorry. I meant to be home sooner."

"No, you weren't at Billy's. He came here looking for you." Temperance held her breath, hoping for her lie to be denied.

Silence again. Then a short laugh. "So that's where he was. I meant John. I didn't mean Billy. I went by Billy's place, but he wasn't there. We must've missed each other."

Oh, dear Lord. I'm right, she thought. I didn't want to be. Her heart thumped painfully in her chest.

"You're not telling me the truth, Mitchell. Nancy Sweeney's mama was here, too. She was very upset. She had walked over to Joe and Nancy's, to see if Nancy was all right by herself, with Joe gone downriver to Darien, and your horse was there."

Oh, God, please let him deny it. Let him convince me I'm wrong. Let him know I'm making up the story about Widow Greene.

Mitchell rolled over and sat on the side of the bed, slumped over, hands on his knees, his back to her. In the thin light of the moon, she could see his bare back, broad and familiar, the indentation of his spine between the muscled planes. Her impulse was to reach out to touch him, to feel the warmth of his skin, so smooth and pale where the sun didn't burn it.

"Well, I stopped by there looking for Billy."

"And why would you do that, Mitchell? Why would you think Billy would be at Nancy's?" She didn't give him time to answer, but went on with her made-up story. "Nancy's mama said she started to knock, but she heard voices, so she peeked through the window."

Mitchell held his silence. Temperance felt a deep stillness inside. "I should have known, Mitchell. I suppose I just didn't want to know."

Mitchell stood up. Temperance propped herself up on her elbows. "Turn around and look at me, Mitchell. You promised me it wouldn't happen again."

She sat up on her side of the bed, and reached for the candle. There were still a few coals smoldering in the fireplace. She walked the few steps to the hearth, her bare feet cold on the floor, and bent to light the candle.

"Turn around, Mitchell. Tell me the truth." She put the candle on the mantelpiece and waited. Mitchell said nothing.

"Mitchell, how long has this been going on? Does everyone know but me and Joe? Or maybe Joe does know. Maybe that's why he's gone so much."

Mitchell turned and looked at her.

Temperance said, with a calmness that came from the dead place around her heart, "No more, Mitchell. You've made your choice. I've closed my eyes too many times. I'm not doing it again. I'm tired."

"I don't know what you're talking about. I don't know what that fat old biddy told you, but it's a lie!"

"I know better, Mitchell. If you want Nancy so much, she can have you. I want you to go now."

"You think you know so much." Mitchell's voice was raised now. "You always think you know so much. You can't tell me what to do. I get to pick whether I go or stay."

"Not this time. I want you out of the house. Now."

Temperance drew herself up as tall as she could and forced herself to look at the angry face of her husband. It was suffused with blood, and veins stood out along his neck.

"You bitch!" He stepped towards her, and she felt the edge of the blanket trunk pressing into the back of her knees.

He grabbed her by the forearms and shook her. "You bitch," he hissed again, spittle spraying her face.

"Take your hands off me," Temperance said quietly, "And don't yell. You'll wake Linney."

"All right. I'll go now. But I'll be back. You're not throwing me out of my own house."

Dropping his hands, Mitchell spun around and stamped out the door, grabbing his pants, shirt, and boots.

Temperance rubbed her forearms. There'd be bruises there tomorrow. A good thing it was still cool. Her long sleeves would cover them. She considered going after him, but what would that accomplish? There was nothing left to say. Temperance walked to the bed and sat down, heavily. Vixen stuck her nose out from beneath the bed and pressed it against her leg. She reached a hand down and patted her. A door banged shut. "It's okay, girl. You can come out now. He's gone."

She got up and blew out the candle, then crawled back under the covers and lay there, tearless. There was a pain in her chest, and she couldn't swallow. The bed felt vast and cold. *What will I tell the children? What will people say? How can I live life without him?*

Towards dawn, she woke from a confused dream of Mitchell splitting firewood while she stood beside him, weeping, and she sat up, her heart pounding.

Swinging her feet over the side of the bed, she grabbed a quilt to wrap around her. She made her way in the dark to the parlor and poked up the fire, adding a log. Vixen followed, tail wagging. She opened the door to let the little dog out, then decided to make the walk to the privy bare-footed.

On the way back to the house, Temperance looked at the sky. *It must be about six.* She went to the kitchen house and, shivering, poked up that fireplace, adding some logs from the pile by the hearth. *Who will chop the wood? Would Sampson and his family leave with Mitchell? Mary was nearly ten and a big help around the house, but too frail to split logs. Darius was eleven. He could help out and bring some wood. Unless he went, too.* Thoughts chased themselves around in her head. She added some water to the kettle from the bucket and swung it over the fire.

Back in the bedroom, she spread up the bed, splashed her face with cold water, and dressed. She ran a brush through her hair and coiled it up on the back of her neck and secured it with pins. She caught a glimpse of herself in the mirror. *Forty-two, and today she felt every day of it. Nancy wasn't raising five children—not even one.* She smoothed the bodice of her blue-sprigged dress over her breasts. *Mitchell had never said anything about their slight droop or the marks on her hips from her pregnancies. But the lovemaking, which had been so all-consuming when they were* younger, was less frequent in the last few years; perfunctory, even. Temperance hadn't worried. They were both tired from expending the energy required to keep food on the table, and the children clean and happy. She had always believed that when the children were older, she and Mitchell would find the time to grow close.

Well, no chance for that now.

Back in the kitchen house, she poured boiling water over coffee grounds in the coffee pot, then added grits and salt to the kettle. The children would be awake soon. She put some fatback into a skillet and started it cooking at the edge of the fire. Phoebe would be coming along the path any minute. Should she say anything? She decided not to, just yet.

EARLY AFTERNOON, the older children were playing in the yard while Linney napped. Linney had been fretful all day, and Temperance had spent the morning with Linney on one hip while she went blindly about her chores.

"Mama, we got company," called Benjie from the yard. The dogs were barking.

"Who is it?" she answered, heading for the door.

"It's me, Miz Griffin. Fred!" an excited voice answered.

She opened the door and stepped out on the porch. Fred Mizell was swinging down from the saddle of an old mare that was about as scrawny as Fred. The mare was sweating, and her bony sides were heaving.

"Miz Griffin, something turrible! Joseph Burch has done been kilt by the Indians, 'n' Littleton's done been scalpt! Get your husband!"

"Fred, he's not here. I'm not sure where he is, but you might try the Sweeneys' place."

"Sweeneys? But Joe Sweeney's gone to Darien." There was a pause, then, "Oh. Yes'm. Thank you!" Fred turned and swung his leg over the saddle of the gray mare and rode off.

"If Captain Griffin comes home, tell him Major Cawthorn's gathering the men at Fort Adams. And tell him to bring his gun," he yelled over his shoulder.

Then, and only then, she thought about what Fred had told her. Joseph Burch dead? He had yet another baby on the way, even though the old goat was sixty, she thought. And Littleton scalped? She went back inside and poured herself a cup of coffee, her hands shaking, and sank down onto a kitchen chair. The men were gathering. They'd be heading off to find the Indians.

The cup was empty when she heard the sound of hoof-beats. Mitchell came barreling through the door, yelling over his shoulder.

"Mary, go get Sampson. Tell him to bring his gun and some supplies."

To Tempie he said, avoiding her eyes, "The Indians attacked Joe Burch and Littleton while they were across the river, building a hunting shed. We're getting all the men together, and we're going across to find the bastard savages that did this."

He headed into the bedroom, where he kept his gun and powder. "Littleton managed to swim across to John Willcox's place, with a good hunk of his scalp gone," he said over his shoulder.

While he was talking, he was pulling his militia musket off the wall and gathering supplies that he threw into a satchel.

"Pour me some of that coffee, and get me some bread or biscuits or something."

Temperance silently complied, handing him the coffee. She split some leftover biscuits from breakfast and added some fatback, then wrapped the biscuits in a napkin. Why didn't you ask Nancy to do this for you, she thought.

He looked at her as he took the food. "We'll talk when I get back. I'm sorry, Tempie. I did wrong. But you can't throw me out of my own house. For now, you and the children need to get yourselves to Fort Adams. Take Phoebe and Portia and her young'uns, too."

She followed him out onto the porch and watched him mount. The sun was up now, and his blond hair gleamed in the sun. From a distance you couldn't see any of the gray, and sitting so confidently in the saddle, he looked like the strong young man she'd married twenty-three years ago. Her heart felt painfully big in her chest.

228

He didn't look back and wave as he rode away, followed by Sampson. The boys, who had come running to the house when they heard him ride up, stood staring after him, then turned to Temperance, full of questions.

Temperance went back into the house, trying to keep the terror out of her voice as she explained what they needed to do. Phoebe and Portia, carrying her baby, were coming down the path, herding the rest of Portia's children ahead of them.

It was nearly dark the next afternoon when Nat Statham rode up to Fort Adams, leading Mitchell's horse. A mule and wagon followed behind, two men sitting dejectedly on the seat, two forms wrapped in a blankets lying in the wagon bed. Other men on horseback followed.

The women and children, hearing the commotion, came out of the gate of the fort. Nat shook his head. "I'm so sorry, Temperance. We were outnumbered. Mitchell got hit right away. He never felt a thing, I'm sure. We've got him here in the wagon."

Temperance walked closer as Benjie and Mary, holding Richard by the hand, came up. Those were Mitchell's boots protruding from one of the blankets.

"What's the matter, Mama?"

"It's Papa. He's gone."

Behind her, she heard a high keening as Phoebe and Portia ran to the second body.

LINN: NINETEEN
Monday night

LINN TOSSED HER PHONE ON HER BED and pulled a tee and pajama bottoms out of the dresser drawer. She met her eyes in the mirror. Weird. She looked the same as she did yesterday. Seemed like she should look older. It had been a long, strange day. She shook her head, remembering Mom complaining about the overuse of the phrase, "It was a real emotional roller-coaster," on reality shows. But Linn thought she understood. How else to describe the sudden ups and downs of the day? She couldn't think of any other ride that gave you those short, deceptively smooth interludes before plunging you down a terrifying slope, leaving you shattered and hoarse from shrieking.

Mom had actually cried when Linn told her about Jake's death. That surprised them both. Mom seldom cried, except during movies and commercials that involved dogs or small children. She had made Linn sit down and had poured her a cup of coffee after she dried her eyes.

"I'm sorry. It's just that I've hated that boy ever since you told us, and now I feel so guilty for hating him. But in a way this is over for you now, honey. I hope you can put it all behind you. And that poor girl, what was her name? Courtney, right?"

"Yes. She won't have to go to court now and be cross-examined. Dad said that could be an awful experience—that Jake's lawyer would try to make it seem like it was her fault. And there won't be any more girls he rapes, or tries to. I'll be okay, Mom. It's just a lot to try to get my head around. Will you tell dad when he gets up? And Gran? Call Gran for me. I've got to get a sandwich made and get out of here. I don't want to be late."

Mom smiled, "I already made your sandwich. I saw the leftover tuna." She got a lunch sack off the counter and handed it to Linn. "You need some breakfast, though, honey."

"I'll be okay, really, Mom. I'll swing through the drive-through and pick up an Egg McMuffin on the way. Bye. See you later. I should be home before six. Oh, did I tell you I'm meeting Phil for ice cream after supper?"

"No. That's nice. Anything special you'd like for supper? I've got to hit Kroger."

"Whatever you decide will be fine." Linn smiled. "Although you haven't made macaroni and cheese since I've been home. Hint, hint."

Ann McKinney smiled back. "Okay. Mac-Cheese it is." Good. Linn's appetite was back. Maybe she'd find those pounds she'd lost.

Linn was out the door by then.

Her first day at work went fine. She was going to like the five-year-old class. She'd reined in the rowdy little blond kid by making him her Assistant in Charge of Towels. His job was to see that no towels got left behind at the pool. Eric took his assignment seriously and picked up the two stray towels, chastising their owners for their carelessness.

There'd been a surprise, but a good one. She'd been asked to help with the water therapy class for children with physical disabilities. She was happy to see Kevin Graham, and she guessed from the way his face lit up that he was glad to see her, too. Kevin had cerebral palsy, and Linn had babysat him some during her senior year. Neat little kid.

When she took her lunch break, she found a message to call her grandmother. She'd been too busy all morning to think much about Jake. Mom must have called Gran. She got her phone from her locker and made the call.

"Oh, Linn, honey, I've been thinking about you. Are you okay?"

"I'll be fine, Gran. I just can't figure out how to feel." Linn looked around. The break room was empty. "I mean, I can't be glad that Jake's dead. But I'm glad that nobody else will get hurt, and that Courtney won't have to testify. And that I for sure will never see him again. So, it's like one part of me is happy, and another part is sad for his parents."

"I think what you're feeling is pretty normal. I'm sure it'll get easier. And remember, Linn, not all men are like Jake. Don't let him spoil things for you. Would you like to come over tonight and talk?"

"Thanks, but I have a date. Phil and I are going to meet at Mickey Gee's—you know, the ice cream place—tonight. I'm trying to decide whether to tell him about Jake and all that mess. I wonder what he'd think?"

"I guess you'll never know until you tell him. But it doesn't have to be now. You two barely know each other."

"That's what's so weird. I feel like I've known him forever. Gotta go, Gran. I've got to eat and get on lifeguard duty. Talk to you later. Love you."

"I love you, too, baby."

THE AFTERNOON PASSED SLOWLY. The pool was open for general admission, and Linn perched on the lifeguard stand, and kept her eyes focused on the pool. There were no real problems. She had to whistle down some rough-housing, but the parents who brought their children did most of the work. She tried to push any thoughts of Massachusetts and Jake to the rear of her brain by thinking about tomorrow, when she and Mom were going to some of the area colleges to pick up application forms and schedules and to make appointments for interviews. They'd decided to go to Emory, with the thought that applying now, even if she didn't get accepted, would put a foot in the door for the following year.

Thank goodness I kept my grades up. That'll help. She'd finished her first year of school with a near-perfect GPA.

And she thought about her room. Wonder if Phil likes to paint? Maybe she was getting ahead of herself. But there'd been a text earlier, while she took her afternoon break. It just said, "Pistachio. 7:30. Be there."

She'd smiled and texted back. "Wouldn't miss it!"

Mom's macaroni and cheese was perfect. All crusty on top the way she liked it. Of course, Mom being Mom, there was a huge salad with lots of veggies to offset the macaroni. Linn turned down a second helping of the macaroni and cheese to save room for ice cream.

PHIL HAD ALREADY CLAIMED A BOOTH when she got there. He stood up, smiling, as he watched her approach. She had decided on the new spaghetti-strapped sundress, and from his pink ear tips and raised eyebrows, she surmised it was a success.

"Wow. You look great. How was your first day at the Rec Center?"

"Fine. Really good. They're letting me help with the class for handicapped kids. That's going to be amazing. One of the boys I already know— Kevin. I used to baby-sit him."

"How old is Kevin?"

"Nine, now, I think. He's just a great kid. Funny. He likes to tease. He calls me "Mrs. McGregor" because I used to read him "Peter Cottontail" all the time. It's kind of hard to understand him at first, but you catch on pretty fast. How was your day?"

"Fine. I'll get us some ice cream. I'm having pistachio, solely on your recommendation. What would you like?"

"I'll have that, too. One scoop."

"Coke, tea?"

"Just water, thanks."

Phil walked to the counter. Linn watched him, appraisingly. Nice build. Not too muscular, but broad shoulders. He wore a freshly-pressed blue short-sleeved shirt with his jeans. She wondered if he did his own ironing. Should she have offered to pay for her ice cream? *I'm not too good at this dating thing.*

He was back with a tray with the ice cream, her water, and a ginger ale.

"Phil, let me pay you for this," Linn said as she took her dish.

"Not this time." Phil smiled. "My day? Pretty boring. I shelved books and worked the circulation desk at the library after class this morning. This pistachio IS good."

"Do you like working there?"

"It's not what I want to do with the rest of my life, but it's fine for now. I kind of envy you being outdoors. Speaking of outdoors, have you been to Stone Mountain?"

"Of course. I grew up here, remember?"

"A guy in the dorm told me about the laser show. He said it's pretty spectacular. Would you like to see that some time?"

"Sure, I haven't been in years. You can take blankets and picnic on the lawn. That would be fun. Wonder if Kaylie and Eddie would like to go?"

"I'll check with Eddie. How about this weekend? The guys can bring the picnic this time. We could pick up some wings or something. Or some barbecue. Do you eat barbecue?"

"I eat almost anything. I'm not all that fond of beets."

"Okay. No beets." He laughed. "So you had a good first day."

Linn put her spoon down and looked at her half-empty ice cream dish. "It got off to a strange start."

"What happened?"

"I don't know if you want to hear the whole story or not, but first thing this morning, I heard that a guy I sort of knew in Massachusetts got killed in a car wreck."

"*Sort of knew?* So he wasn't like a boyfriend or anything?"

"No, I only went out with him once."

Linn still hadn't looked up from her ice cream.

Phil waited for her to go on. After a silence, he said, "What aren't you telling me?"

Linn lifted her head and met his eyes. "He tried to rape me. And he did rape another girl. And now he's dead." Her face crumbled, and tears slid down her cheeks.

"Hey." Phil got up, came around the table, and slid in beside her. He put his arm around her shoulders. "Are you okay?"

"Everyone keeps asking me that. Well, Mom and Gran. I don't know how I am. I guess I'm luckier than Courtney. That's the other girl. Maybe I'm stronger. I punched him pretty good."

"I'm really sorry that happened to you. I don't know what else to say. I know that's lame." He handed her his paper napkin. "Here, dry your eyes. Are you finished with your ice cream? Let's get out of here."

He put their glasses and dishes back on the tray and left it on the stand. "Come on. We can walk a few minutes." Phil steered her out of the shop. "Which way?"

"If we go right, we'll come to the park."

They walked silently until they reached the park. Phil led her to a bench, and they sat down. His arm went around her again. "Good thing he's dead, because I feel like killing him. I'm sorry he hurt you."

"It's over now, and I'll be fine. Don't worry about me, and don't hate him. I didn't mean to ruin this evening."

"You haven't ruined anything. I'm glad you told me. Honesty is important."

"Okay. Let's talk about something else. Please."

"What does the rest of your week look like?"

"I'm off tomorrow, and Mom and I are going to make the rounds of the schools with nursing programs. I'm pretty excited about that," she confessed.

"What about tomorrow night? No, wait, I have to work. What about Wednesday? Want to go to a movie or something?"

"Why don't you come over and we'll watch a little TV. Dad's got a two-day conference in Augusta, and Mom's going with him. We'll have the house to ourselves." She blushed. Would he think she was suggesting something? "We'll have to make an early evening of it, though. I have to be at work at 8:00."

"No problem. I have class first thing. What time do you get home?"

"A little before six."

"Okay, I'll pick up a pizza on the way over, and see you at six. What do you like on your pizza?"

"Most anything. No onions." Would he make something of that, too?

"I wish I could stay longer, but I need to get you back to your car. I've got a quiz tomorrow I have to study for."

Phil took her hand as they walked back to the ice cream shop. When they stopped at her car, he leaned in, and this time, his kiss was right on target. He pulled her closer and kissed her again, more deliberately.

"I'll see you Wednesday, lovely Linn. Sleep well."

"Good night." Linn, her head spinning slightly, got behind the wheel and backed out of the parking space. Phil was watching as she drove away. He waved. She smiled and waved back. Wow. She touched her lips with her free hand.

IN PAJAMAS NOW, she turned on her computer. Family Tree Maker came up where she'd left it, on the children of Mitchell and Temperance Griffin. The youngest was Linney, who married a Reverend Bedell. My name, she thought. I wonder where they got that? James the Jerk Griffin had a daughter named Martha Linnie. And then there were Linnies or Linneys in every Griffin family after that. I never knew that. I know I was named for GeeGee, but I didn't realize there were Linnies before that.

"Lovely Linn." He called me that! She switched off the computer and climbed into bed, turning off the light. Her phone alerted her to a text.

"Thanks for being honest with me. Sweet dreams."

She texted back: "Sweet dreams to you, too, Phil."

Was this what it felt like to be in love? Like floating on a peaceful river, with the warmth of the sun beaming down. She drifted into sleep as she passed under the shade of an ancient tree on the banks.

It was GOING TO BE A GLORIOUS DAY! Tempie pushed the curtains back to let the morning sun claim a little more of the front bedroom. Downstairs, she could hear Richard's voice, followed by laughter. He sounded so much like his father. She spread up her bed quickly and checked her hair in the mirror over the dressing table, tucking a stray piece into the neat bun on the back of her neck. Fifty-six, and it showed, she thought. My hair is almost completely gray now. And it was a muddy gray, not white as she would have wished. Susan's hair had turned an enviable snowy white. At least I have all my teeth. The last time she'd seen her, over a year ago now, she'd noticed that Susan kept her lips closed over her teeth, and when an unexpected laugh at something Mary and Jim's little Betty had said had caught Susan by surprise, Tempie had realized that Susan was missing several teeth. No matter. Granny Susan was well-loved by her growing family in Attapulgus.

Mary had her hands full these days, with Betty, Lucy and baby Len, and the most recent letter from her said that a fourth was on the way. Jim was tobacco-farming, like his brothers. Only Dred had stayed in Twiggs County. The rest of Susan's boys had moved on and settled in Decatur County, taking Susan with them. Ben was there now, too, river-boating on the Flint.

She missed her older children. Betsy, calling herself by her first name now, Temperance, wrote occasionally from Ware County, where she and Stephen lived. She, too, had three children, but all three were boys. Johnny, Lewis, and Jimmy. Tempie had never met them, but perhaps next spring, she'd make a trip to Waresboro. Richard was already talking about joining his brother and sister and his Griffin cousins in Decatur County.

She'd have some decisions to make soon. She could stay in Telfair County or relocate to Decatur County. Her inheritance from Jonas had been a godsend after Mitchell and Sampson had been killed. She and Phoebe and Portia had been left to manage. She'd sold off Mitchell's share in the logging business, but had kept the farmland. Betsy—no, Temperance—and Stephen Williams had left for Ware County soon after Mitchell's death, and Susan, who had become such a dear friend over the years, had gone with her boys and daughter Martha to Twiggs County within the year.

And she'd bought this house. Two stories. There was room for company should any of the children or grandchildren care to visit. Travel was becoming easier, with roads being built linking some of Georgia's towns. There was even talk of a railroad connecting the Ocmulgee and the Flint.

Tempie would be forever grateful for the loyalty and determination of Phoebe and Portia. Wherever she decided to go, they'd go with her, she knew. Portia's older sons were, Tempie stopped and thought, Darius was twenty-five and Dick twenty-three now, with Reuben not far behind at eighteen, Richard's age. They often hired out to neighboring loggers. Peach was seventeen, working nearby at the parsonage. And Billy would turn fifteen soon. Phoebe had come to her after the death of Mitchell and Sampson to ask her if she planned to sell any of them off. "No, never," she'd assured their anxious grandmother. "I couldn't do that."

"Not even if times git hard?"

Tempie looked into Phoebe's worried eyes. "No, I promise you." She thought a minute, biting her lip. "Phoebe, do you remember the last time Jonah came to see me?"

"'Course I do. He didn't live much past then."

"He brought me something when he came. Money. A fair amount. I still have most of it."

"Why'd he give *you* money?" Phoebe's voice dropped. "Oh."

"That's right. Because I was kin to him. I'm going to ask you not to say anything to anyone, but please don't worry about money. As long as we're careful, we'll be fine."

"I won't tell nobody, Miss Temp. Ain't nobody's business, anyways."

So they had carried on, a household of women and children. Temperance community had rallied around them, and Tempie was grateful for the support, but new people were moving in all the time, the community was changing, and with Susan's family gone, it would be easy for her to move on, if that was her decision.

It wasn't that she didn't have choices. Ben had urged her on her visit to Decatur County to join him there, bringing Richard. Mady and William, living now in Montgomery County, Alabama, had written her often, inviting her to join their household. James and Polly had recently moved to Wyatt, in Mississippi, together with some of their many children. And both Winnie and Philip, after talking about relocating for years, had uprooted their families and moved to Denmark, Tennessee. She'd be welcome there, too. She shook her head, thinking. Perhaps she should just stay here. She was comfortable here, and she knew Phoebe and Portia would prefer just to stay put, especially as Portia's sons were of an age to marry and start families of their own.

A recurring thought pushed itself to the front of her mind. What if she gave Phoebe and Portia and the children their freedom? She could afford to pay them wages if they wanted to stay on with her, but they'd have the choice of remaining or going with her should she decide to leave. She had a feeling she knew what Richard would think. He was bringing all his powers of persuasion to convince her to move to Attapulgus. There were fortunes to be in made in tobacco farming, and Portia's sons were ready-made field hands.

Jonas had been free. She smiled, picturing the faked document of manumission drawn up by her brother John. Jonas had kept it in a safe place all those years, but no one had ever questioned him. She'd have to free her slaves legally, of course, dealing with all the paperwork at the courthouse. Everyone here knew the black Griffins. No faked documents would do. Slavery had been abolished in the northern states, but here in the rural south, most of the white plantation owners saw abolitionism as a dangerous thing, leading to slave rebellion.

Something else to think about, but more and more this was on her mind. It would be her decision, with or without Richard's backing. She shook her head. This was a matter for another day, not today. Today was Linney's day.

The little Methodist church down the road, where her sister and her daughters had married, and where Mitchell and William Carroll were buried, had called a new preacher last year, just after Christmas, a young man named Lucius Mahlon Bedell. The Reverend Bedell divided his time between the Temperance community and two other small churches in Telfair County. Linney, not yet fourteen at the time, was instantly smitten. Tempie would have written it off as a schoolgirl infatuation until she noticed young Mahlon eyeing her daughter in return on Sundays. Still, she was surprised in late April, soon after Linney's birthday, when Reverend Bedell had taken her aside after the Sunday service, to ask if he might speak to her.

"Of course, Reverend."

"Please call me Mahlon, ma'am."

"How can I help you?"

"It's about your daughter, Linney. I'd like your permission to call on her."

"Reverend—Mahlon—you know she's just turned fourteen."

"I know. I was waiting until then. I've watched her and talked with her. She's a lovely young woman, quiet and kind. Well-mannered. You've raised her well."

Tempie thought quickly. She'd heard nothing but praise for the young minister. He was from a good family in North Carolina, and at twenty-five, was certainly old enough to think about marriage and a family.

"Let me talk to Linney to see if she's agreeable." She smiled, realizing how unnecessary that would be. "Perhaps you could come to dinner next Sunday."

"Thank you, Mrs. Griffin."

"Just let me say one thing, Mahlon. I won't have her marrying before she's fifteen."

He nodded. "I understand."

The courtship had proceeded with decorum, in full view of the community. To everyone's delight, with the possible exception of several of the young unmarried women in the congregation, Mahlon had announced their engagement on Easter Sunday, April 22nd, with a June wedding to follow, calling a pink-cheeked and beaming, newly-turned-fifteen-year-old to the front of the church.

Linney was unable to contain her joy. With her mother's help, and Portia's, she had sewn her trousseau. The house designated as the parsonage was small, but already furnished. Linney and her mother had gone there, with Mahlon's willing permission, to measure for new curtains. Those were hanging now, and there was new linen on the marriage bed. Mahlon's housekeeper was Peach, Portia's daughter, an arrangement Tempie had made with the church. Peach would stay on and help Linney with the heavy cleaning, but Linney was turning into a good cook, and enjoyed producing treats for Mahlon when he ate dinner with them. Her pecan pies were much appreciated by her husband-to-be, whose dark eyes lit up when one appeared on the table.

Mahlon was a handsome man with a slender build, not much taller than Tempie, although he topped Linney by several inches. Tempie thought him a little vain. He was very particular about his glossy brown hair, keeping it neatly combed, and unlike most of the men in Telfair County, he was clean-shaven. His hands were smooth and uncalloused, and he kept his nails clean and trimmed. Not that personal cleanliness was a bad thing, Tempie thought. She had raised her children to bathe regularly and to wear clean clothes, but she knew that was the exception.

She turned away from the window, smiling, with a sudden memory of her determined mother, dark curls tumbling around her face, wrestling a yowling and twisting plump baby Philip into a tub of soapy water, while her father leaned against the doorframe of the boys' bedroom, laughing. It's how you're raised, she thought. Mitchell had left the raising of the children in her hands, so she had carried on her mother's standards of cleanliness and good manners. It had not been easy in the early years, but her perseverance paid off, and her children, at least the ones she could observe, she admitted to herself, were tidy and well-mannered.

She crossed to the dresser, remembering the errand that had sent her upstairs. She pulled out the tray of the carved wooden jewelry box, another of Jonah's gifts, and took out her sister Elizabeth's pearls. Linney would wear them today, with her white dress and a veil covering her golden curls. Linney would be the fourth bride to wear them. I hope her marriage is a happy one, like Mady's and Betsy's, or, at least, a content one. She wondered as she often did, if her own marriage could have been patched up, had Mitchell not been killed. In some ways, he cared about me, she thought. Perhaps he loved me as much as he could. He never asked to leave, in spite of his what? Infatuations? Romances? He just was unable to be faithful. Not a problem I ever had. Tempie had been approached by widowers several times after Mitchell's death. She was reasonably attractive and reasonably well-off, and most men, after the death of a wife, immediately sought a replacement, to raise the children and keep the house. But she was already doing that, raising children and keeping house, and adding the burden of looking after a man she didn't love seemed absurd to her. She had no problem turning away prospective suitors, with a smile and good wishes.

She'd had a talk with Linney about a husband's expectations in marriage, but suspected from Linney's blushes and evasions that the picnics and buggy rides that she'd gone on with Mahlon following the announcement of their engagement had involved more than food and admiration of the countryside. If Mahlon had been a little forward, Linney seemed to have taken it well. That was good. Perhaps if she'd had courtship time with

Mitchell, her own wedding night would not have been as frightening.

She glanced at the clock on the mantel. Time to go downstairs.

In the dining room, Phoebe was setting out dishes and silverware in preparation for the dinner to follow the wedding. She was already dressed in her best, since she and Portia and their family would attend the service. There was a balcony for the slaves at Providence Church, and the front row upstairs was reserved for Phoebe's group today. Phoebe, Portia and Peach would hurry home afterwards to bring in the buffet dinner, already prepared and waiting in the kitchen house. There'd be ham and fried chicken, tomatoes, white peas, and okra from the garden. Several varieties of pickles. Cornbread with fresh-churned butter. Pies, including Mahlon's favorite, pecan. And a glorious cake, made by Portia. No one would go away hungry today!

In the parlor, Richard was waiting. He'd have the honor of walking his sister down the aisle. He was still growing at eighteen, and Tempie had commissioned a new dark blue frockcoat with extra fabric so it could be let out if he continued to grow. She smiled at her younger son. He did look handsome. He was very much his father's child, blond like Mitchell, and tall, with broad shoulders.

"Where is Linney?"

"She said something about picking some roses to carry."

Tempie glanced at the mantel. The white pitcher was filled with yellow and pink roses from the garden. She had planned to cut some of the white roses for a bouquet. "Here, hold these for me." She handed Richard the pearls.

She found Linney in the side yard. "Let me help you with those, Linn, honey. I don't want you pricking your fingers and bleeding on your gown!"

She took the scissors from her daughter's hands and quickly clipped half a dozen roses from the bushes in the bed that ran alongside the house. "There's a piece of white satin ribbon I left in the parlor to tie these up. Sweetheart, you look lovely."

Linney's golden hair, gleaming in the sun, was parted in the middle, with ringlets alongside her cheeks and the rest pulled up and pinned on the top of her head. Tempie recognized Portia's deft touch in the arrangement. Her white cotton gown had a modestly scooped neckline, full sleeves gathered at the wrist, and a snug bodice. Crocheted lace edged the full skirt and the neckline.

"Come inside, Linney. It's time to put on your veil, and I have my sister's pearls for you to wear."

There'd be other rivers to cross, Tempie thought, as she followed her daughter into the house, but they could wait. Tomorrow would be soon enough to think about all the days that would follow this one. But this day, this day, was filled with joy.

Drew and Elizabeth Smith—These are the parents of Temperance Smith Alston. Drew's death date is surmised by the writing of his will and the date it was probated. His parents were Nicholas Smith and Mary Blow. His grandfather John Smith came to America from England. Elizabeth Smith is one of the many women of those times whose existence is known only because she was named in a will, as in "My wife, Elizabeth." We don't know birth or death dates or even her maiden name. Temperence's siblings were:

> **Priscilla Smith**—Married Thomas Hunter, produced children.

> **Millea Smith**—Married Jacob Barrow, produced children.

> **Ann Smith**—Married Thomas Blount Whitmel, produced children.

Joseph John Alston and Elizabeth Chancy Alston—These are the parents of Philip Alston. Joseph John's vast holdings are a matter of public record. We don't know when Elizabeth was born, and her death date is a guess, only because we know when her last child was born and when Joseph John remarried. The will giving freedom to "Lucy, the cook wench" sent me on an imaginative flight of pure fiction. Philip's siblings were:

John Alston—Married Ann Hunt Macon, produced children

William Alston—Married Anne Yeargan, produced children

Martha Alston—Married Henry Meroney, produced children

Philip's half-siblings (children of Joseph John Alston and Euphan Wilson) all married and produced children:

Willis Alston married Elizabeth Wright.

Mary Alston married William Palmer.

Euphan Wilson Alston married John Cooper. She died in a shipwreck off Charleston in 1810.

Joseph John Alston, Jr. married Martha Kearney. He was called "Chatham Jack" and had extensive land holdings in Chatham County, as well as many slaves.

Temperance Smith Alston—She died at 61, in 1837, and is buried by her husband in the Concord Methodist Church Cemetery near the Tempereance settlement in Telfair County, Georgia.

Philip Alston—We don't know when he was born. His adventures at the Battle of Brier Creek and his escape from the Roebuck, the attack on the House in the Horseshoe, his political quarrels, his escape from the Wilmington jail, and his murder in Georgia are all well-documented.

Philip and Temperance Alston are the parents of the eight children that are named in the story. There were two five-year gaps in her child-bearing, and I can guess that these represented children lost to the family, but Rachel, William, and Dinah are imaginary.

James Alston—His birth date is unknown. He married Mary Jane Willcox. They relocated from North Carolina to Georgia to Mississippi and died there. There were children. One of their daughters, Elizabeth Caroline Alston, married Thomas Goodwin Mitchell in Telfair County.

John Alston—His birth date is unknown, as are his death date and place. It is unknown if he married. He died sometime after 1806.

Elizabeth Alston—Her birth date is unknown. She apparently was dead, unmarried, by about 1789, probably in Moore County, North Carolina.

Philip Alston, Jr.—Married Nancy Ann Ramsey and died in 1867 in Madison County, Tennessee. There were children of the marriage.

Winifred Alston—married William Waddell and died in Madison County, Tennessee in 1857. There were children of the marriage.

Mary Drew Alston—married first William Carroll, and after his death, William Harris, in Telfair County, Georgia. She died in Montgomery, Alabama in 1841.

Drew Smith Alston—is called variously "Drewry" and "Drury" on deeds. He died about 1813, but his place of death is unknown. There is no record of a marriage.

Dave—Dave was owned by Philip Alston and was accused of shooting George Glascock. He disappears from history after being bonded out of jail by Philip. Nothing else is known of him. We don't know his age or parentage. They are my invention.

Temperance Alston Griffin—Her birth date and death date are recorded in her daughter's family Bible. She is buried near the settlement of Temperance in Telfair County, Georgia. We know the names of some, but perhaps not all, of her children.

Benjamin Mitchell Griffin—He first appears as a "chain carrier" (surveyor) in Washington County, Georgia, in the 1780's. His birth date, birthplace, and the names of his parents are all unknown, as is his relationship to the other Griffins and Mitchells in Telfair County. I feel sure there *was* a relationship, but whether it was as brother or as cousin, I don't know. His death by the guns of Creek Indians is documented. I am assuming he was illiterate, since he signed an "X" on deeds. His wife signed her name, "Temperance A. Griffin," on the same deeds. He is buried beside her.

Temperance Alston and Benjamin Mitchell Griffin were the parents of several children. We know of five of them:

Temperance Griffin married Stephen Williams. There were children of the marriage.

Benjamin Mitchell Griffin, Jr. married Eliza Ann Hull. There were children of the marriage.

Richard Griffin married Nancy Guyton. There were children of the marriage.

Mary C. Alston Griffin married James Griffin, Jr. who was probably a cousin. Among their children was Len Mitchell Griffin from whom I am descended. The "C." in her name probably stood for "Catherine."

Linney W. Griffin married the Reverend Mahlon Bedell. It is their family Bible that records her mother Temperance's birth and death dates. There were children, but Linney died young. I don't know what the "W." stood for, but I like to think it may have been "Winifred."

Slaves

Besides Dave, who belonged to Philip Alston, and Lucy "the cook wench" who belonged to Joseph John Alston, I have used the names of some of the slaves bequeathed in Drew Smith's will to his wife and daughters: Lucy, Rose and Mingo. (Others were Dick, Jacob, Hannah, and Olive.) All other slaves I have invented, sometimes using names found in other family wills. The early censuses list slaves only by number. In fact, it was only beginning in 1840 that white women and children were given names in censuses.

I have tried to tell the story of Temperance and her daughter as it would have been told by people of those times. However I personally may feel about the morality of owning people, few Southerners then seemed to have had difficulties with it, and many seemed to have been no more attached to a slave than to a dog or a horse. Slaves were often treated as cruelly as some people treat livestock. I hope, therefore, that some would have been treated as lovingly as some pets were treated then.